Praise for
J.L. Bourne's

DAY BY DAY
ARMAGEDDON

"There is zombie fiction and then there is crawl-out-of-the-grave-and-drag-you-to-hell zombie fiction. *Day by Day Armageddon* is hands down the best zombie book I have *ever* read. J.L. Bourne blows all other zombie writers away. *Dawn of the Dead* meets *28 Days Later* doesn't even come close to describing how fantastic this thriller is. It is so real, so terrifying, and so well written that I slept with not one, but two loaded Glocks under my pillow for weeks afterward. J.L. Bourne is the new king of hardcore zombie action!"

—Brad Thor, #1 *New York Times* bestselling author
of *The Last Patriot* and *The First Commandment*

"*Day by Day Armageddon* is a dramatic spin on the zombie story. It has depth, a heart, and compelling characters."

—Jonathan Maberry, Bram Stoker Award–winning author of
Ghost Road Blues

"*Day by Day Armageddon* claws at the reader's mind. Bourne's journal is a visceral insight into the psyche of a skilled survivor."

—Gregory Solis, author of ~~Ri~~

Also by J.L. Bourne

Day by Day Armageddon

Day by Day
Armageddon
Beyond Exile

J.L. Bourne

GALLERY BOOKS

New York   London   Toronto   Sydney

Gallery Books
A Division of Simon & Schuster, Inc.
1230 Avenue of the Americas
New York, NY 10020

First Gallery Books trade paperback edition July 2010.

GALLERY BOOKS and colophon are trademarks of Simon & Schuster, Inc.

For information about special discounts for bulk purchases,
please contact Simon & Schuster Special Sales at 1-866-506-1949
or business@simonandschuster.com.

The Simon & Schuster Speakers Bureau can bring authors to your live event. For more information or to book an event contact the Simon & Schuster Speakers Bureau at 1-866-248-3049 or visit our website at www.simonspeakers.com.

Designed by Davina Mock-Maniscalco
Illustrations by Jason Snyder

Manufactured in the United States of America.

10 9 8 7 6 5 4 3 2

ISBN 978-1-4391-7752-5
ISBN 978-1-4391-7753-2 (ebook)

For more information about Permuted Press books and authors, please visit www.permutedpress.com.

Author's Note

The first volume of *Day by Day Armageddon* took us deep into the mind of a military officer and survivor as he made a New Year's resolution to start keeping a journal. The man kept his resolution and brought to us the fall of humanity, *day by day*. We see the man transition from the life that you and I live to the prospect of fighting for his very survival against the overwhelming hordes of the dead. We see him bleed, we see him make mistakes, we witness him evolve.

After surviving numerous trials and travails in the first volume of *Day by Day Armageddon,* the protagonist and his neighbor John escape the government-sanctioned nuclear annihilation of San Antonio, Texas. They eventually find themselves holing up in an abandoned strategic nuclear missile base known by the former occupants as Hotel 23. After their arrival they receive a weak radio transmission: A family of survivors are taking refuge in an attic, with untold numbers of undead below. A man named William, his wife, Janet, and their young daughter, Laura, are all that remain of their former community. After a miraculous rescue, this family joins forces with our protagonist to stay alive. But that may not be enough in a dead world, an unforgiving postapocalyptic place in which a simple infected cut, not to mention the millions of undead, can easily kill them, adding them to the overwhelming undead population.

The situation brought out the worst in some . . .

Without warning a band of brigands, seeing targets of opportunity, mercilessly assault our survivors inside Hotel 23, planning to kill them for the shelter and the vast supplies inside. Narrowly pushed back at the end of the novel, the survivors fear these men might return in much greater numbers—unless the countless millions of unrelenting undead close in around them first.

This novel begins where the first novel left off, with our narrator and a few survivors of an unimaginable worldwide cataclysm taking refuge inside Hotel 23. Follow them as they continue their journey into the apocalypse and just imagine for one moment that any one of them could be *you*.

Welcome back and lock your doors . . .

J. L. Bourne

Aftermath

I started feeling physically better the day of the twenty-first. The attack from the raiders had really busted me up. I got out of bed, drank a gallon of water (over the course of a few hours) and stretched a bit. I asked John what it looked like topside. He didn't want to say much of anything so I followed him up to the control room to look for myself. The previous night John had rushed out in the darkness and pulled the bag off one of the cameras and dashed back inside. There were undead about and he didn't wish to be out for long amongst them.

More undead inhabit the area around where the fence was damaged. They are like water, flowing to the point of least resistance. My painful burns are healing, but they were not that awful to begin with. Just a few blisters on my face and other places. Our victory in the last encounter with the insurgents was largely due to chance. What if they hadn't been convoying cross-country with a fuel truck? We would have probably been executed, unable to overcome their numbers. Outnumbered not only by the undead but by those who wished us dead. I feared the insurgents nearly as much as the creatures. In theory they could at least outstrategize us by putting their heads together and brainstorming on ways to force us from this compound. We do not know how many tangos remain; however, I am sure they still dwarf our numbers.

. . .

On camera number three I could see the charred bodies of men walking about the wreckage of the diesel truck and trailer . . .

Men that I had killed.

That night we went outside and put them down. To avoid muzzle flash, I snuck up on them from behind in the darkness with NVGs, selected single fire on my carbine and popped them in the back of the head with the barrel almost touching the skull. After every depression of the trigger I saw them react to the noise and start moving toward the sound, blind in the darkness. They could still hear, even though many of them had nothing that resembled ears. I repeated this seventeen times before they were all laid to rest.

We noticed that three vehicles had not been harmed badly in the fuel blast from the other night. There was a Land Rover, a Jeep and a late model Ford Bronco a hundred yards from the charred grass zone. John and I approached with caution. Upon closer inspection I discovered that both of the Jeep's front tires were blown and the window glass was spiderwebbed and concave.

Fifty meters farther were the Land Rover and the Ford. As I approached the Land Rover, I noticed that it appeared to be in very good condition and had no previous owners inhabiting the interior. Bonus. John and I walked up to the door; I opened it and checked the interior more closely. It smelled like pine, probably from the tree hanging on the rearview mirror. We got in and carefully shut the doors just enough for the latch to catch. I reached down to the ignition and turned. It roared to life. I suppose I would leave the keys in it too in a world like this. I looked down at the flimsy plastic tag on the key. It read: Nelm's Land Rover of Texas.

I suppose the marauders had acquired this vehicle after everything collapsed. The gas tank was three-quarters of the way full and it had three thousand miles on the odometer. Not even broken in. I put the vehicle in gear and sped off back toward the perimeter fence of the compound. When we neared the raider-covered cameras we got out and took turns pulling the bags off them while the other covered.

The hole in the fence was about the same size as the length of the Land Rover. I didn't feel like doing any fence repair tonight so I brushed up on my parallel parking skills and maneuvered her in front of the fence gap to discourage any of our cold-blooded amigos from getting inside the perimeter.

John climbed out the passenger side; I climbed over the console and also climbed out the passenger side. I hit the lock in the door and slammed it shut, putting the key in my pocket. Who was I kidding? I'm still not leaving the keys in it.

1248

I woke up a couple of hours ago after another painful, sleepless night. My blisters are starting to pop, causing some respectable pain. I have a few blisters around my eyes where my skin was unprotected by my nomex gear. The lump on the back of my head is starting to shrink, and more recently I am noticeably sorer than I was right after my little incident with the tanker. This is a good sign. I am healing.

I have given up on the internet. It is down for the count. The websites that I had been checking to test things out are down, i.e., military bases in the four corners of the United States. No internet activity. It is probably safe to assume that if anyone is out there to log on to the net, it won't matter. The backbone is shot and it looks like all the IT guys are out to lunch for the next hundred years. The Land Rover has GPS navigation. I went out to check things over and it appears the GPS is only acquiring three satellites for purposes of position finding. I don't know how long those satellites will remain in orbit without ground control station support as well as the birds we are using to take photographs. We are fast approaching the Iron Age. I keep fighting off the mental urge of self-destructive behavior. I don't mean this in a "wrist-slitting" way; I suppose I'm just feeling the need to take more risks because I'm tired of being in this predicament . . . but so is everyone else, so I remain. Heading out in a bit with John to attempt to quietly repair the downed fence.

24 May

2344

John and I repaired the fence with the scrap metal and parts left over from the debris from the raider attack. We also retrieved the Ford Bronco. It had four full gas cans in the back. I filled the Land Rover up with one of the gas cans in the event we would be using it in the future. I don't know why I didn't think of this before but I had totally forgotten about the aircraft throughout all of this. I remembered just as John was pulling up in the Bronco. John and I went to the tree line to see if it had been tampered with or possibly damaged by stray fire. It was just as I left it. The foliage I had placed on the plane to hide it was withered and brown, making it stand out a little. John and I gathered more branches, improving the overall camouflage of the aircraft before we left it to its solitude.

The undead in this area have been scattered. The marauders neutralized many of them as they herded them back and forth around the compound. The cameras only show a few stragglers at the front blast door. The rock-bearing freak is still shambling about there and has been for over a month. It is banging on the blast door, marching to the beat of its own drum. The empty missile silo is a mess; John and I don't even want to bother with it. I don't know what is causing these things to get up and walk around after death and I don't wish to be shuffling around down there and accidentally cut myself on an infected jawbone. If I had a cement truck, I would fill up the fucking hole and just forget about it.

28 May

1851

We are still alive, but our scenario echoes of those that were in the hospital on life support before all of this happened. They were living on borrowed time, doomed to die. We are one and the same. Eventually the averages will catch me. It's the *when* that is the real clincher.

I wouldn't mind getting my hands on another fuel tanker (and not blowing it up) so that we would have fuel for any expeditions we may need to undertake. I could park it a safe distance from the compound, learning from the raiders' mistake. It would definitely be worth the risk to have an overabundant source of gasoline. I am not sure how much those tankers hold; however, I am sure one of them would supply enough fuel for our two vehicles here for an extended period. Finding one should not be that difficult, as we could cherry-pick one from the interstate up north a few miles.

2105

More *code* language on the radios. This time they are switching the frequency every minute to what I assume is a planned order. Good COMSEC.

31 May

0118

I cannot sleep. Tara and I talked for a few hours today. I feel like I have no more purpose, and I'm not alone in this. Many of us miss normal, we miss when punching a clock and doing a job was boring. At least before all of this happened I had a job and goals. My only goal now is to stay alive. The adults got together today in the recreation room and drank some rum and had a good old time. I almost forgot about our situation in my alcohol-induced euphoria. I needed the release. We have been eating the compound's packaged meals since our arrival here. I would like some variety in my diet but shopping is getting more dangerous by the day.

It has been Memorial Day for an hour and a half. Tara and I went outside yesterday to pick some wild Texas flowers as sort of a memorial to everyone we have lost. I personally don't think there are enough flowers in the world. It pains me to no end to think of my mother and father walking the hills of our land like those creatures. I'm almost tempted to go home, just to see for myself and put them to rest like a decent son should.

Laura's schooling is coming along. Jan asked me to teach Laura some world history since I enjoyed it in my former life as an officer. Laura's eyes grew wide when I told her the stories of how the United States came about and how men walked on the moon

5

and such. She has never known a world without smart phones, HDTV or the internet and she's far too young to have ever seen *Schoolhouse Rock*. I'd give just about anything to be sitting in my living room on an early 1980s Saturday morning singing about being *just a bill, sittin' on Capitol Hill*. I feel a bit of guilt that she has no peers and that there is no little boy to pull her pigtails in school.

I really need my sleep as John and I have a little trip planned in the aircraft tomorrow. We are going out to find some fuel for the plane and do some reconnaissance. This time we won't be flying so low as to invite small-arms fire. I have my charts from our trip to Matagorda Island that cover this area's airports. I would also like to find some sort of synthetic camouflage netting to better disguise the aircraft.

Hobby

John, William and I took off early yesterday morning toward the west. We snuck out to the aircraft just before the sun came up on the eastern horizon. We pushed it to the grassy strip where we would take off. In the distance, we could see some shambling stragglers moving about. It wasn't long before we were airborne. It was a last-minute decision to take Will. He insisted that he go. We were able to establish a communications link with Hotel 23 via the VHF radio on the Cessna. If the girls were to get into any trouble, we would be able to communicate with them. We were looking for a large airport outside a major urban center. Before forcing myself to go to sleep last night I picked out William P. Hobby Airport. It was just south of Houston, outside the center of the city.

It was not a long flight. En route we flew over numerous small towns, all with the same speckles of walking dead dominating the streets below. It wasn't forty-five minutes and already we were in sight of Hobby Airport. I thought it safe to lower my altitude, as I would be able to see any living human figures below trying to shoot at me from the open concrete. Approaching the large expanse of paved runway and taxi area I saw yet another symbol of death.

A Boeing 737 was on the tarmac with severe fuselage wrinkles indicating a hard crashed landing. It was the only large plane in the airport. There were other, smaller aircraft—executive jets and smaller props similar to the Cessna—but this was the last of the large passenger jets here at Hobby. We circled around once more to make sure we had the proper assessment before we landed. I could see a fuel truck in the distance near one of the aircraft hangars. The hangar was large compared to the others and was most likely for Boeing aircraft just like the one that is forever disabled on the runway.

Our curiosity propelled us and we decided to land the plane near the large aircraft to see if anything of value might be inside. One advantage to this was that it was out in the open and not adjacent to any buildings that would leave us an easy mark for someone or some thing to sneak up on us. William would stay outside near the aircraft to keep watch as we found an entry point. All of the window shades were down on the 737. It wouldn't really matter since the windows were nearly fifteen feet off the ground anyway. The over-wing escape hatches were secure and we were not successful in getting them open as the fuselage ripple stresses had jammed them tight. That left the co-pilot's escape hatch on the starboard side of the cockpit glass.

I looked up, ten feet into the air on the right side of the cockpit, and saw how we were going to gain entrance to this aircraft. Using a grapple that Will and I had previously constructed from the rope and some metal left over from last month's tanker explosion, I was able to climb up to the window. First, I supported John's weight on my shoulders as he reached up to open the emergency access latch, releasing the airtight seal to the cockpit.

I almost dropped John when he carelessly fumbled the unattached piece of cockpit glass to the floor inside the plane. I cursed when I finally realized what he had done. I grunted under his weight on my shoulders and asked him if he had heard any reactions to our noise from the interior of the aircraft. He replied no, but also said that the smell coming from inside was beyond terrible and that the cockpit access door was closed. Using the pitot tubes jutting from the aluminum skin of the aircraft, John climbed back down off my shoulders and we made a decision.

This was enough for me. I wasn't going to risk my ass trying to squeeze through the tight emergency opening only to get it bitten off as I tried to regain my balance on the inside. This aircraft was a tomb and it was going to stay that way. I can only dream of the horrors that are waiting inside. Buckled passengers writhing to be set free from their belts, dead flight attendants carefully walking the aisles, still performing their duties even in the afterlife.

We returned to the aircraft to continue formulating our plan for getting the fuel and any other supplies we deemed necessary. The hangar was our goal. I doubted we were going to be able to move the fuel truck to where the aircraft rested so we all climbed back in and I started her up and taxied toward the hangar and the fuel supply. The closer we got, the more we knew the value of "ground truth" intelligence. We could see movement inside the airport through the aircraft windows. Dead, all of them. I gave them no more thought when I saw the horror spilling out of the open hangar that we were quickly closing on.

I stopped the aircraft and left the engine running as I jumped out, rifle in hand. John was out quick and Will followed, spilling out on my side. He started to walk past me when I reached my hand out, the way my mother used to reach out across my chest when our car was about to make a quick stop. He was fixated on the creatures and nearly walked himself into our aircraft's spinning propeller blades.

We fell back and began our task of killing them. There were roughly twenty that I could see. I could see shadows of movement dancing underneath the belly of the fuel truck. I screamed out over the engine for the men to kill the ones approaching the propeller first to avoid any aircraft damage. We needed the fuel and we needed to keep the engine running until we were safe from them. It was a Catch-22. I began firing and they followed suit. I killed five before number six refused to go down. Two shots to the head and it still came at me. I gave up on the head and shot its legs out from under it.

John and Will were making short work of the others as I picked off the remaining undead behind the fuel truck. We were clear for now. I checked the fuel truck to see if it was in working order. Using the butt of my rifle, I struck the tank. The sound that resonated indicated that there was fuel inside. One thing seemed odd. Why would a small prop aircraft fuel truck be parked in front of the Boeing hangar? I now began to think that I was not the only pilot that had visited this airfield since things went crazy. I wondered if this truck had been used recently/reused, or if I was just overthinking.

I climbed up to the driver's window and peered in before I

opened it up. Nothing. Keys were inside and it appeared to be in decent condition. I turned over the ignition and it coughed to life on the first attempt. Either someone had been maintaining this vehicle or I was just especially lucky with the battery charge. I flipped the switches for the pumps and got out. Before shutting down the aircraft, I checked our perimeter to make sure we weren't about to be blitzed. As the prop spun down and the engine noise abated, the unnerving clicking sound of jewelry hitting the terminal glass a couple hundred yards away filled my ears and grabbed my attention. The undead almost seemed to protest our taking of the fuel. *They* could see us from the inside and *they* were thrashing the glass in protest. Watches, rings and bracelets sounded like loud rain on the tempered glass even from this distance.

I unplugged the fuel caps and walked over to the truck. When I opened the control box to flip the switch, a yellow piece of folded legal-sized paper fell out and started to drift downwind. I ran after the paper, caught it with my boot and unfolded it to read:

Davis family, Lake Charles airfield, Louisiana. 5/14

It was a family . . . survivors. It was brilliant of them to leave this note inside the exterior fuel pump control switchbox. Davis had shown himself to be an intellectual with this single gesture. He didn't overtly spray-paint the runway with his name and location; he left it in a place where another pilot could find it. Aircraft fuel is useless to automobiles, rendering an aircraft fuel truck the same. I took the note and put it in my pocket. Walking up to the aircraft, I could tell John and Will were edgy. I filled the aircraft tanks to the top as I watched them. Will's skin seemed to be getting lighter in color in anticipation of what I was going to say next.

Time to check out the hangar.

I don't know why they were afraid. The hangar doors were wide open and anything that wanted us could just walk out here and try. After all the gunfire, I was nearly certain that there were no more of those things inside this hangar. I was right.

As the three of us broke the threshold of the large rolling hangar doorway, I almost pissed my pants. Something swooped in out of the darkness and nearly hit me in the head. It seems that a family of swallows had a summer nest just above the entryway and the mother didn't like me near her young. I could hear them chirping above. Makes me wonder how many undead eyes she had poked out in the previous weeks. I steered clear of the nest and made my way back to the supplies. The hangar had numerous Plexiglas skylight openings. It was a nice sunny day. The smell of death was in the air, but the smell of rot had followed the undead outside the hangar to their demise at the hands of our small team. It wasn't long before we found the door to the large supply room.

Slowly, I opened the door with a long pole commonly used to clean out-of-reach aircraft windows. Nothing but the smell of mothballs rolled out to meet us. This room was clean. I was acclimated to the smell of the undead but I could surely tell when their smell was absent. The supply room could almost have been considered a mini warehouse. The shelves were lined with superfluous aircraft parts and equipment. This was the Boeing supply and maintenance hangar. However, I wasn't looking for jet engine parts, I was looking for survival radios and equipment. It was then that I came upon something that I couldn't leave home without. There were rows of black briefcase-looking devices labeled "Inmarsat." We had stumbled upon aviation portable satellite telephones. I had no idea if they were still operational. However, four of them on the right side of the shelf were still sealed in plastic. We took those four and moved them to the door. Continuing our loop around the supply locker we found numerous portable distress radios, inflatable life rafts and other things of that nature. We took the satellite phones and portable VHF maintenance radios and made our exit.

We were full on fuel, had four new satellite phones, some portable VHF radios and had also made a startling discovery that a family had headed out to an airstrip in Louisiana weeks ago. It was time to leave. We all loaded up the aircraft and began our journey home. This time I stayed above seven thousand feet until I was almost on top of Hotel 23. I didn't want to take the chance of any stray weapons fire shooting me down. As I approached the compound I called out over the radio to Jan and Tara, telling them,

"Navy One is three down and locked for a full stop." I mused at the use of the presidential call sign, but no one got it. I bet Davis would get it. We landed and hid the aircraft once again. I entered the complex thinking of the Davis family and wondered if they ever made it to that airfield.

Tower of Charles

I have been arguing with our group over the past three days about whether I should attempt to find the Davis family at Lake Charles. I have checked my charts and it is not that far. Of course if this becomes a reality, I will calculate the exact distance and fuel required to make the journey. The others seem to think that the risk far outweighs the benefit of finding them. John is neutral but Jan, Tara and Will are adamant that this could swiftly develop into a suicide mission.

We were able to charge up the satellite phones but unfortunately, as previously determined, there is no one to call with them. They seem to work fine, though, when we use them to dial up the other phones. It didn't take long to figure them out. I just don't know how the billing works. I know the phones belong to the airlines and I know that no one is left to send a bill for the satellite usage; I am just worried that there may be some sort of automated system shutoff when the phones reach a certain number of minutes.

I wonder what they are doing at Lake Charles airfield right now. I wonder if they even knew their note would be found. I feel the need to establish communications with them, even if it means just dropping one of the satellite phones out of the aircraft door with a makeshift parachute. At least it would be something. We could communicate with them, get more information, more ideas.

08 Jun

0226

I am leaving this morning. John and the others are staying behind in the event I bring someone back. I don't want to terribly overstress the aircraft. I hope they have stayed near the airfield at Lake Charles. As I sit here and stare at the yellow piece of paper that is almost a month old, I wonder if they still live or if they were taken under siege as John and I that day at the tower. William almost begged to come with me but as I mentioned before, I may be bringing back survivors. I have no way of knowing, so I cannot take the chance on extra aircraft weight. I am bringing two fully charged satellite phones and my usual load out of one pistol with fifty 9mm rounds and carbine with a few hundred rounds. A couple days of food and water will also make its home in the avionics bay of the aircraft. In this journal, I thought I would write something pithy and creative in the event they would be my last written words. Since I am neither pithy nor creative I shall borrow great words from a man long (really) dead:

"To the last I grapple with thee; from hell's heart I stab at thee; for hate's sake I spit my last breath at thee."—Melville/Ahab

Off I go to the Pequod.

2201

One hundred and seventy miles as the crow flies, that was the distance to Lake Charles. It wouldn't be a straight shot for me, as I had decided to fly over Hobby airfield again to see if the fuel truck would still be available in the event I needed it on the way back. I had five hundred nautical miles before my aircraft would start dropping out of the sky, very permanently.

As I buzzed the Hobby at two thousand feet, I could see the fuel truck below just as we had left it. I could also see that one of the terminal windows had shattered and numerous undead were streaming in and out of this new opening, which spilled out onto a rooftop roughly twenty feet above the concrete taxiway below.

I couldn't see any of them near the fuel truck area. However, I knew that they had no fear of heights and would walk freely off the roof if they thought they could make a meal by their efforts. Satisfied with what I saw, I headed northeast toward Lake Charles. The sun was up fully and shining right into my eyes as I leveled off at seven thousand feet. After thirty minutes I could see the remains of the city of Beaumont in the distance. I decided to go lower and possibly find survivors. According to my chart this was a medium-sized city.

Smoke and fire swirled about and inside the taller buildings. They looked like large matchsticks of varying height, each with its own unique shape of fire and smoke. This trip could have been avoided if the satellite photography system in the compound was working properly. We lost the Louisiana pass (satellite footprint) two weeks ago. I would have loved to have typed in the coordinates of Lake Charles and found my answer without ever having to leave.

Power was off in this area. All of the red anticollision beacons installed on the tall radio towers were out, compounding the fun. I was flying low and slow, scanning Beaumont's city streets and buildings that were not on fire. I strained my eyes best I could but saw no survivors. The only things out walking on this nice summer day are them . . . those that are not us.

After three passes over what I thought was the center section of the city, I was convinced that no survivors remained. At least none that had any way of signaling. Lake Charles airfield was roughly fifty miles east of Beaumont. At current rate of speed, I would be there in twenty-eight minutes. This turned out to be a very long wait. I was apprehensive about meeting new survivors. I had no idea what to expect. The note in my pocket clearly says "Davis family," but I still didn't know if this Davis fellow would turn out to be friend or foe. Hell, the note was dated for the fourteenth of last month, I had no guarantees they were even still vertical or at least living vertical.

It didn't take long before I could see the boot-shaped lake getting bigger off the nose of the aircraft. On the chart, this lake was just south and a little west from my destination. I had to find them. Having another pilot in the event anything happened to me would be useful to the others. At least having Davis around would be sort of an insurance policy. The sun was still high in the sky. It was almost two o'clock when I arrived in the area of the airfield. It took a little window shopping to pick it out over the clutter and smoke of the urban areas below. Lowering my nose, I slowed to seventy knots and began my descent. I could see numerous figures below near the runway.

From where I was it appeared that there were numerous survivors. I could see their brightly colored clothing even from this distance, unlike the soiled, worn clothing of the undead. It even seemed that they had people working, as I could see someone carrying signal cones—the cones that have a flashlight attached to them and are used to signal the flight deck to a parking spot.

I don't know what had caused me to see what I wanted, but I soon realized that I had been fooled. This airfield was overrun. A large section of fence was out on the eastern side of the airfield and the undead had overwhelmed the area. Leveling my nose, I attempted a pass at the tower in the event they had made a stand inside. Nothing. Nothing but them. They were everywhere, even inside the tower. As I neared the departure end of the runway I could see a small aircraft sitting below. The doors were open and there were bodies strewn all around the aircraft. I lost count of how many. Several of them were gathered around the propeller section of the aircraft as if they'd walked into it and were sliced up on the spot. I could also see numerous body parts, arms mostly, around the forward section of the aircraft.

My suspicions were confirmed as I began my climb out of the area. Practically the moment I had decided that it was time to leave and go back home, I spotted them. I could see two people waving frantically from the catwalk that surrounded the airfield's main water tank tower. Waving for their lives below were a young boy and a woman. I made another pass and rocked my wings to signal that I had seen them. There was a sleeping bag and some boxes sitting on the tower with them. It seemed unlikely that they had survived after being exposed to the elements for who knows how long, trapped on the tower. I was moving too fast to be able to get a good look at them, but slow enough to know that they were alive.

The tower was positioned off the airfield on the other side of the broken chain-link fence. I would have found them sooner by the masses of undead that were pawing on the pillars below if it were not for the bottom of the tower being shrouded in trees and smaller undergrowth. I could see the undead, relentlessly begging upward, when I flew nearly on top of the water tower.

Landing at the airfield was not an option. With the break in the fence the scores of undead gathered below the survivors would pour in and easily swarm me. They would be drawn to the noise of the engine. An even bigger problem would be taking off again without hitting one with catastrophic effect. I wanted to figure out a way to tell them I was coming back for them but with my adrenaline rushing at the prospect of dealing with the undead, I could not.

I brought the aircraft up and departed the airfield, searching for a suitable landing strip. I cruised east, flying as low as possible looking for anywhere within ten miles that I could set her down. According to my chart and the view from the cockpit, I was flying directly over Interstate Highway 10. I could see cars all over the highway in the eastbound lane. However, the westbound lane was relatively empty. I kept a mental note of how long and how fast I was flying so as to anticipate my hike back to the water tower.

As my mental calculations kept spinning in my head, I noticed yet another post-apocalyptic odyssey on the ground. A large section of I-10 was missing, along with an adjacent overpass. There was a green military vehicle parked near an explosion crater and numerous "Danger" signs posted around the area. I suppose that either the highway was intentionally blown in the days after the outbreak or the bridge collapsed and chronic erosion took the rest of the highway. Either way this was my opportunity and I had to commit. I commenced an emergency landing on the interstate. I remembered driving this very strip of highway two years before when I was transferred for military training and now I would be landing an aircraft on it.

It was clear. I could see some debris in the distance, but I would be well clear of it before it became an issue. I brought her down, but not without complications. I began to apply my brakes to slow my speed down the strip of road. One, two, then four of them shuffled out of the high, grassy median of the highway. Not as many as I would have thought. As I pressed the brakes a little harder, I felt a jolt in the pedals and the aircraft turned sharply to the right. I had lost one of my brakes. I had no choice but to apply opposite rudder to straighten the aircraft out and just ride it out until the aerodynamic drag stopped me.

Now, the debris that I thought would not be a factor suddenly became a big one. I tapped the good brake while applying opposite rudder to straighten my yaw, each time kissing the grass on the right side of the highway. I stopped barely short of the debris that would have resulted in a likely fatal crash. The obstruction and mess blocking my roll fifty meters in the distance was nothing more than another blast hole, a green army truck and collapsed overpass. I doubted that two overpasses would coincidentally collapse like that. They were likely a result of professional demolition. I barely had enough room to turn the aircraft around and get it set up for takeoff. That is, if I made it back. I shut the engine down, taking special care to keep an eye on the small numbers approaching as I readied my pack for the expedition.

I reached into the backseat of the aircraft and pulled out my carbine and magazines. I stuffed the extra magazines in my pack and put the other four "go-to" mags in easily accessible pockets. My sidearm was already at my side. I placed four bottles of water and two MRE packages in the pack also. I had no idea how long they had been surviving on the tower or if they had been without water for very long.

I shut the aircraft door and turned around, shock-startled by the snarling, decomposing face of one of the creatures. I struck it in the temple with the butt of my rifle and kicked it hard in the knee, bringing it to the ground. That one wasn't worth the bullet or the byproduct of the loud rifle report. It didn't move again as I walked away from the aircraft.

I walked perpendicular to the interstate into the woods. I would shadow the road from here, safer from their ever-searching, always vigilant gaze. I could see them through the trees intermittently as I passed. They seemed confused, knowing something of interest was near, but unsure how to benefit from it. It was hot and humid but I kept on; my soul had no choice. I finally made it to the point where the first demolitions had occurred. I hadn't noticed the undead soldier on my first flyover, as he was in my blind spot on the other side of the truck when I made the pass. It wasn't difficult to tell what happened to him. The back of his green coat was shut in the driver's-side door, prohibiting movement. His coat was zipped up to his chest and he was wearing a Kevlar helmet strapped to his chin. He was missing large chunks of flesh and muscle from his shoulder and neck. It was apparent that he had rushed out of the truck only to shut his coat in the door, inviting catastrophe. I suppose the Darwin award had a winner for this month.

No point in letting him see me, as he would only pound on the truck like a drum and invite more creatures. I needed to leave him just as he was. Part of me wanted to put him out of his misery, as he was a fellow military man. I quietly walked around to the passenger side of the large truck and had a look inside. Sitting in the seat was an M-9 pistol. The window was rolled up and the door was locked on my side. I only had my rifle and pistol and it wouldn't be a bad idea for the survivors to have a weapon for the rescue operation. I changed my mind and made the decision to kill the soldier as a trade for the pistol. I stepped down off the running board of the truck and walked to the rear. It was a transport truck with a canvas-covered wagon-type bed. I peered into the bed. I could see nothing of use in the back of the truck—just wooden crates full of God knows what. Probably explosives. That wasn't my field of expertise.

I picked up a large chunk of leftover interstate and tossed it on the concrete near the creature's feet to make it look the other way as I advanced. It worked. I quickly approached the thing and shoved the muzzle of my weapon underneath the helmet, getting around the Kevlar protecting its head. I squeezed off one round. The creature went limp and just hung there until I opened the door. I checked its pockets. Nothing of value. I took the M-9 and left the scene.

I didn't have much time to figure out a way to get them off the water tower. We needed to be out of here before sundown. Neutralizing the creatures was not an option. I had the advantage of a brain and firepower, but there were just too many of them. I needed another way. It seemed the only option was to run up to them and start screaming or shooting, drawing them from the tower, which was similar to the way I extracted the Grisham family. That was also too dangerous, as I did not have a working car to lead them away. More lack of planning. I had planned only to land at Lake Charles, make contact and possibly transport survivors to Hotel 23. I didn't plan for another ridiculous rescue effort.

The water tower was in view. I could see one of them on the catwalk. I tried to wave my arms and signal but there was no response. It almost made me second-guess myself. I wondered if I had gone through this trouble only to be saving two corpses. It was then that my efforts were reaffirmed. I could see a small male figure urinating off the edge of the railing onto the corpses below. Although I could not see the corpses through the undergrowth, I knew what the boy was doing. He was mischievously aiming for their heads.

I briefly chuckled to myself and got back to business. The water tower was only about ten meters from the airport perimeter fence. The top of the fence was not barbed and I could easily climb over it, so I jogged to a section out of view of the creatures and did just that. As soon as I hit the ground I started running toward the hangar. I saw a row of electric-powered luggage carts plugged into a charging bank behind the hangar. I slowly moved over to them. I had no idea how long the power had been out in this area so I didn't know if they would still operate. I unlatched one of them and pulled it out to the side of the hangar so that I could get a good look at it. I had drawn a curious corpse on the other side of the fence. It must have seen me jump over.

There were no keys for the small luggage cars, I suppose to avoid foreign object debris (FOD) damage to the aircraft engines in the event the keys were dropped on the taxiway. I turned the switch to the on position, sat down and pressed the accelerator. The electric engine jolted over but the cart did not move. I tried another. There were several, all in a row behind the building. On the third cart, I was successful. It hummed to life and I immediately hopped on and drove toward the broken section of the fence near the water tower. I stopped on the center of the runway and got out, leaving the luggage cart on. I shouldered my rifle and began shooting at the base of the tower, taking down as many as I could before every undead eye in a two-mile radius looked my way.

I kept firing until the mass of them started pouring out of the opening in the fence, arms outstretched and wanting me. I waited until they were fifty meters distant before I got back into the cart and drove away, drawing the undead away from the tower. As I sped down the runway I reloaded my magazine. I couldn't tell but if I were to guess I would say there were at least two to three hundred of them behind me.

I was at the end of the runway. I got out and started shooting at them again. They were about three hundred yards away at this point. I had some time. I killed the ones near me that were already inside the airport perimeter first. Then I started selectively picking off the large crowd, aiming for the ones most distant first. That would buy me more time before they caught up to me when I made my transition back to the tower.

They were now at one hundred yards. There were so many flies buzzing around the mass it was sickening. I could easily hear the flies' collective buzz over their moans. I would have to say that the worst thing about them is their dried, decomposing faces. Their lips locked in a permanent snarl with bony hands reaching for purchase. It was time to roll. I jumped back in the cart and circled around the mass and put the accelerator to the floor. This thing had limitations on its speed for safety. I was only going ten or fifteen miles per hour at best. As I neared the tower I screamed for them to get ready. I couldn't tell if they heard me or not. The bulk of the creatures were almost one thousand yards away. We had time, but I still had to take care of the dozen or so that had remained at the base of the tower. The battery in the cart was beginning to show signs of drain.

I was at the break in the fence. The foliage was restricting my view and I had no way of knowing exactly what was hiding inside. I opened fire on what I thought was a head. I gave up on this tactic and carefully walked into the undergrowth under the tower. The ones that were left behind were probably deaf, as they were in advanced stages of decomposition. They probably didn't even hear my gunfire. Many of them had only one eye, or none at all. They were easy targets. It was not long before the base of the tower was secure. I called up to the survivors to get down as fast as they could.

I heard a woman's commanding voice say, "Danny, do as the man says."

Then the boy replied nervously, "Yes, Granny."

The boy went first. He was about twelve years old with brown hair and dark brown eyes with a light complexion. Then came the female. She looked to be in her late fifties or even early sixties. She had red curly hair and was slightly overweight. They were both on the ground holding what few belongings they had, looking to me for answers. My confidence seemed to drain along with the golf cart battery after seeing so many of the creatures. I mustered up what acting ability I had (Abraham Lincoln in kindergarten) and feigned confidence, telling them to follow me. Before we left I took a zip tie out of my pack and went over to the luggage cart.

They were closer now, about six hundred yards, and closing fast. I climbed into the luggage cart and put it into reverse. A loud warning beep sounded. I zip-tied the pedal down so that it would go until it hit something or the battery was completely depleted. I jumped out and rolled to avoid injury as the cart drove off, beeping loudly, in the direction of the undead mass. We headed back to the aircraft the same way I had come in, taking special care to remain undetected as we clumsily traipsed through the foliage parallel to Interstate 10. I could hear loud moans coming from behind us from the direction of the airport. We were upwind from them. No doubt they could somehow smell us, even though I admit I never bothered to examine one closely enough to see if it even breathed.

As we journeyed through the woods in the general direction of the aircraft, I handed the woman the M-9 that I had stolen from the army transport truck earlier. She told me that her name was Dean and that this was her grandson, Danny. I shook both of their hands and pulled out the yellow handwritten note that I had found hidden in the fuel truck at Hobby Airport.

The woman looked at the note. Her bloodshot eyes began to tear up and she stopped for a moment, looking into my eyes. She reached out her arms and hugged me while she cried. My first thought was that Mr. Davis was a close friend and family member of hers and that the note had somehow surfaced painful recent memories of his untimely demise.

"I know you are unhappy, but we have to keep moving. There

are many of those creatures around. The golf cart won't fool them for long," I told her.

She insisted that she needed a minute or two to get her bearings. What could I say? If my mother ever found out I had disrespected my elder I'd get my ass kicked.

I asked the woman what had happened to Mr. Davis and his family.

She replied, "Danny and I are the Davis family. I left the note at Hobby Regional last month, right before we flew here."

Puzzled and feeling the ever-so-slight sting of sexism in the back of my mind, I humbly inquired who flew the plane.

She smiled and for a brief second looked a little younger and said, "I did. I am a certified pilot, or used to be, when being a certified pilot meant something."

Holding back my look of jackassery, I scanned the area for any threat and continued talking to the woman named Dean. Danny sat on the ground in front of her feet, his small head scanning all around for threats.

I felt peaceful as I spoke to this woman, almost as if she was the last grandmother left on the planet and I wanted to hear her stories. . . . Now wasn't the time.

My main reason for stopping was to give them an emotional rest from what had just happened at the water tower. Although the woman was more than capable of handling herself, she was still an older woman and I felt that they had needed this brief break in the action. The woman called Dean showed obvious signs of malnutrition. Loose skin hung from her arms and legs as a testament to her love for her grandson. Danny didn't look great, either, but I could tell that food had been given up for his survival.

With guilt and a little sorrow in my voice, I made the suggestion that we keep moving and get to the aircraft as soon as possible. It would be very difficult to find the fuel truck at Hobby if we were forced to fly at night. As we walked, I tried to keep Dean's mind off today's events by quietly asking her why she learned to fly. She was eager and happy to talk about it. As she whispered, I kept glancing past her face into the breaks in the trees that intermittently revealed the interstate. From time to time during our move to the plane I saw them.

She quietly spoke as she walked of how she was a retired pilot, formerly of the New Orleans Fire Department, and how she missed flying and helping people in need. She also mentioned her age in the conversation, saying that she had retired ten years ago when she had turned fifty-five. I couldn't believe that the woman had survived as long in this, keeping this young boy alive. I was truly in awe and fully respected this woman's will to survive.

There were a few creatures up the interstate toward the airfield between the aircraft and our group. The moans of the dead were almost to the point of imagination at this distance. I told Dean how I had lost my left wheel brake in the landing and said that I hoped we wouldn't have to abort takeoff because there would be a nice, big, green army truck waiting for us at the end of this strip of interstate. She didn't seem to worry and never questioned where my piloting skills came from. She just seemed thankful to be alive. After arriving at the aircraft, I opened the door and almost caught myself shielding Danny's eyes from the corpse I had killed near the aircraft earlier. What was the point? The boy had probably pissed on more of the undead than I had ever seen.

After inspecting the aircraft and strapping in we started the takeoff checklist. Both Dean and I put on the internal communications headsets and she helped me run the checklist, as she had over two hundred hours in this particular model aircraft, much more than I had. The engine started with no problem. I gave the aircraft power and began my forward roll. There was no use testing the brakes. The area was clear; I kept my roll to fifty knots. A single corpse was approaching the concrete of the interstate from the grassy median separating I-10 east and west. I wasn't sure if I was going to make it.

I then felt the yoke controls of the aircraft being pulled back to me. Dean's voice over the internal communications said, "We can make this climb." I couldn't believe it. This climb was even steeper than the time John and I had to fly out of the dirt track back before San Antonio was rocked off the map by nukes. It was not the engines that pushed me back into my seat. It was gravity. We had missed the corpse and taken off nearly a thousand feet before I would have. I had to buck up and admit to myself she was better at flying this plane than I was.

As we passed the truck, crater and collapsed overpass, the airport once again came into sight. Out of pure curiosity I asked Dean to take us over the airfield. As we flew over I could see them huddled around the electric cart at the opposite end of the airfield. It was wedged into the fence and I assume was still beeping, because the corpses were quite interested in it, trying to rip it apart. Maybe it was the smell, maybe the noise, maybe both.

She asked where we were headed. I told her to fly us to her fuel truck. She did.

Curious how she came to be on top of the water tower, I began asking some questions now that we were safely in the air. They landed at Lake Charles on the night of May 14. She didn't go into detail, but her hands started to shake on the controls as she spoke of how she had to leave the aircraft running and both she and Danny had to run as fast as they could to the tower to avoid being eaten by them. All they had on the tower was what they could carry in one trip. I asked why she just didn't escape in the aircraft. She answered my question with another by saying, "Didn't you see all the bodies lying around the aircraft near the propeller when you flew over?" I could see that she was uncomfortable talking about it.

She told of how she used her sleeping blanket to get water for the both of them. She had climbed up to the top of the tower from the catwalk on the side at day six, one day after they had run out of their rationed potable water. Somehow, she unscrewed the plug on the top of the tower that was commonly used to test the water inside the tank. Using the blanket, she dipped it down into the tank and was able to get it submerged approximately six inches into the tank without dropping it in. She and Danny had lived off "freshly squeezed Louisiana blanket water" for nearly a month while enduring the endless moans of the dead below. She cried again when she spoke of this.

Over Hobby, we were in need of fuel. We might have been able to make it back to Hotel 23 on fumes, but I didn't think it necessary to take the risk. I knew the fuel truck worked, I had used it recently and I knew it had plenty of fuel. The sun was approaching the western horizon as we circled Hobby to take a look. There were undead on the roof adjacent to the shattered terminal window and

I did see a few of them on the ground below the roof. Some of them had rendered themselves immobile from the fall. Kinetics is a bitch.

I landed the aircraft and taxied it dangerously close to the fuel truck and told Dean to stay inside. She didn't like this idea and wanted to help, but I could see in her eyes that she knew I was right. She wasn't one hundred percent after starving, baking and freezing for a month on that tower, which is why, despite her high flight hours, I kept my hands on or near the controls the entire time she flew. She may have been a better stick, but she was worn down to the wire.

Leaving the engine running, as is my standard operating procedure for a situation like this, I made my way to the fuel truck. It wasn't long before I had the tanks full and the aircraft positioned to take off again. At the hold short line on the Hobby runway I realized that I hadn't checked in with Hotel 23 for nearly ten hours, nor did I have the headsets tuned to the VHF radio. Dean and I were talking on the way to Hobby and we were out of range of Hotel 23 anyway, so I'd switched the VHF off after taking off from the interstate to avoid the static. Dean was using the copilot's controls to get the aircraft airborne in the same manner that she had used them to give control inputs to avoid the corpse on last take-off. I kept my hands on the pilot controls, shadowing her.

On a side note, as we were taking off and as I began to tune the radios to contact Hotel 23, I noticed a corpse hanging out of the large Boeing aircraft cockpit window that John, Will and I had attempted to explore weeks ago. It was obviously stuck at the waist and I could see its arms moving in a futile attempt to drop itself to the tarmac. All of the recent activity at this airfield must have excited the undead entombed in that large, multi-million-dollar sarcophagus.

I keyed the microphone: "H23, this is Navy One, over." John came back. He was borderline frantic. Using the proper radio discipline so as to not reveal any names or locations, he came back. "Navy One, this is H23, we have been trying to reach you for hours. It is not safe to land at H23 at this time." I asked John what was going on. I was instantly worried that the only enemy more dangerous than the dead was attacking again.

He came back and told me that there had been a recent influx of undead to the landing area and the area surrounding the back fence and that it would not be safe to land as there were currently over one hundred of them standing where I would be attempting to touch down. I asked him if there was any way he could clear it out, as I was coming back with "one plus two souls onboard." He replied that it would be too dark to do anything in twenty minutes. I agreed. It would be suicide to go out there at night and attempt to herd them out of the way, and even then there would be no guarantee that it would work. It would only take one of those things to hit the aircraft at eighty knots to cause terrible structural/engine damage and quick death to all onboard. We had to find somewhere to stay tonight, fast.

Eagle Lake airfield was out of the question for obvious reasons. I would not be willing to take a chance and land the aircraft in an unknown field. I had to find an airfield. I began scanning my chart for any possible candidates. On the chart was a very small airstrip called Stoval about fourteen miles southwest of H23. That would have to do. The sun would be down by the time we were there, so it was going to have to be another NVG landing.

This time I was not willing to cut the engines, as we had no guaranteed shelter to escape to if this went south on us. We had to take our chances with the engine noise. Not knowing how Dean would react, I asked Danny to reach into my bag and pull out the hard plastic green case. He did. Dean was at the controls. I began to explain to her what we had to do and that we basically had no choice in the matter. I asked her to cut the exterior collision lights and be prepared to give me control when it became too dark for her to see any detail on the ground. I pointed out the airfield we were heading for. She slightly altered heading and we made way.

I pulled the NVGs out of the case and strapped them on my head. I wanted to give my eyes plenty of time to adjust, just to make sure. I turned the intensity down so low that the goggles were acting more as a blindfold than a night vision aid. It was getting very dark outside. I asked Dean for the controls just as I adjusted the NVG intensifiers. The landscape below came alive in the familiar green color to which I had become so accustomed.

I began searching for the airfield. It wasn't there. I kept searching and searching, checking the chart. I was looking for an airstrip with a tower. It took twenty minutes before I realized that we had flown over it several times. This field was abandoned, and didn't have a tower. The strip was almost grown up to the point that the aircraft could nearly cut the grass with the prop as it landed. I could, however, still see the concrete and make out the strip. There was nothing in the area of this field except one lone hangar. I flew near it to see if any of the doors on it were open. It seemed secure. I brought the plane around for the landing. I had become acclimated to the depth perception problem I was having with the NVGs and made a better landing this time. I positioned the aircraft for tomorrow's takeoff, cut the engines and kept a vigilant watch.

They are sleeping right now. We landed at about 2100 hrs. I contacted John and told him our coordinates. He said that he and Will would take care of them in the Land Rover tomorrow and not to worry. He laughed and told me to make sure that I turned the radio on in the morning and said that he would be up monitoring his all night. I asked how Tara was doing. John said that she was sitting right next to him and that she said she misses me.

9 Jun
0218

I see movement in the distance at the outer perimeter of the airfield. Not sure what it is. The cabin doors are locked and I am sleepy but refuse to nod off. Dean is awake. I am not telling her what I see.

0354

The movement in the distance turned out to be a family of deer. I could tell they were living creatures by the mirrorlike reflection of their eyes caused by the effects of night vision. The undead do not share this comforting quality.

0622

The sun is up and the radios are on. I have already spoken to John and he will be giving me the go-ahead within the next hour. There is no movement in this area and the family of deer has moved out. Dean and Danny have already eaten much of the food that I have brought. Can't say that I blame them.

0740

Call made; John says it's clear. We are taking off shortly.

11 Jun

0940

We arrived at Hotel 23 on the morning of the ninth without incident. Jan stayed in touch via the VHF radios and relayed John and Will's position to us in the air as they herded the undead mob safely away from our landing spot. Before we touched down at H23, I told Dean not to expect much of our shelter and that there would now only be nine of us (including Annabelle). Danny was wearing a headset in the backseat. It was too big for him and I found it funny how it kept slipping off as he asked the question, "Who is Annabelle?" I told Danny that we had a puppy at Hotel 23 and that her name is Annabelle and she loves little boys. Danny began to tear up in happiness at the prospect of touching something truly good again and not having to look at the "ugly people," as he had been calling them.

I saved Laura as a surprise for him. I can't imagine the joy in his heart when he saw another child to play with, even though she was a *girl*. Although it only comes to me once in a great many years, a flash of memory, a familiar smell from an old cedar chest of keepsakes . . . I still remember what it was like being twelve.

Crude

We had a meeting today. All nine of us attended although Laura, Danny and Annabelle did not pay attention. They were quietly playing in the corner as we talked. Dean is looking much better. I caught her up on the recent events at Hotel 23 regarding the bandits and basically gave her a rundown on everyone here and how we came to find each other.

She had a few stories of survival herself regarding the months leading up to her imprisonment at the "Tower of Charles." She spoke of how she and little Danny had been in New Orleans and had heard the warning that the Big Easy would be a target and how they had taken off in her aircraft for the nearest safe zone. She never found it. They had spent months bouncing from airport to airport, scavenging food, water and fuel until their luck finally ran out.

Dean has become the resident grandmother around here, taking care of the kids and offering advice. She even approached me yesterday in private to tell me that she could see that Tara was fond of me. I had known this for a little while but have been too preoccupied with staying alive to do anything about it. She asked me what the purpose of survival was if I had no one to love and be loved by. I didn't really answer that. I was in no mood for emotion. We were still in some serious trouble and I felt like I have no time for love or romance.

I asked her if she had run across any survivors in her airport-hopping campaign. She told another grisly tale in which she and Danny attempted to rescue two survivors signaling for them from a field below. They were being flanked by hundreds of undead that they could not see over an adjacent hill. Dean had tried to warn them by flying over the area where the dead were advancing. However, it was too late. By the time they realized what was going on, the dead had topped the hill. The sheer number of them picked them clean like African driver ants.

Dean had felt guilty about that incident and often wondered if they were in that field solely to signal her and Danny. I tried to comfort her by saying that they were probably already there and that she had just flown over at the right time. Odds are, she probably did draw them out into the open to signal her, but what would be the point in presenting that gruesome thought?

I have gotten into a pretty good routine of exercise lately. The undead numbers have greatly declined around the complex since the raider attack. I have installed a pull-up bar in the control room. I constructed it out of scrap, using twine to secure it to the overhead beams.

John has been monitoring the radios and has had no sign of encrypted comms, or any chatter for that matter. Dean seems to think that we could be safe here as long as we keep aware of our surroundings. I informed her that there is more than one way in and out of the complex. I will be giving her a full tour of Hotel 23 in the coming days. She is no novice with firearms and I feel that she could handle herself if need be. She is a tough old bird, a product of old-fashioned upbringing. She lost her husband to natural causes years before the undead walked. She is no stranger to death, just a stranger to death walking.

17 Jun

2106

GPS is gone. I'm sure the satellites are still up there, but without ground station intervention to regularly recalibrate them they cannot transmit properly and I cannot get a receiver lock. The internal DVD/GPS navigation system in the Land Rover is useless. Because of the loss of GPS, I was eager to test the SATphones. They worked fine. John and I went topside with them and I dialed the number imprinted on a barcode on the side of the phone

John was holding. It rang through and John did the same with the phone I was carrying. Although an excellent means of communication, they could not be considered reliable. The same goes for any communication that depends on complex third-party mechanisms. I have been sleeping in the environmental control room as I have given up my living quarters to Dean and Danny.

It is a little cooler in my new quarters. There are plenty of other compartments to choose from; I just like being somewhat close to everyone else. There is even a rather large compartment with lockers and folding cots. I am sure they are probably for civilian survivors that would encounter this place during and after a nuclear exchange. I just wish I had something useful and positive to accomplish, besides staying alive.

I pulled my wallet out of my personal belongings today and looked at my Armed Forces Identification Card. The man depicted on that card didn't look like me. Sure, it was my face, name and Social Security number, however . . . the eyes. They were different. The eyes in the photo didn't have the same gaze as those of the man I see in the mirror now. I will keep it. Keep it as a memento of what I once was; a cog in the wheel of something greater. It has been six months to the day since the first time I saw one of them eye-to-eye. They still have the same chilling effect. I am certain they always will.

20 Jun

2309

It is raining very hard right now. The weather is playing hell with the closed-circuit TV, causing static and loss of v-hold. The undead in this area are pretty spread out, but I can still make them out during an intense lightning flash. Still no joy on the radios. There is no one out there, or at least no one in our range. I have been flipping through the watchman's diary to pass the time during the storm. I sort of forgot about it due to the current events at Hotel 23.

I had gone to my old quarters last night to pick up the last of my personal effects when it resurfaced. Dean had packed my cardboard box for me and told me how nice I was for giving up my space for her and Danny. She told me that she had found my personal diary, but wouldn't dare take a peek. I explained to her that it wasn't mine and that it belonged to a person who was formerly posted here. I told her that I was keeping it for him. She understood and handed it to me, trying to figure out whether she had said something wrong.

I gave her a reassuring smile as I took the diary out of her hand, threw it into the box and started walking to my new quarters in the environmental control room. It wasn't until tonight that I reopened Captain Baker's personal log. January 10 was dogeared, as I had remembered reading it before. I turned the page, and began reading January 11.

January 11

As suspected, according the recently received message traffic, we will not be permitted to leave for quite some time. This facility will be more than adequate for extended habitability, but staying here underground really takes a mental toll on you. Unlike myself, he is married and I am not sure how long he will remain sane if this order to stay underground continues. He is constantly daydreaming and writing letters to his wife, letters that he cannot even mail until we are cleared topside by high command.

I have received official communications involving the situation in Asia. It is above the classification of this log and will not be included.

I know we will be secure down here no matter what and that is what is important to U.S. strategic deterrence.

The only other thing on this page was a freehand doodle of a missile flying through the air over what appears to be the United States.

23 Jun
2150

I have a splitting headache. Normally I force myself to drink enough water to remain hydrated, but today I just didn't get around to it. I have a dehydration headache and no matter how much water I drink at this point, it won't matter. It will just have to run its course. On the morning of the twenty-first, John, Will and I went out scouting. Instead of heading in the direction of the crucifixes, we went westerly, toward the small town of Hallettsville. We didn't take the Land Rover, as we wanted to remain quiet and avoid detection. For all we knew there were still bandits in the area.

We walked through fields and undeveloped farmland. It had been over six months since anyone was alive to maintain the land, so it wasn't a surprise when we stumbled upon them. We had jumped yet another fence into derelict farmland when we observed the sentinel symbols of United States greed and power. There was a large refinery field and the skeletal hulks of the large ground pumps were just sitting there, unmoving. Grass was overgrown all around them and it was obvious that they had been dead for months.

I suppose the bright side to the living population being annihilated is the fact that our oil reserves should last thousands of years longer. Of course, the downside is the fact that no one is alive who knows the art of refining the crude oil, hence making it as useless as a Hadron collider. John and I have long since discussed the need for technical manuals on everything from farming to medicine to things like refining crude. The information we require would be in countless abandoned libraries throughout the United States. However, getting to the information and getting it back to Hotel 23 could prove most fatal.

Passing the second large oil pump, I made yet another macabre discovery. I suppose when the world ended back in January the pumps were still running for a while. It looks like one of those bastards was crushed by the pendulum arm of the pump and its lower torso was caught in the machinery. I couldn't tell if it was still reanimated. I gave it no mind as I walked past. Obviously, birds had done their thing to this rotting monstrosity.

William had to force himself to look away from the creature as we passed. We kept on, seeing no signs of life. Our tactic was avoidance, as we had no suppressors or silent weapons to use. We would open fire only if our lives were in danger. We dodged three walking dead in the field before returning home. They were quite mobile, but still too slow to keep up. They would follow. However, I doubt they could ever make it over the many fences that separate our compound from this oil field. John and I have had further discussions about the need to gather some reference books, so we will be planning and executing this operation in the days to come.

Semper Fi

During our normal monitoring of the parking lot area of the compound, we noticed movement on the road beyond it. It looked much like an eight-wheeled USMC light armor reconnaissance vehicle. There was only one. It was moving at a high rate of speed, headed northeast relative to the compound. I wish I could have recorded the image so that I could maybe enhance it and catch a better glimpse of the gunner. My only conclusion would be that this is a scout and he/she was sent as a forward observer only to return and report the situation to the person in charge. I could be totally wrong and this could just be a rogue unit, running and gunning in the LAV across the country. I don't know much about these vehicles and I have only seen one once. They are amphibious and capable of taking some serious small-arms fire.

This could be one of the last remnants of the Marine Corps in this area. Who knows if they are still loyal to the cause? If I were, I would not be writing this.

Dean and I took the children topside to play a few hours after the LAV sighting. I told her of my plan to take John into an urban outskirt area for the purpose of retrieving some vital technical manuals. She seemed to think it a good idea. However, she told me that she had already known my plan. Tara had told her about it after talking to John. Tara seemed to think it was a crazy plan. She hadn't mentioned her feelings about me, but it seems that she is able to talk to Dean about anything. Dean just warned me that she might be upset that I choose to leave the safety of the compound for something as trivial as books. After seeing the military vehicle

37

go by earlier today, I am not certain what to do. I know we need specific medical manuals, as we have two children and an older lady at the compound. I am no doctor. Jan is the closest thing we have.

29 Jun

1913

It all began last night. It had started as simple radio garble. That night, it intensified. I could hear a frantic human voice, drowned out by automatic-weapons fire. Only bits and pieces were discernible. It stopped at nightfall. During John's watch that night, it began again. It was 2300. The weapons fire had lessened to a frequency and sound that reminded me of microwave popcorn in the waning phase of popping. The voice identified himself as Lance Corporal Ramirez of the 1st Battalion, 23rd Marines. He and his crew were broke dick and trapped inside their ride. He claimed to have six souls onboard. They had a mechanical malfunction and were stranded in a sea of undead. There was screaming in the background and I couldn't tell if someone had been injured or was just delirious. These Marines were most likely the same unit sighted yesterday speeding past our compound.

John called me into the control room at this point, and I made the decision to initiate communications with the Marines. I keyed the microphone and said in a calm cool voice:

"To the Marine unit transmitting a distress call . . . transmit your latitude and longitude, over."

After a few seconds of static, we received a reply:

"Unidentified station, we are in need of assistance and extraction. Please repeat your transmission . . . over."

I then repeated my request four times before the radio operator finally came back with the latitude and longitude of their position:

"Station calling, our position is believed to be N29-52, W097-02. Your transmissions are weak and nearly unreadable, two by five. We are out of crew-served weapon rounds and have closed the hatch on our vehicle. Situation is dire, please render assistance."

I really had no choice. I couldn't leave those Marines to die there. Those things couldn't get into the LAV, but the Marines couldn't get out either. I marked the position on the map and John, William and I began our hasty preparation. We left as soon as we could that night, to take advantage of the cover of darkness. I took one of the handheld shortwave HF radios, the M-16 with the M-203 launcher, my Glock and NVGs. I pointed out where we were going on the map and William suggested that we take one of the Geiger counters. I agreed. Before leaving, I asked John to help me cut the rank off of my shoulders. I couldn't risk these men finding out that I am or was military. We also grabbed several pillowcases in the event we had to bring them back here.

If I could land a plane at night with NVGs, I could definitely drive the Land Rover. The only problem that I found was the need to stick to the paved roads to avoid getting stuck. This vehicle was made for off-road use, but, unlike the LAV the Marines were trapped inside, it was not designed, if stuck, to repel hundreds of dead fists and bloody stumps.

We were out the door by 0030 hrs, and headed northwest to the rendezvous point. As I walked out of the compound, I reached over to my left shoulder and pulled off the Velcro American flag that I had worn on my uniform since the start of this. Once again, I couldn't risk being discovered and forced back to active duty for a futile cause or worse, sent to the brig. I made my bed when I decided to leave my unit and survive. I believe I'm the last one left. There was no way to defeat our foe. We had to wait them out. According to the chart, we had just over thirty miles of dangerous territory to cover.

Judging by the information they had given me, they were eight miles west of La Grange, Texas. Once again the map indicated this was a very small town. The Marines were less than a mile southwest of the Colorado River. The area they were in was technically deep inside the radiation zone and was also the closest I had been to a fallout area since rescuing the Grishams. I was apprehensive about this as I remembered transmissions from the Louisiana congressman last March. We could be going into the lion's mouth. We had lost the broadcast from Louisiana and I had often wondered what had happened there. Did the scouts that the congressman dispatched only draw a legion of radiated undead to their position?

We ran into no trouble until we arrived at I-10. Of course the interstate was a war zone, and tall grass had grown up between the east and westbound lanes. For all we knew there could have been an army of them behind the grass wall. All this projected a very surreal feeling, and made me realize how quickly things fall apart with no human intervention. Approaching the on ramp that would take us to 71 North we came upon a four-car pileup. There was no way to go around the wreckage, as a tall concrete wall had put the wreckage between a rock and a hard place. We were going to have to pull one of the cars out of the way with the Land Rover. We had removed the bulbs from the tail/brake lights a couple of weeks ago. With the headlights turned off, we would show no lights no matter how much I pressed the brakes. We also took the bulbs out of the blinker lights just in case one of us accidentally bumped the turn signal.

Of course . . . there was always human error. John and William got out of the vehicle to attach the chain to one of the wrecked cars. I could see through my NVGs that William was signaling me to back up. With the grainy green resolution I couldn't see beyond John and William into the darkness of the on ramp behind them. I shifted the transmission into reverse . . . instantly the light from the rear and side view mirrors induced whiteout in my goggles. In all our attention to detail, we had overlooked the bulb that illuminates when you put the vehicle in reverse. The light shone like a phoenix. Yanking the goggles off my head, I checked the mirrors again. Something was moving behind my friends.

I backed into position, quickly put the vehicle in neutral and put the parking brake on. I called out to John and William to drop the chain and get back in the vehicle. I was the only one who could see in the dark, so it was only logical that I be the one to face whatever it was that was moving in reaction to our light. While fumbling with the NVGs to get them back on, I could hear John and Will drop the chain. I heard their smacking footsteps and the sound of something more distant.

I stepped out of the vehicle and lightly shut the door, causing it to barely latch. Hoping for the familiar reflection of the living eyes of an animal through the NVGs, I stepped forward. Rounding the back of one of the wrecked vehicles was the corpse of some sort of builder or contractor. His leather tool belt still held a hammer in place. All the other tools must have fallen out. He wasn't badly decomposed. He could not see me and could not negotiate a path through the wreckage, so he just stood there, trying to sense where I was.

The former builder's hair wasn't long. He didn't have much facial hair. It was a common myth that when people die, their hair and nails continue to grow. This was not true. Upon death nothing grows . . .

Unless you count the undead hunger.

I wasn't sure, but judging by the tool belt, the short hair and the apparent clean shave, this man had been one of the first to go six months ago.

Aside from a large chunk of meat missing from his shoulder, he was very well preserved. As I got a closer look, I noticed some skin and hair stuck to the claw of his hammer. He likely had killed the creature that bit him with the tool now holstered on his belt. Since the creature was standing still and posed no immediate threat, I went back to the vehicle and grabbed the Geiger. I had spent some time reading the directions, as my recent new quarters was the environmental and equipment room of Hotel 23. I had learned all about the restrictions for the MCU-2P gasmask, as well as the limitations of the chemical, biological and radiological protective gear. I had even devoted a whole night to Geiger counter operations.

I turned the Geiger on and placed the ear bud in my ear. After giving it sufficient warm-up time, I used it on John. The Geiger indicated a normal RAD level. The static clicking sound in my ear was random. As I neared the vehicle wreckage the static picked up intensity. I was sure these vehicles had absorbed some radiation, being inside the zone. They were still within safe exposure levels, as long as I didn't sit in them for a prolonged period.

I reached over the wrecked hood of one of the cars to get a reading from the corpse. The sound in my ear sounded like that of an old dialup modem. This corpse was hot far beyond safe levels. Looking down at the meter, I saw that it read 400R. I definitely did not want a hug from this one. As I pulled my hand back over the hood, the corpse must have caught the smell, as it walked violently forward into the car, shaking it on its shocks. It was jerking erratically, unlike any corpse that I have seen so far. It moved laterally to the car and then I caught a glimpse of its feet. The creature's boots were nearly worn away; it had likely been walking on them for months without pause. The soles were gone and its maimed feet were visible under nothing but strips of leather and dangling bootlaces wrapped around its ankle.

The corpse was visibly excited, possibly by my presence. It moved back and forth like one of those toy robots. It would bump into a section of wreckage and turn and try another spot. If it kept doing this, eventually it would make it around the wreckage. I couldn't afford contact with this creature, as it was soaked with radiation. Picking up the chain, I kept a close eye on the robot corpse. I attached the chain around the axle of the vehicle I intended to move. I silently moved back to the Land Rover and got in. I told John and Will that we had a *hot* one outside. I planned to pull the car out of the way, unhook the chain and leave without dealing with the corpse. I put the vehicle in gear and slowly pulled forward. I felt the tension on the chain and heard it pop taut. I gave it some more gas and felt the car give way. I kept going for at least fifty yards before getting out and executing my plan.

Once out, I trained my eyes on the place where the car used to be. The thing was approaching. It was trying to run, but obviously lacked the coordination to do so. It fell, got back up, and kept coming. It had no idea where it was going but as luck would have it, the thing was headed right for the Land Rover. I immediately unhooked the chain, opened the back door and tossed it in without looking. I heard William curse as the fifty-pound chain hit his feet. Just as I got back into the vehicle and locked the doors, I heard the corpse bounce off the back window. I floored the Land Rover and turned it around, speeding through the hole I had just made in the wreckage. In my rearview mirror I could see the corpse attempting to give chase as it clumsily half-jogged behind, homing in on the sound of the vehicle.

I can't lie to myself. I thought for a brief second about canceling this mission and heading home. What could the three of us do against an army of poisoned dead? We were closer now. Will attempted to make contact via the radio. He keyed the microphone and called out. We heard nothing, but this radio set wasn't as powerful as the one at Hotel 23. They could still be alive. After imagining what it would be like to be them, I pushed the thought of mission abort out of my mind.

Only minutes after Will first tried the radio, they came back. Again, the lance corporal identified himself as well as his unit. I pulled the vehicle over and grabbed the radio from Will. I asked the corporal if he had an update to his coordinates and if he had any small arms inside the LAV. He replied that they were still at the previous position and they were all armed and had small-arms ammunition. However, there was no way to fire outside the vehicle accurately without the top hatch open. He also commented that they were out of ammo for the crew-served weapon and that was the reason they had to close the hatch. I asked how many undead were at his position. After a pause (it seemed he didn't want to tell me), he informed me that he was a Marine and couldn't count that high. I asked him, *"Hundreds, Corporal?"*

He replied, "Yes, sir."

Both John and William cursed loudly and shook their heads in apprehension of what was about to go down. It was about to get real.

We only needed I-10 for two miles. We exited north on 71 and sped toward the Marines. The only tactic we could possibly use is the one that I had executed with the Grishams and one that I had seen performed by the raiders. I had to try to herd them away from the broken-down vehicle. Maintaining radio contact, I tried to make some small talk to keep their minds off of the immediate surroundings. The corporal informed me that they had left the highway for the river because the sheer number of dead on the highway was overpowering them. Their vehicle experienced mechanical failure near the river. They were going to attempt to cross the river and escape the undead using the amphibious capability of the LAV. Initially it wasn't the corporal's beacon light that enabled me to find them, it was the overwhelming moans of the dead.

I told the men that I would attempt to lead the mass of them away with the noise of our vehicle and the horn. We established a rally point and I told the Marines to escape the LAV and evade to Highway 71 at the same spot they initially left the highway. They agreed. After saying a little prayer in my head, I asked John and Will if they were ready. Giving them no time to reply, I hit the gas and sped toward the moat of undead that surrounded the stranded Marines.

The ground was littered with corpses, victims of the LAV's crew-served weapon barrage. I was maybe one hundred meters from the moat when I rolled down my window and opened fire. John and Will were on reloading duty. The flash suppressor was helping keep my goggles relevant, but it was almost more advantageous to just use the muzzle flash without the gogs to see my targets as I was firing very rapidly at the dead.

I must have killed twenty of them before I had to relocate the vehicle another hundred yards down track. Will handed me a fresh magazine and I popped out the empty, handed it to John and quickly slapped another in the receiver. The dead were advancing quickly, as they were very attracted to my rifle muzzle flash and loud report. Like the undead builder we had avoided earlier, many of these corpses were coming at us in jerky, erratic movements. The way they approached was reminiscent of a line of police searching for a body. Ironically, the dead bodies were now searching for me.

I kept shooting them, kept moving the vehicle. John and Will kept reloading. After moving the vehicle for the fourth time and opening fire again, I could see movement on top of the LAV. I stopped firing for a moment to allow my eyes to adjust. The Marines were taking their opportunity for escape. Exactly as planned, they were moving as a squad toward the pick-up point. I emptied my sixth magazine on the mob and then handed the very hot weapon to Will. I honked my horn and led the dead just a little farther away from the Marines before speeding back for the pickup. The six Marines were in a defensive posture, weapons aimed outward into the darkness. They were in uniform, including flak jackets and Kevlar helmets.

I rolled down the window and told them to get in. Out of courtesy, I closed my eyes and turned on the dome light so they could see us. They jumped in the Land Rover. Three of them had to sit in the very back, but I'm sure they didn't mind. We sped off toward I-10 and then back toward the Hotel. Every Marine in the vehicle sincerely thanked each of us for their lives.

While driving back, I asked John to check them with the Geiger to see if they were fine. The meter indicated that they were giving off some ambient radiation from the mass of the dead, but it was insignificant. We really had no way to tell how much they had absorbed without their wearing dosimeters. We could only measure how many RADs they were now giving off.

Just before reaching the point where we had had to pull the car wreckage out of the way, I stopped the vehicle. I looked back and asked who was in charge. The lance corporal sounded off that he was in command of the others.

I commented that he was a pretty low rank to be in charge on a remote reconnaissance mission like this. He was coy in his remark: "Wait until you meet our commanding officer."

One of the others elbowed him to shut up. This was the moment I picked to lay down the law.

I stated, "Lance Corporal, I can take you to a safe place with water, food and a place to sleep, but you have to follow my rules. You will not be prisoners and you can leave when you want."

I could see him nod in the rearview in acknowledgment that he was ready to listen.

I said, "You are going to have to surrender your firearms and submit to wearing a hood over your head until we get inside our home and can sort things out."

Reluctantly, the Marine gave the order for the others to comply. John confiscated all the weapons and placed them in the front with us. William checked them for pistols. I told William to let them keep their knives. With six Marines wearing pillowcases over their heads, I sped off. Passing the point of the wreckage I saw no sign of the radioactive builder corpse.

It didn't take long to return to Hotel 23. As I approached the compound, the infrared lamps on the cameras shined brightly in our direction. The girls were watching us. We parked the vehicle and led the Marines through the fence and down the stairs into the large berthing area. I told them that they could take their hoods off. We took the magazines out of their weapons and gave the M-16s back to them, bolts locked to the rear. I told them that they could have their mags back when they decided to leave. It was late and I showed them where the cots and extra blankets were stored. I informed them that they were safe in an underground bunker and that they could sleep tight tonight and we would talk things over when they woke up.

Early this morning the lance corporal appeared at my door wanting to talk. He was reluctant to tell me where his unit was located, but he did say that there weren't many of them left. I told him that he was welcome to use our radios to contact his commanding officer. However, I would not allow them to know where this compound was located. I suggested to him that he should stay another day and get his thoughts straight and some food and water in him before making the decision to leave. I don't know the names of the other Marines, sans the last names embroidered on their uniform tapes. They are playing cards in the berthing area right now. I overheard one of them commenting on how nice this place is compared to base camp. I wonder just what is left of the military. Part of me wants to tell these men who I am.

01 Jul

2224

Corporal Ramirez and the five other U.S. Marines departed this morning. I sat and talked with the men for a few hours last night. They were all young men. Ramirez, Williams, Bourbonnais, Collins, Akers and Mull were their names. I didn't bother with first names, as I did not see the point. When asked about their commanding officer and base location, they declined to comment. Ramirez brought up the point that we didn't want them knowing the location of our stronghold, either. I agreed, as it was only fair.

I asked Ramirez about the government and if there was any form of it left. He told me that the last official government orders from the top were received in early February. Ramirez didn't think there was any formal civilian government left. He had heard rumors about the president's underground haven being infected from the inside. That would explain the First Lady's final transmission after the president's death.

I asked how a large unit like his could survive this long aboveground. The lance corporal just smirked and said, "We are Marines, we just do." I was trying to get a bead on the size of his force by the wording of that question. He knew it. He was young, but he was intelligent. At around 1030 this morning, the Marines, John and I departed in two vehicles. We put the hoods over the men and led them to the Land Rover. John followed in the Bronco. We drove in circles and did our best to deceive our passengers. I was almost certain that they were honest men, but I had no idea what type of commanding officer they had.

It didn't take long to get to the point that we agreed we would take them to, a point from which they knew they could find their way back home. When we arrived at the drop-off point, we took the pillowcases off their heads and gave them back their magazines. John left the Bronco running. We said our good-byes to the men and they all piled into the Bronco.

One of the youngest Marines rolled his window down and said, "Thanks for the hospitality, *sir*."

It was the way he emphasized the *sir*. I felt that he knew something. Perhaps it was just my paranoia and guilt kicking in. Following the young Marine's example, the other followed suit, and I could have sworn that Ramirez saluted me before stomping on the gas and heading off into the void of the undead badlands.

Klieg Light

It has been busy here at Hotel 23. The day after the Marines departed, we started picking up chatter on the UHF band. Then on the morning of the third we picked up a convoy of LAVs and Humvees going in the same direction Ramirez was headed days earlier, before we rescued them.

I don't know what to make of it except that they may have attempted to go and retrieve their abandoned vehicle, as it is quite valuable and irreplaceable in a world like this. On more than one occasion I had thought of attempting to retrieve it myself. This idea was shot down, as the vehicle weighs literally tons and it would have been impossible to fight my way in with the Land Rover, attach the chain and crawl in low gear back to the compound. The Marines could do it. From the looks of the military convoy, they had plenty of torque-abundant vehicles to make this happen.

The radios are still busy but the transmissions are not voice. It sounds like an old dial-up modem trying to connect. I am almost positive they are using encryption on the radio. I would, if I had it.

We keep seeing part of the previous convoy passing in front of the complex as if searching the area. I hope the Marines made it back to their base. One of two things can be deduced from what we are seeing. Either they are searching for their Marines or they are searching for us.

07 Jul
2038

Just received a radio transmission from the military. They are calling out to the civilians in the underground compound that rescued the Marines. At least we know they made it back. They say that the commanding officer requests a meeting with the man wearing green coveralls. We have not answered this transmission and I bet that they are just randomly transmitting every few miles to see if we will pick it up. I am very apprehensive about the intentions of the Marines, due to their understandably cryptic answers when I probed for information. I really don't know what we are up against here, but I am certain that sooner or later they will think to check the chain-link fence area that they have passed by so many times . . . Hotel 23.

11 Jul
2121

The military is still in this general area. From the information we have gathered from radio chatter on nonsecure lines, it is safe to assume that they have put up a forward camp in this vicinity to find us. They have recorded a message and have it playing on most frequencies, including the distress frequency. We all had a meeting a couple of days ago and decided it was best to stay out of the military's path and eyes. They could easily find us, and I am sure they could eventually get into the compound using the same tactic as the civilian marauders. They would simply blast their way in using high order explosives (in lieu of cutting torches).

The undead are slowly building numbers at the front blast doors again. A week ago there were only ten or fifteen. Now, scores of them cluster around the heavy steel doors around the front of the complex. We have been leaving off the IR mode of night vision at night to reduce the chances of the Marines' seeing our infrared camera beam on their own night vision devices. This has forced us to monitor living activity via thermal mode. This was the only thing that allowed us to see the small group of Marines pass within four hundred yards of our complex last night. They are getting closer, but for some reason have not stumbled upon the field of chain-link fence and open silo door that marked Hotel 23. Something in the back of my mind tells me that perhaps they know what this place is and that they could be just casing the area to determine weak spots to exploit.

Normally John only monitors a few HF channels at night. He cycles through them on a random schedule so that he can possibly catch a transmission that he normally would not. Last night, he did. It was severely garbled, but John swears he heard the words "Andrews Air Force Base." Andrews is very near D.C. I had assumed that D.C. had been nuked along with New York.

I don't know how much longer we will be able to hold out before the military finds us. I suppose they might give up, but I find that prospect unlikely. Another haunting thought is that they refuse to mention the commanding officer's name and rank in their recorded transmissions. Perhaps he wishes to be anonymous, as I do.

Siege

We have been discovered by what is left of the Marines in this area. Fifteen military vehicles are parked nearby and shots are again being fired outside Hotel 23 directed at the undead. They have made no attempts to disable our cameras, so we have been watching them carefully. Of the fifteen vehicles, six are LAVs. There are some military Hummers and even a four-wheeled ATV. I didn't count the ATV or the olive-drab dirt bike as part of the fifteen. They all appear to be in Marine issue digital camouflage, which tells me that some order still might exist within the unit. The radio has been playing the same loop. I cannot get an accurate head count on them, as the dead are amongst them attempting to converge.

The creatures that the Marines are dealing with outside are not the same as the one I had to avoid when on my last rescue mission. I have a feeling that if I were faced with an overwhelming army of the radiated dead, I would eventually fall to either their slightly faster mobility or their extreme radiation. The small numbers outside at this moment should not be a problem for the men dealing with them.

We can escape now (via the alternate exit) and leave Hotel 23 forever, never knowing if the military outside are our allies, or we can stay and fight or maybe attempt communication. We still maintain our radio silence and do not plan to break it unless absolutely necessary.

They are making no attempts to gain entry at this time and have made no gestures toward the cameras. The sun will be down in roughly two hours and if they plan to gain forced entry, I feel they will do it in the dead of night.

One thing is absolute . . . defeating foolish raiders with a lucky cheap shot is one thing, but going head to head with a couple of dozen well-armed U.S. Marines is quite another.

17 Jul

_2236_

Negotiations at first were civil, then turned to threats that in turn led to violence. They began with radio transmissions directed "at the ones in the bunker." Then came the explosives. They set the explosives but did not detonate them. They wanted to get in without resistance. After seeing block after block of explosives being carted down into the silo hole, I had no choice but to break radio silence with the Marines.

I keyed the microphone and said (to the best of my recollection):

"To the men trying to take this facility by force, please cease hostile actions or we will be forced to retaliate."

I thought for sure I would hear laughter on the radio, but they were professional.

"No one wants hostilities, we just want the complex. It is U.S. government property, and we have rightful claim to such properties, in accordance with applicable federal laws and executive orders. We ask that you allow us to gain access and no one will be harmed."

That was the moment when I wanted to laugh at _them_ on the radio. We were at a standoff. I had to speak to the person in command of this unit. I requested to do so and was met with evasive wording and lip service.

"The commanding officer is at headquarters and will not be present."

I asked for the person speaking to identify himself. He refused.

I asked, "On what real authority do you claim this compound?"

He replied, "On the authority of the chief of Naval Operations."

"Don't you mean the Commandant of the Marine Corps?"

At first there was silence, and then the tinny voice came back and said, "The commandant is missing in action. It is our best guess he is with his fellow cadre of the chairman of the Joint Chiefs at some *secure* location, along with most of the nation's leadership . . . dead."

"So you are under naval operational control at this time?"

"We are the Marine Corps, Department of the Navy." There was audible laughter at this point.

I didn't see any point in hiding that we were the ones who had saved Ramirez and his men.

These Marines probably knew that we were the same people, so I asked, "What about Ramirez and the other men that we saved from the disabled LAV?"

"They are fine and one of them is with us now. Ramirez is back at base camp on perimeter defense duty but wanted to pass something along face-to-face."

With as much sternness as I could muster on the radio, I yelled into the mic, "Let me speak to a commissioned officer now, Marine!"

"I can't do that."

"Why not?"

"We don't have any . . . er, I mean we don't have any *here*."

The Marine had slipped. I began to wonder who exactly was in command of these men. More banter went on until I finally convinced the Marine on the radio to put me on with the senior noncom present. Gunnery Sergeant Handley answered the call.

The Gunny bellowed, "Now listen down there, we need the complex as a forward command center, as there's still a little bit a' hope. A plan is being formed for the remnants of the U.S. military to attempt reclamation of the United States from the creatures."

I asked him how often they had communicated with the Chief of Naval Operations (CNO).

"We got regular but sunspotty HF comms with his carrier and they're still flyin' very maintenance-limited sorties off the boat doing airborne reconnaissance on the mainland in an attempt to give accurate intelligence to what's left of the men on the ground.

Hell, they've even dropped some iron a time or two for us when things got real bad."

I asked him, "So, I suppose much of the Navy has survived the plague?"

He replied, "A lotta ships turned into floatin' caskets in the beginnin'. Of the ten carriers in active service at the start a' all this, only four were not infested and overrun by the dead. You might also wanna know that there is a ballistic missile submarine that has been under for seven months. They're livin' off powdered eggs 'n' dried fruits 'n' meat. That boat is the last normal piece of the lifecycle. . . . People can still die in peace there and not come back."

I asked the gunnery sergeant what he meant by that.

He said, "The boomer sub was under before all of this happened, so somehow they're unaffected by whatever is causin' the dead to rise. They radioed in on the very low frequency band that they had suffered one natural death in the month of February but the corpse didn't rise. After a twenty-four-hour observation, their doc put the corpse in the freezer and had it restrained with riggin' web. The thing has been there since, motionless. Of course, they will have to surface sooner or later or they'll run outta food, but for now they are the last unaffected humans known to exist. All the other boomers and fast attack subs didn't hit the right time gate to avoid exposure. I guess we all have some form of this plague dormant inside us . . . waitin' on the day our heart stops beatin'. The whole thing's fucked up as a football bat."

Then came a chilling silence, interrupted only by the random report of 5.56 rounds being fired at the creatures.

"Sir, we don't wanna blow a big hole in your clubhouse and then take it from ya. Isn't there some sort of peaceful agreement we can come to? There are civilians at our compound that are happy to be there."

I replied, "We won't be happy there, Gunny, we aren't cattle. We have been surviving on the run since the beginning and much of it was before we found this place."

"That is impressive, but it doesn't change the fact that this complex falls under military jurisdiction."

"Gunny, you still haven't given me proof that you all aren't some rogue group of military survivors with no government leadership backing your actions."

"Sir, government guidance and hesitation are what brought us into the shithouse and to the point of extinction."

"Yes, Gunny, you may have a point. However, we found this place and we don't want to live under any iron fists, even if they belong to the U.S. military."

He just replied with a "very well" and then came more radio silence. This was the night of the sixteenth. Two hours after the last radio call they detonated their first charge in the silo. It had no effect save for a barely visible crack in the eight-inch-thick window glass of the blast door. Then another detonation, and another. The already damaged camera in the silo was disabled at this point, not even returning any variance of visible signal. The explosions were having no effect.

Thinking of this, I wondered if the civilian marauders had even had a chance at getting in with their cutting tools before I killed them. The alloy and fiberglass embedded concrete that made up Hotel 23 was very strong. I suppose it would need to be to withstand a nuclear blast. I felt an ever-so-slight sting of guilt at the possibly needless killing of the civilian raiders. Perhaps they would have given up when their torches turned out to be ineffective. Maybe I didn't have to see them as walking, burnt men. Rationalization tells me that they deserved it . . .

Every synapse ping of pain.

I snapped out of this thought at the sound of another explosion. I felt a slight pressure change. This change caused me to pinch my nose, close my mouth and blow to equalize the pressure between my ears. The explosion did not damage the structure of the complex, but it did vibrate the alloy enough to induce a quick change in pressure inside. Jan and Tara were very upset at the thought of being captured and taken to a military-controlled camp. For all they knew at this moment, they would be used as breeding vessels; I would never let that happen. The explosions weren't making anything better. Laura was crying and Annabelle yelped in fear and stuck her tail between her legs every time another went off. After thirty minutes of this, the explosions ceased. They must have been fresh out of plastique.

The radio once again crackled.

"Had 'nuff yet? Why not just open the doors and come out peacefully? You will not be harmed."

I asked the gunnery sergeant to give us until sunrise to pack our things before we opened the door. He bought it.

I gathered the adults and we began brainstorming on what cards we could possibly play in this scenario. Options were limited. We could go on the run again and try to find another defensible location, but nothing would compare to Hotel 23. It would take us years to build anything as durable and safe.

Jan suggested we take off in the aircraft. I explained to them that the Cessna could not possibly hold us all, let alone our gear, and that that option was out. Besides, the aircraft was not in excellent condition; the brake on one side was out. It was midnight and we had six good hours to come up with something. I turned to John, who would normally have an "outside the box" answer to give me. He claimed that there was no logical answer.

I was not sure that they knew the alternate exit existed, but there were vehicles parked in that area near the fence. They probably knew about it. The front door was a decent option, but there was a growing group of undead there, still banging on the door. The other option was to trust the Marines. If they kept their word, they would simply let us go after they seized the compound.

I had no desire to be on the run again with an older lady, two small children and a dog. We would be dead before the month ended at the claws and maws of those things. I just didn't know what to do. I sat in my living quarters pondering on any possible solution to our conundrum. If only I had possessed some sort of leverage.

I hadn't put my belongings away since I let Dean have my other living area. A small box of what I had was still sitting in the corner of the room, waiting for the day I got tired of looking at it. Now it seemed that day would never come. I stared at the box for a few minutes, thinking of how we were going to transport all of our gear with us cross-country and survive. Walking over to the box I began to inventory its contents. Two extra flight suits, gloves, kneeboard for flying, Glock 17 handgun, three small family pictures, six boxes of 9mm ammunition and my Velcro name patch with, of course, my name, rank and wings embroidered into the fabric. I hadn't worn this patch since civilization fell. What was the need? Finally, I pulled my wallet out of the box . . .

Looking inside my wallet, I found numerous cards. I was an NRA member back when it existed. It wasn't that long ago. I also had a card for what seemed like every video rental chain. Would I be exempt from the late fees if society ever rebuilt itself? I am sure the server that housed my felonious late fees data would long be rusted by the time the power grid was restored. If ever.

Then came something that changed everything. Last month I had remembered looking at my military identification card with a feeling of nostalgia. It was two years until it expired. I stood there looking at it, running my thumb across the microchip embedded in the front. My data was on that chip, along with the data that was embedded in the barcode on the right side of the card. Again there was my photo. A clean-shaven, naive version of myself who would have never thought the dead would walk.

If these men were still U.S. Marines, following the Uniform Code of Military Justice, then I was still a commissioned officer and still their superior. If anyone still followed the rank structure of the military, it would be a Marine. In all my limited encounters with the Marine enlisted men in my military past, they had always stood up to address me when I spoke to them. The gunnery sergeant had said himself that there was no officer available topside and that he was the senior man present.

He was lying and didn't know it.

I was, in theory, the senior man present.

As I stood there with my back to the door, staring at the card in my hands, I saw Dean reach over and take the ID card and look at it. She carefully examined the military ID and looked at me.

She said, "Looks a lot like you, sailor."

I smiled back at her and said, "Yes, it used to be me."

She replied, "It's still you, it's just that you lost your military bearing and it looks like you need to shave!"

I thought for a moment that she could be right. I had done some bad things since January, but that didn't change the fact that there were military units still active and I was still a military officer. My unit was destroyed, probably with no survivors. I knew this; I had flown over my base and seen it with my own eyes. The base had been overrun, then later nuked. Game over. For all I knew, I was the only one left.

I called the group together and discussed what I planned to do. They all gasped at the thought but eventually agreed that it was the only real way to handle the situation.

It was 0500 hrs this morning before I woke up and switched on the lights. I took my shower kit and began the laborious task of getting myself together. As I passed my old quarters, the door swung open and Dean stepped out with a pair of scissors from the control center office.

"Can't have you going topside without a haircut."

I laughed and made sure my towel wouldn't fall off in front of her.

"I suppose not, Dean."

She had cut Danny's hair when he needed it, and she made sure to tell me that he had never complained. My hair had grown long and far out of military regulation in the past months. I had shaved it off three months ago, but I had not touched it since and it was rather long. It was unlike me to let it get this way. The end of the civilized world was a decent excuse, I thought, but Dean wouldn't have it. Like a master barber, she restored my head to unwritten aviation officer regulations (just a little longer than that of the enlisted men).

As I finished up in the shower and hacked my thick stubble off, I looked in the mirror. I looked presentable for what I was about to do. I had no dress uniform or officer's sword, but I would make do. With my towel wrapped around me I walked my way back to my quarters. Outside my door were my boots, shined to perfection with a note in child's writing: "I hope you like I shined my dad's boots before—Danny."

He must have come in and retrieved them while I slept. I leave the door open so that I can hear if anything is going on in the walkway. I must be losing my edge, or he must be a very quiet kid.

I thought back to when I had seen Danny urinating on the undead at the tower. What a funny sight.

I put on my clean flight suit, with rank on my shoulders and name patch on my chest. I pulled my garrison cap out of the leg pocket where it had been for six months and put it on my head. I walked out of my quarters in uniform, prepared to meet the Marines. It was 0550 hrs and I could see on the cameras that the sun was coming up, making the clouds to the east shine with an ominous orange tint.

I keyed the radio. "Gunny, are you there? . . . over . . ."

After a short pause, a tired, haggard and perturbed voice came back, "Yes, I am here, and I have been here all damn night."

"Good, now clear your men away from the silo opening, I am coming up."

"We'll be waiting on you at the top . . . out."

Armed only with a sidearm, I went to the access hatch that led directly into the silo. John and Will covered me with their weapons. It took three of us to spin the wheel and open the hatch, as all the heat and explosions had expanded and contracted the alloy. As soon as the hatch opened, a flood of light shone down from above and dust billowed in. John and Will quickly dogged the hatch. I hadn't seen the inside of the silo close up for quite a while. There were bits of burnt bone and clothing all over the bottom. Lots of teeth were scattered on the deck. There must have been quite a few creatures down here when the marauders started burning them. The walls were blackened from all the explosives that had been detonated during the past twenty-four hours.

The men at the top could not yet see me, as I was near the bulkhead at the bottom. With cold anticipation I stepped into the light and began climbing up the ladder to the top. The ladder was covered in ash. I kept climbing. The sound of "Holy shit!" signified that I had been sighted. I kept climbing until I reached the top. The gloved hand of a USMC gunnery sergeant reached out to help me over the lip of the silo doors. I stood there and looked him in the eye. He squared off in front of me and rendered a sharp salute. I returned it with the same bearing and he dropped his. He immediately led me to his tent and a handful of staff sergeants followed.

"Sir, we had no idea, I . . .

"No need for that, Gunny, you didn't know I was an officer and I wasn't going to tell you until I had to."

A question-and-answer session followed, and I told him my story from day one. I left out the part about my XO ordering me to report to the base shelter. I told him that I was probably the last surviving member of my squadron and that I had been surviving and picking up others when I could. It was then that he ordered the staff sergeants to leave the tent.

He leaned in close to me and with a very quiet and nervous whisper said, "Sir, I have not seen an officer for months. All of our ground-pounder brass was ordered to an undisclosed location months ago and we have not seen nor communicated with them since. Basically, they left us to die in the open out here. I have been tellin' the men that the commanding officer was alive and issuing orders directly to me via secure radio. It is not really lying, considerin' I have been receiving orders from an Admiral Goettleman, onboard the flagship USS *George Washington*. They are starting to doubt my word. I had to keep the men's morale up. How would they fight or even work as a team knowing their unit's superior officers left them in the open to die and were probably dead themselves?"

We both sat there. I pondered what this implied. My concentration was broken intermittently by gunfire as the men fended off the undead.

"What are you telling me, Gunny?"

"Sir, I'm telling you that you are the first officer I have seen in a long time, and we need you, if only as a mouthpiece leader for the men. Leader or not, I just need you to play the part or this whole thing is going to unravel quick-like and blow up in everyone's face."

"Gunny, in that case, this place, Hotel 23, will be *my* command. You will need to stay and send most of your men back, along with your most trusted staff sergeant." He agreed. I told him that I would address the men while he decided who stayed and who didn't.

Over the next half hour, I stood on an ammunition crate and watched the faces of the young patriots who looked on and listened.

"I am the commanding officer of this stronghold, and I need a few good men."

This was met with aggressive applause.

"About six and a half months ago, something really rocked our world. Now no one really knows what it was that happened, but it doesn't really matter what it is."

I didn't think I sounded that great, but the men disagreed with their whistles and clapping.

"The way I see it, we may run out of rounds, but we still have sharp sticks! It may take a long time, but we won't give up. We're going to save as many as we can and we are going to put the hurt on those *things*.

"I want you men to never forget that you are in the United States military. I don't want to hear any talk of there not being a United States. That is nonsense. Our Constitution may be sitting there in D.C. just fine or it may be burned up, but that doesn't mean it's dead like those things out there. We will still support and defend till the end."

This was met with cheers and claps and also led to a crowd of men gathering around the Gunny, volunteering to stay here at Hotel 23. The sun was now rising over the tree line on this summer morning. My simple address was over and I could already see a visible boost in their morale. The compound was buzzing with purpose.

The Gunny said, "One more thing, sir. Ramirez wanted me to give you this."

He handed me a fixed-blade knife with a heavy-duty leather sheath. The sheath had a small pocket containing a sharpening stone. I pulled the knife from the sheath and noticed that it was a very high-quality combat knife with a black micarta handle. The knife appeared to be stainless steel and had the words "Randall Made Orlando FL" stamped into the blade near the handle on one side. I laughed as I thought to myself, "They don't make 'em like this anymore." Hell they don't make anything anymore.

After all was said and done, three LAVs and a covered supply truck stayed here along with twenty-two men, including the Gunny. We were topside when the staff sergeant and his convoy left for base camp with the news that they had found an officer to help with the cause. Two military radios, loaded with crypto key-mat code from KYK-13s (small cryptographic storage units), were taken down into the compound and set up in the command center. The Marines quickly set up their berthing below.

Most of the afternoon was spent returning Hotel 23 to an operational military combined operations center.

C4I

18 Jul
1605

We have established communications with the USS *George Washington*. The acting Chief of Naval Operations is currently away from the carrier on one of the small boys planning with one of his commodores. I am certain there will be more to come in the following days. I'm told they are sending someone out to reprogram my common access card (CAC) chip on my military identification card in the next anticipated supply run, but I'm not sure what good that will do or why it matters to me here.

22 Jul
1720

I have opened a Pandora's box. I now have more responsibility than I know what to do with. The twenty-two new Marines have been busy militarizing the perimeter and standing security watches. I now have a full-time radio operator with direct links to the carrier strike group. Message traffic has been heavy with updates to the status of the Gulf and eastern coastlines. Even daily threat assessments are being received indicating large undead swarm movements in some areas. I was curious about how the carrier was getting food for the three thousand plus skeleton crew they were running. One of the young Marines told me that they had units of Navy strike teams stationed onboard supply vessels and they used these teams to infiltrate and exfiltrate, via zodiac boats, the government coastal supply centers to identify good targets so that the larger cargo choppers can get in and air-lift the food.

I listened to the battle group radios for a few hours today, monitoring Navy and Air Force aviation communications, in particular voice traffic from a U-2 reconnaissance aircraft flying over the eastern seaboard. I was curious to know how they were able to keep the DRAGON LADY airborne with the hefty maintenance and long airfield requirements.

Apparently the U.S. Army didn't fare very well, and according to a report received day before last, they have suffered a loss of over 70 percent of ground troops in CONUS. There just wasn't enough room for them on the ships. The sailors and Marines took priority and the U.S. Army units were left to defend themselves inland. They were given advance warning of the nuclear strike, but many of them were overcome by the radiated undead that were pouring out of the radiation zones after the strike.

Some of the voice communications I was monitoring indicated that there were still search teams out surveying the ground for military survivors. One particular communiqué received was from a surveillance aircraft flying over the Virginias, in search of a lost tank convoy. Apparently the convoy met its demise after one of the lead tanks crushed an overpass under its massive weight. The structure of the ill-repaired overpass gave way and took four tanks with it. The convoy was being pursued by thousands of "hot" un-dead, and it only took a couple of hours before the swarm caught up with them. Three tanks were disabled in the fall from the overpass and their occupants were left to die in metal tombs with countless bodies pounding on the heavy armor and squirming over the turrets and tracks like maggots over roadkill.

The remaining tanks scattered to the winds and got the hell out. Location unknown.

The crew in the back of the aircraft commented on the radio that the occupants of the disabled tanks might already be exposed to high levels of radiation due to the sheer number of dead below. The aircraft sensors indicated that the horde was emitting deadly amounts at ground level. After surveying the situation, the aircraft headed back to base, reporting that they were on *bingo* (emergency) fuel.

One thing is for sure, the number of new inhabitants here will force us out soon to find a water tanker to fill Hotel 23's tanks back up to maximum capacity. Hitting the tank with my rifle today revealed that the level is down to the bottom eighth. We are already rationing water and have set up numerous rain catches around the compound to help fill the critical need.

A technician showed up at the command center after flying in today to reprogram my identification card. There is a chip embedded in the card. The technician inserted my card into a reader/writer connected to a laptop and instructed me to enter a pin number at least six digits long. I thought of a number that I knew I'd never forget and entered it into the terminal. The technician informed me that I would have full control over all sensitive systems at the compound by using my card and pin at the computer terminals in the command center. He warned that I am the only person that would have this access until I was relieved. I asked him why this mattered and he stated that he didn't know but that his instructions from headquarters were to give the ranking officer at the compound this access. The only way to designate another person would be for my card to be used in the command center to give permission for the transfer of authority to another officer designated by higher authority. If my card or pin number were to be lost or destroyed it would take ninety days to reprogram another, as the system has a time-lock fail-safe to avoid the unauthorized transfer of power.

The technician said nonchalantly as he walked out the door, "Too bad you are empty, this authorization would have given you nuke launch authority. Although *I* wouldn't want it."

26 Jul
1422

I cannot be certain that having men topside standing watch is a good idea. The men are firing fifty rounds per twenty-four-hour period and I feel this may be a cycle of waste and danger. Last night I ordered them inside to see if not having them up there would lessen the undead activity in the area. It seemed to work better. This morning, there were ten undead at the fence. Killing ten is better than shooting fifty. The men are using bayonets to dispatch the undead at the fence, then dragging them near the tree line fifty yards off using ATVs and webbing that they wrap around the corpses' chests so that they avoid any chance of getting scraped inadvertently by the inanimate body.

Communication from the aircraft carrier has been sporadic, as our ground unit is an insignificant speck compared to what the rest of the military is dealing with. Andrews and D.C. apparently were not hit (according to message traffic), and there is currently a team of scouts on the ground surveying what it would need to retake the District of Columbia. Another option discussed is moving the capital out west, but little is known about that region of the country. Communication with the other Marines is constant and steady, with the noncommissioned officer in charge checking in every hour on the hour.

I have made it clear to the Gunny that having the other men and civilians closer to our position may not be a bad idea. I tried to connect to the internet backbone again today. Down. This would have been an excellent means of long-range communications with other countries and units, since our main enemy cannot read or use a computer.

The water supply is getting dangerously low and a team is being assembled and briefed for deployment tomorrow in the A.M. I will be accompanying.

30 Jul
1934

Our small unit left in search of water on the morning of the twenty-seventh. John was the temporary appointed civilian leader holding down the law at Hotel 23. He promised he would take care of our folks while we went looking for the H$_2$O. Our path took us north, lateral to the radiation zone outskirts. We took three LAVs and thirteen men. Our goal was simple; we were headed toward the interstate to find a water truck or any truck that could hold water. Hotel 23's tanks were nearly dry and it was going to take ten thousand gallons to fill the reservoir up to capacity. I was informed of the location of the original Marine base camp days ago. Our journey took us within forty miles of their location. Forty miles equaled eighty miles round trip, so a visit was out of the question for now.

After an hour of pulling wreckage out of the way and dodging pileups, our LAV convoy finally made it to what remained of Interstate 100. This stopped being fun before it started. I hate doing this with the white-hot intensity of a thousand suns. I could see a group of them walking about, weaving in and around the abandoned cars. They were four hundred yards off, and if I imagined and concentrated, I could make myself believe for a few minutes that they were not dead. Soon our scent (could they really smell?) would be carried on the wind to them and they would start the slow but determined march toward the living.

It seemed like a balancing act. I sometimes think of the living and the dead as chromosomes, only the dead are the dominant chromosomes. No matter what, all you get in this world are brown-eyed babies. They are dominant if numbers dictate. In this day and time they seem to do just that.

Dean really wanted to come along with us. She could probably handle herself, but I quickly made up another important task for her to accomplish so I didn't have to tell her it wasn't a good idea. Tara and I are probably considered an item now. I suppose I knew it was coming. That is in itself another story. Perhaps I will write about it someday. Jan, Will, John and Tara are showing the Marines at Hotel 23 the basic operation of the facility as well as the escape routes in the event of the worst-case scenario.

I was thinking of Tara as we closed on the interstate . . . I was two hundred yards out when I saw a surrounded vehicle. Reminded me of her. I truly thought she was dead back at the dock that day we found her. We advanced closer and I had to see what was in the car. I could tell the window was cracked on the side visible to our convoy by the undead arms that were reaching in, only to be stopped at the elbow by the partially opened window.

One LAV ran interference and drew the group away from the car so that we could have a look inside. Of course, it worked. The radiation measurement equipment onboard indicated that this area was nearly free of radiation. Some residual radiation remained and would for hundreds of years if no cleanup was done. We were closer to the car now. The men covered us as myself and two other Marines jumped off the vehicle and headed for the car.

I was pleased to find a mother bird and her chirping babies safely nestled in the backseat of the vehicle. I was sure that those creatures were making it extremely difficult for the mother to leave and find food, but she seemed to be doing all right. I thought of rolling the windows up just a little more to make it more difficult for the creatures but much to my disappointment the windows were electric and the battery long dead. Looked like I was leaving this one up to *unnatural* selection.

We radioed the herding LAV to rally with us one mile east of original position. The highway was thick with undead, but a strange sense of security came with riding in these capable vehicles. We had plenty of weapons and ammunition, as it would be dangerous not to. We searched east along the interstate until we were perilously close to the outskirts of Houston. Houston was not hit in the offensive months ago and it most assuredly had an abundance of undead at its core. We had found numerous eighteen-wheeler trucks with fuel trailers probably full of gasoline. It was too bad we couldn't drink fuel. Reminded me of the real world, before all of this, when a bottle of water was much more expensive than its equivalent in gas. Either way, we did find a truck that held a lot of water and it made me feel a little ignorant for not thinking of it before.

I don't know why we didn't just seek out a small-town fire department rather than risking our asses on the interstate. I didn't let on I was thinking this in front of the men, but it would have been much safer the other way. Sitting in front of us was a nice (dirty) fire truck marked "San Felipe Fire Dept." It was a large truck, but not the largest I had seen. We attempted to start the truck. No joy. It turned out to be a difficult task to turn the vehicle around and get it hooked up to one of the LAVs, a task that has aged me a few years.

Continued soon//

• • •

The fire truck was a tomb. Inside were two dead firemen, who actually were dead and not moving. I was not close enough yet to know how they took their own lives and avoided reanimation, but it seemed they succeeded. The interstate was thick with them but they were not the ultra-deadly variety of undead that would have been found nearer the radiated zone west of this position. The only other option besides towing the vehicle would be to attempt to trickle-charge the battery from the equipment onboard the LAVs. First we needed to quietly clear out the immediate danger in the area. From my perch on the crew-served weapon of number two LAV, I counted thirty-eight undead. I radioed Gunny and he claimed to count thirty-nine.

When we left Hotel 23 the Marines had regular M-4 and M-16 carbines not unlike what the Hotel armory held when we first opened it months before. I knew that this was not a unit composed of all original members.

The Gunny had relayed to me in the first days of their arrival that the unit was made up of surviving Marines of several units that followed radio signals and ended up in Texas. Of course, not all of them found the surviving military cell in this way, as many times when the core of the unit went out to find supplies they found survivors. Many times the survivors were military or former military. This explained the weapons that the Marines in LAV number one pulled out of the vehicle. Four Marines that I had previously remembered having dive bubbles and jump wings on their chest pulled out suppressed H&K MP5s. I would have loved to have even one of these weapons in the first months of the end of the world.

I held my fist up in the sign to hold fire while I radioed the Gunny. I asked him how many suppressed weapons the unit had. He told me that the recon Marines had raided their local armory before they had bugged out and took all the suppressed weapons that they could, likely in preparation for a quiet guerilla campaign.

I radioed LAV number one (point) and gave the men permission to fire suppressed rounds at the undead surrounding the fire truck. I hadn't even finished my radio call when I started hearing the eerie sounds of the action of suppressed submachine guns. One by one the undead fell. Many times the Marines missed. During the shooting the Gunny read my thoughts and informed me that these suppressed 9mm weapons were not nearly as accurate as the M-16 but they *were* quiet and didn't draw unwanted attention.

The sound was very nearly the same as if you were to pull the charging handle on a regular M-16 quickly, in succession. A barely audible popping sound was heard. It took four minutes to clear the area around the fire truck. We parked the LAVs around the truck, and we all got out. The Marines had restowed the suppressed weapons, as firing them too much would render the suppression ineffective in the long term (according to them). Eight men set up a defensive perimeter in the LAV gaps. I approached the fire truck and reached up to open the door. It was locked. Same story, the pus marks of dead arms were present on the doors of both sides, indicating that the dead firemen inside had held out in the abandoned truck until they had apparently taken their own lives.

Using a large wrench taken from one of the vehicle's tool bags and some hundred-mile-an-hour duct tape, I quietly broke the glass so that I could open the driver's-side door. I reached in to unfasten the door lock and was grabbed on the wrist by one of the firemen. I tried my best to pull my hand back through the broken opening. The thing almost had his mouth on my wrist when a Marine opened fire and shattered the creature's head. Both of us had thought the firemen were dead. The loud noise must have awoken the creature from some sort of undead hibernation.

The passenger-side fireman inside really was dead, as most of his upper body and head were gone, probably rotting in the other creature's throat and stomach. After opening the door and pulling the driver's-side ghoul to the ground, I nudged the passenger with the barrel of my rifle. No movement. He still clutched a blood-stained axe.

The advantage of having a unit of variously skilled and capable military men became apparent when I realized that I knew nothing of large-engine vehicles. One of the Marine mechanics went to work, popping the engine compartment, checking the salvage potential. Low on oil, dead battery and no fuel was the prognosis. The fuel was no problem. We used some of our LAV reserves to partly fill the tank. The oil would have to wait as neither I nor the mechanic knew what oil we needed without taking the time to read the manual. That was not an option now, as I could hear the perimeter guards shooting a small group of dead that had been drawn here by the sound of the fireman's execution.

The last thing to handle was the battery charge. The Marine was not certain of the battery's condition, sitting out in the elements unchecked for six months. We attempted to charge the battery. A waiting game began. It would take thirty minutes to charge the large battery enough to turn the stagnant engine over. In the meantime, we all stood defensive duty, sans the mech working on the fire truck. He was also charged with setting up the towing chains needed in the event the battery would not charge. Shot after shot. There was a virtually unlimited supply of undead. The city was in view on the horizon, smoke still spiraling up to the sky from fires left unopposed. I wondered which one this fire truck was meant for. Probably one long burned out. Another shot . . . then another . . .

They were coming . . . thicker, heavier . . . faster. Just ten more minutes . . . The sound was droning ever louder. Moans on the wind and intermittent sounds of metal banging or falling in the distance, those things tripping over road debris. Looking back over my shoulder I could see the mech attaching the chains to the underbelly of the rig. He didn't run the other end to the waiting LAV. He simply wrapped the length of chain around the hooks that were welded to the front bumper of the fire truck. Then came the sound of the engine sputtering and turning over. It worked. The engine turned and brought a new noise variable to the problem. Looking back, I saw smoke rise from the exhaust pipes; the huge red behemoth was waking up, waking up to a world very different from what it had known before.

The mechanic was grinning. I shot him an approving look and told the men to return to their vehicles. I sprinted to LAV number two, waving the men past me, and then I jumped in, screaming, *"Last man!"*

I could not be sure about the mechanical reliability of the fire truck. I radioed the mechanic to take the third position in the convoy. LAV one, two (I was in two), then the fire truck and last, LAV three made up the formation. I didn't want the large truck to break down, entombing another poor soul. I know the truck was probably fine and had just run out of fuel sitting in gridlock on the interstate. The poor firemen were surrounded with no way out. The rest is pure speculation.

We were on the move, headed for H23. Along our route, the Gunny and I took note of the numerous fuel tanker rigs by marking them on our maps. We would eventually need a lot of diesel fuel. That would be for another day. I don't think the power drain is affected by the recent population boost back home. The generators only run a few hours per day to power the batteries for the lighting, air, water circulation and limited cooking that is done. We have been surviving on MREs and limited dried goods since the beginning and they are getting old, but I know these Marines have probably eaten them longer in *normal* peacetime conditions.

We made it to the same point at which we first encountered the interstate. The sun was getting low, and that was a catalyst for something bad to happen. It did. The fire truck died. I sent two men from my LAV to attach the chain to our towing point. This vehicle had no problem in the torque department. I was sure one of the younger Marines probably knew every nut and bolt of this machine, but I only knew one thing . . . It was tough.

The large steel chain jerked and popped every time the tension did not balance the weight of the massive emergency vehicle towed behind. I felt our vehicle surge and the independent gearing kick in, dispersing the traction to the wheel that needed it. The undead were here in force. I could not count to five without hearing our vehicle impact one of them with a commanding *THUD*.

Looking through the thick armored glass window I observed them bouncing off the vehicle, some of them thrown nearly twenty feet into the overgrown ditches along the road. We were only half an hour out from H23 when I radioed the mech, asking him to check the water gauge on the truck. The mech couldn't read the gauge, as the water control panel had no power. I hoped that the truck at least had enough water to last us until we could repair the truck and find another water source. I was certain that the compound's water would run out any time, if it hadn't already.

Using the night vision capability of the LAV, I was able to pick up H23's camera beacons. We were on course and tracking. We made it back home with the truck in tow. The fire truck had a five-thousand-gallon capacity, and was one-quarter full. This would be enough to last us until we could find another water source. With the medical kits we have at H23 as well as the kits the Marines have, we should be able to purify the water using iodine. It would be wise to kick in a few suburban doors and grab some household bleach at some point.

Messages are constantly coming in from headquarters, most of them only for our information and not calling for action. I have had to send in one status report concerning Austin, Texas. The brass on the carrier needed the data to update their all-important status boards. I have a feeling we could soon be sent into a radiated area for the same type of *status* information. I suppose I will cross that bridge when it falls out from under me.

Cutter

I was inside Hotel 23. Trapped. The dead Marines outside were pounding on the door to the environmental control room. Sliding the steel peephole to the side, I could see her . . . Tara was there, bloody, dead, wanting. John was behind her pawing at the door. I couldn't remember how I had gotten here; I only knew that I *was* here. Surrounding the familiar faces were the Marines. Many of them were riddled with fatal bullet holes. My radio operator was there also. He still had his headset strapped to his head . . . then . . . he talked. The dead radioman talked! He said . . . "Sir, wake up . . . I have some important information for you."

I am not certain of the nature of the message that arrived last night while I was sleeping. I woke up to the sound of the radioman tapping on my door. The message stated that we were to deploy to the coastline to help out a wrecked Coast Guard cutter. They were in no immediate danger and were anchored off the coast of Texas, only eighty miles up the coast from where the *Bahama Mama* probably still rested on the shore. After I had read the message and discussed its contents with the Gunny, we decided it would be best to leave tonight.

Shaken from the dream, I told Tara what I had seen in my vision. She was more than a friend and I felt I could tell her anything. Also, Dean was a rock. Her wisdom helped me deal with the demons that racked my soul more often than not these days.

The feeling was similar to coming off a long vacation to find that work had piled up in my absence. As I write this, my third in command is charting our course overland to rendezvous with the cutter that is dead in the water. In any other situation we would have departed already, but since the men onboard were relatively safe, we were taking the time in planning and provisioning to ensure a safer trip.

I would like to keep this excursion to a maximum of forty-eight hours. There is still much that needs to be done with merging the two camps. Hotel 23 cannot accommodate all the people, but I feel that with the right heavy equipment and some concrete dividers taken from the interstate, we could form a large wall around the perimeter outside the chain link fence. It could take months to gather the needed barriers but it might be worth it.

On another note, Danny hurt himself today playing with Laura outside. They were chasing Annabelle and Danny tripped in a small hole in the ground, spraining his left ankle. They are getting to go topside more these days, but the Marines are under strict orders to ensure their safety whenever they are aboveground. I have already packed my equipment into LAV number two. I have affectionately (and secretly) named this LAV "bumble bee tuna." I don't know why, it just fits for some odd reason.

It is very hot outside today and we will be bringing some extra water along with us in order to stay hydrated and alive. I know our water situation is not as good as it should be and neither is our fuel situation. This is a problem that will need to be resolved between official duties. In a way, I am happy that Hotel 23 is a small drop in the strategic command bucket. I am taking the same Marines with me on this mission. I didn't notice any huge screw-ups from any of them on the last mission, so I don't see the need to fix something that isn't broken on a mission with such short notice. Perhaps I will mix them up on the next mission, if there is one.

11 Aug

_2228_

The departure from Hotel 23 was uneventful. It was very humid outside and it felt as if we were entering a sauna when we opened the hatch leading topside from the compound. The vehicles were already fueled up and ready for departure.

The roads were in severe need of maintenance that would never be given. The concrete was cracked and I hadn't seen roads this bad since my overseas duty in Asia.

We continued east to the coastline until we came across what used to be a major roadway. Now it more closely resembled a field with wrecked cars lined up pointing east. It wasn't what I was used to seeing. The rusting hulks were the only indication of the direction and curve of the road.

We crept along beside the wrecks in the general direction of the road, making sure to keep a safe distance from them to avoid any problems. The undead were not intelligent and this was not a known radiation zone, but the rolling hills of Texas could hide them easily in the troughs between here and our destination.

Another thing in the back of my mind was the difference in the big picture. In the old world, there were only a handful of animals that could deliver a fatal bite, such as some breeds of snake. Now the pendulum of deadly creatures to vulnerable humans has swung toward cataclysm. At least with a deadly viper one might have a possibility of survival. From the stories I am hearing from the Marines, these creatures that haunt the world have no antidote. The Gunny claims to have seen hundreds of men, strong men, who succumbed within thirty-six hours of being bitten or scratched. There is even a documented case of a few victims' being infected by the accidental transfusion of saliva to open wounds.

Something still haunts me about them. Where do they get their energy? They seem to have unlimited supplies of energy in death. I secretly hope that someone or some think-tank is working to assess the strengths and weaknesses of these things, which most likely outnumber us by millions in the U.S. and billions abroad. These were among the thoughts swimming around in my mind during our mission to rescue the cutter *Reliance,* dead in the water. We were quite a few miles from our destination when we saw the first group of them in our NVGs.

I carefully outlined the unit's rules of engagement (ROE). They knew to only use force against them when absolutely necessary. The loud engines of our LAVs triggered the undead to jerk on their axis and move toward us as we passed. They were conditioned and knew that any loud noise most definitely meant food.

I just glared at them from the gunner's turret, then stared ahead into the night. The goggles were good, but one could see only so far with them, unlike the naked eye in daylight. It was sort of like having a huge green torch that lit up the night out to nearly eight hundred yards.

It was the same thing, corpse after corpse, wandering in the areas around their respective demises. Traveling with eight-wheeled vehicles had its advantages. We were fine trekking off-road until we came to bridges or overpasses. Approaching these structures meant that we would have to either pull the clogged arteries of the highway free from the vehicles that blocked them, or descend into the depths of the riverbeds. Sometimes it wasn't a riverbed that the overpass was hiding, it was an interchange, or a smaller highway that ran underneath. That is what we happened on the night of our trip to the cutter.

LAV number one radioed back two hundred yards before reaching the decision point. They also knew never to stop. They idled forward as the radioman's crackled voice came through: "Sir, we are approaching an overpass, the road is congested, what do you want to do?"

I asked, "What types of vehicles are clogging the pass?"

He replied, "Sir, I see a couple eighteen-wheelers."

I had no choice but to order the men down into the embankment that lead to the perpendicular road below. I told the men to take it diagonally as they descended, and to stop for nothing. As much as I hated to think about it, these machines were still in need of depot-level maintenance (professional civilian maintenance), and on more than one occasion they have been known to sputter and die when coming to an abrupt stop.

Just as LAV number one disappeared fifty meters ahead of me into the abyss below, the radio keyed up, and then only static.

I keyed the microphone, asking for the station calling to repeat.

LAV one came back, "Sir, you might want to step on it and get around this. There is a school bus full of those things and there are quite a few of them around it."

I gave thanks for the warning and asked the sergeant to keep me updated. We were almost on the crest of the hill and in view of them.

The radio again crackled. "Sir, we got active Geiger . . ."

I sat there for a minute, stunned. We were further away from radiated zones than Hotel 23. Why were we getting Geiger readings this far out?

As the nose of LAV two (mine) tipped over the ridge and began heading down the ravine to rendezvous with the highway, I saw the school bus. It was nothing special at first, until I took a second look.

The bus was ready for battle. Its windows had chicken wire and chain-link welded to the sides and a makeshift snowplow attached to the front. Our Geiger was now going off as we neared the big yellow bus. The bus was giving off high amounts of radiation. There were numerous undead occupants. On a more disturbing note, I could see nearly a dozen corpses on top of the bus, permanently dead.

I could not even begin to speculate on this one. The bus was hot, but the undead surrounding it were not nearly at the same level. The Geiger counter indicated the bus was giving off radiation levels that would make it deadly for prolonged exposure. Some of the occupants of the bus appeared to have very traumatic wounds, but some of them looked unscathed. They were very excited at the sound of our vehicles cruising by. The last sight I had of the bus was the second-to-last window on the right side. A young boy was hanging out of the window by his right leg. Nothing but bone was left on his left leg. His face was full of lesions and blisters. He didn't appear to be dead, or undead.

Maintaining radio contact, we eventually skirted the wreckage and eluded the undead as we began climbing the hill to return to our easterly course. Something about the bus disturbed me. I wondered if the bus had been filled with survivors attempting to reach a safer area. They obviously came from a radiated zone and knew that to stay meant death.

I wondered how those on the roof of the bus had taken themselves out. I didn't see any guns there with them. It was a few hours before I could think of anything else. We went on, all through the night, towing, skirting, avoiding. The only other complete stop we made was when we arrived at a fuel tanker that was at a safe distance from any bottleneck of pileups and traffic jams.

Since we didn't have any time to figure the vehicle out, or to try to bring it back to life, one of the men simply attached a cloth-wrapped chain to the valve of the vehicle and yanked it from the tank. Diesel began to flow onto the ground. We all knew that diesel was not very volatile, and posed no real threat as long as we were smart about handling it. Using one of the k-bars, we cut one of the rubber hoses from the side of the tanker and taped it to the broken valve with hundred-mile-per-hour tape. It wasn't pretty, or watertight, but it did the job. We filled the vehicles and the exterior fuel tanks with the fuel. One of the mechanics tested the fuel and claimed that it was still okay, but it probably wouldn't be in a year or so, without treatment.

We stuffed the broken valve with cloth that we cut from the seats of the vehicle, a large 120-ounce drink cup and a piece of rope.

It dripped a little, but it would take ages to leak dry. We marked it on our charts as a possible refuel point if needed on the way back. The prospect of having a known fueling point made me feel a little better, but with the shoddy maintenance on the vehicles, coupled with questionable fuel quality, any positive feelings were diminished.

As the sun came up, we arrived at Richwood, Texas. The sign indicating the name and population was partially obscured by graffiti crossing it out. I could smell the salt air. We were not far from the Gulf. We had been attempting to contact the cutter via radio all night. No joy. The men were tired and movement during the day was risky. We were in an industrial area and it didn't take long to find a fenced-in factory in which to play hide and sleep.

The factory was called PLP, and judging from the equipment sitting outside the main building, they had something to do with industrial piping. One of the Marines knocked the lock off with an axe that was strapped down to the exterior of LAV three. We drove through, shut the gate and reattached the chain using tape and spare tent stakes. We parked the LAVs around back and set up a watch rotation as well as defensive perimeters using the stacks of pipes that littered the exterior.

We got very little sleep that day, because of the incessant banging from inside the factory. The undead workers knew we were out here and wanted to be also. By the time we woke up and cleared the heavy stacked pipes out of our way, we had an audience at the fence near our area. Not many, but enough. One is too many. Another random thought . . . how many humans could one of them infect if victims walked in a line, allowing the creature to bite everyone? Unlimited? Fifty?

We sent four men to distract the undead audience so that the rest of us could open the gates and exfiltrate the factory. The sun was hanging low. It was thirteen hours since we had stopped. We needed the extra time to allow full sleep rotation. We could have saved four hours by just letting everyone sleep at the same time, but that would have been foolhardy. We were out of the area quickly and on our way to the coastline. It had been a bit since I had seen the ocean. The familiar smell brought back memories, like the smell of old cologne found in the back of a medicine cabinet.

Once again, we tried to establish communication with the cutter. Our HF radios could easily reach Hotel 23 if tuned properly and should have been able to reach the cutter even more easily. The only thing I could think of was signal bounce, a phenomenon well known to radio operators. Being too close or too far from the intended recipient of a transmission could put the signal in a position to bounce over the receiving radio antennas. There was overcast, and sometimes this was a factor in a signal bounce problem.

We checked in with John and the rest of the Hotel originals. I told them of the school bus and the fuel truck and factory. I asked John if Tara was in the room and he said that she wasn't. I then told him to tell her not to worry and not to mention the school bus to her. The main purpose of my call was to get an accurate position for the cutter. John said he would have the radioman send out a message and would get back to me within the hour.

As we idled along toward the ocean, her green color came into view. The vast expanse of the Gulf lay before us. Her palette of color had been long missed. Judging by the reactions of the men, they too missed the view of open waters. Approaching the marina, John came back over the radio and relayed the response from the carrier. Carrier intelligence had received the last Link-11 datalink update thirty minutes prior. The cutter was at 28-50.0N 095-

16.4W. According to our charts, this put the ship four miles off the coast.

We were close enough to the marina to see the details. Only small sailboats remained there. This area reminded me of Seadrift. Why wouldn't it? It was not far from there. I wondered if the pickled onions were still sitting on the deck of the *Mama*. She wasn't far from here either.

We were going to need awhile to plan this amphibious rescue mission, so we pulled our three-vehicle convoy into the parking lot of the Fair Winds marina. I radioed John again and asked him to get a message to HQ requesting updates if the cutter's position drifted more than half a mile. He told me to be careful and he would see me in a couple of days.

With the lack of communication between our convoy and the cutter, I wondered if this was in fact a rescue mission or a salvage mission. I was startled from this thought by the sound of carbine fire. I cursed under my breath and wondered which man had broken the ROE. I picked up the microphone and keyed out, asking who had fired and why. The senior man on LAV three came back asking me to turn the scope directly to six o'clock and see what was approaching.

I complied and saw probably fifty of them pouring out of the urban area a quarter mile from our position. Fifty was better than five thousand on any day, so I wasn't too worried. The sergeant wasn't shooting at the undead fifteen hundred feet away; he was shooting at the ones pounding on his back doorstep! I don't know why, but the group of four corpses behind LAV three looked familiar. I couldn't place them. I had seen thousands of these things since they first walked, and I was probably just being paranoid.

I signaled the men to prepare the vehicles for amphibious travel. These Marine LAVs were just as seaworthy as most small boats. They were large, heavy and slow, but they could move in the water. They have two small screws in the back, boosting the vehicles to speeds approaching ten knots. We opened up on the ones in our area and the chain of them that popped up between the water and us. Our path was clear and our vehicles ready so we barreled into the Gulf of Mexico, undead hordes behind in pursuit.

The water that splashed up onto my face was warm. Water

began to spill into the troop compartment, and I shot a worried glance over to the Gunny. He smiled and told me not to worry, that if it weren't leaking *he* would be the one worried. I trusted the man and popped my head back topside to observe the activity on the shore. I told the other LAVs to cut to idle and form a line one hundred yards from the marina. The inside of my vehicle had two inches of water, but it showed no sign of sinking.

I climbed out onto the top and just watched them gather on the shoreline like ants. It was then that the radio beeped again with another voice message incoming. It was the familiar sound of crypto syncing up. It sort of sounds like an old computer modem, until the voice comes into recognition. John came back and told us he had a position update on the cutter. Even though we had only requested updates in the event of a drift greater than a quarter mile, HQ felt that the news of the cutter's not moving at all would also be valuable. I had to agree. The ship had no significant movement since the last time an automated update was sent from the antenna on the mast of the ship.

The moans from the dead carried well over the water and into my microphone. I heard Tara's voice and a struggle for the microphone back at the compound. She came on and asked if everything was all right. I explained our current situation and informed her that we were in no immediate danger. I asked her to put John back on and she reluctantly did. I told John that we were about to head out into the open water in search of the ship. Fog was beginning to roll in. The light of the moon, as well as the cold of the night, magnified the fear that every man felt.

We left the gaggle of undead at the shoreline and headed for the coordinates given to us by the carrier battle group. As we slowly advanced, the moans were drowned out and we forgot about our enemy for the time being. I tried not to think about the undead that were lurking on the ocean floor or floating with neutral buoyancy just below the surface. I wished them the worst, as those were the ones I feared most.

The LAV's onboard optic was much better than my goggles, so I scurried back in the hole and deployed the sensors. I could still see the shoreline. The undead were still there. Again, like ants they swarmed. I swung the viewer back around toward the front of the vehicle. My feet were wet from the salt water that had leaked or splashed into the compartment.

We were now one mile off the coast and I could see a small shining object on the horizon. It almost looked like a candle. When we reached the two-mile marker, the radio came alive again with a position report. John claimed that the Coast Guard cutter had again remained stationary since the last update. That was fine by me. The less hunting for it in the open water the better.

I grabbed a strobe light from one of the survival kits and clipped it on the cargo net topside. I wanted to do everything I could to get indications that the crew was alive before attempting to board. I still could not see the silhouette of the cutter. We were now at the three-mile distance from the shoreline. The source of the candlelight became apparent. The light was the flame from an offshore oil platform. At her base was the cutter. It appeared to be moored on the southeast support column of the rig. There was no sign of life from this distance.

As we approached the rig, I could hear living human voices in the distance. They appeared to be yelling. I was nearly certain that our strobes could be seen from their vantage point on the vessel. As I got closer, I began to realize that the voices were not coming from the ship, but from the platform. I listened and went back inside to use the LAV optics. I could see the green outline of men on the platform waving their arms. We were now close enough to make out what they were saying. They were telling us not to board the ship.

It was overrun.

I wondered how a mechanical malfunction had turned out to be an infestation onboard this warship. The Gunny and I were the first to touch the ladder of the oil platform. On my way up, I could make out figures on the boat. It was a long climb to the top, even longer than the ladder in the missile silo of Hotel 23. As I reached the top rung, I was helped to my feet by one of the crew. I counted roughly thirty men on the platform. They all appeared to be in good health.

I asked who was in charge, and one of the men replied, "LTJG Barnes, sir."

I asked to speak with the LT, but the men quickly informed

me that he had sealed himself inside a compartment on the vessel and had no way out. I had a feeling that my next question had been anticipated, as, when I asked them how the hell those rotting shitbags could take over a warship, they started to explain the situation piece by piece.

I was talking to a petty officer. He was one of the ship's information systems technicians, who ran the ship's automated systems and networks. He seemed to have it together. The petty officer explained that they had run aground near the offshore rig. The updated charts they would normally have onboard were not available and they were not sure how deep the water was in this area. It wasn't bad, but they ended up damaging their screw while getting themselves off the sandbar. The boat could be operated but that would cause too much stress on the engine and shaft because the screw was not functioning at 100 percent efficiency.

There would be no time like the night for us to retake the vessel. I knew for a fact these things could not see in the dark any better than the average living person.

Despite the petty officer's explanation of how they came to be nearly dead in the water, the question remained about the undead and why they were present on the cutter in sufficient numbers to cause the crew to abandon the vessel. I ordered him to explain this. He was hesitant at first, but I explained to him who I was and under what authority I operated.

After lowering his head so that his eyes were hidden below his ballcap, he said: "Word came down from the top to get and transport specimens of *them* for research on the flattop [carrier]."

Insane . . . really? Would the people in charge actually want these things onboard their command ship, no matter how critical the research? Bringing them onto a cutter was one thing, but onboard the acting U.S. military command ship?

I know that the carrier had a full onboard medical staff and decent equipment for research, but this research could be done somewhere else, anywhere else, away from the military's leadership. We were getting thin on active-duty military personnel or so I estimated.

"Why the Gulf of Mexico?" I asked.

He replied, "Because command wanted the radiated ones."

I nearly slugged the man right where he stood for agreeing to follow those orders, but I restrained myself, and he went on to tell me that many smaller ships had been dispatched with extraction teams to the radiation zones of destroyed cities to find specimens for study. I agreed in my mind with the intentions, but not the means or storage of these things. Why did they need them from different areas? This man did not know the answer to that and I was betting the only people who did were on that aircraft carrier. I asked the man how many radiated corpses were onboard; he told me that they had acquired five of them from the New Orleans hot zone.

I asked him how only five of those creatures could effectively mission-kill the cutter. He stared off into the night and sat there for a minute, not knowing what to say. I snapped my fingers in front of his face, pulling him out of his trancelike state. He then began telling me what I had feared and suspected.

"These aren't the same as the others, sir. They don't decay like the others, they are stronger, faster, and some say more intelligent. I don't get it. The radiation does something to them, preserves them. The doctors on the carrier think the radiation is some type of catalyst for preserving motor function and regrowing dead cells. Oddly, the regenerated cells are still dead. They don't understand it, no one does. They won't admit it, but I know they made a mistake when they dropped the nukes.

"The creatures on the ship broke out of their restraining straps and killed the three men guarding them. Those men turned and it was all we could do to secure the bridge and get the ship moored alongside this oil platform before we were eaten."

He estimated that the ship housed nearly fifteen undead now.

It was time to act, I supposed. I told the man that I was sorry and that the carrier would not be acquiring their specimens from this ship. We were going to kill them all.

We lost a Marine in the assault. All in all it took forty-five minutes to secure the ship. It was dark and it would have been suicide for our whole squad to board. I took the Gunny and a seasoned staff sergeant with me. He would have had it no other way. I have recently been informed that he had a spouse back at the original Marine base camp. I can say that he fought valiantly and probably saved both the Gunny and me.

We carefully boarded the ship by jumping over the mooring lines onto the weather deck. Staff Sergeant "Mac" had the only suppressed weapon in the group. We left the others at home in the event they needed the weapons to defend themselves.

I was not familiar with the weapon's handling, so I left it to the Marine. I would have loved to take more than three, but unfortunately we only had three sets of night vision goggles. Mac wasted the two creatures on the weather deck. Those two were part of the original crew. We piled them on the forecastle and proceeded to secure the ship. Using the ship's 21MC bitch box we were able to establish communications with six surviving crewmembers holed up in the galley. I could hear the sound of the undead in the background through the speakers, relentlessly striking the steel roll-down galley shutter.

This partition was the only thing keeping the culinary specialists and the ship's senior officer from being eaten.

They proceeded to tell us that they had taken down one of the radiated undead with a fire extinguisher and a fire axe. One of the men who had downed the thing was vomiting and weak, probably from exposure. The sailors wore radiation suits inside the New Orleans zone to acquire the specimens, which were no doubt very radioactive and dangerous to be near. The lieutenant told me that the other two were outside the galley partition pounding on the bulkheads. He seemed to think that much of the undead crew was there with them but wasn't sure if all of them were present on the other side. We crept through the passageway, down the steep ladders. The galley was in the center of the ship, deep below the waterline. As we approached the main deck, Mac whispered that he was going to destroy one of the bright passageway lights so we could continue to have the upper hand. He shot it out, and this change in atmosphere triggered one of those things to move into the open in front of his weapon.

Mac took it out with two shots. The first shot hit the creature's left shoulder and did nothing but spatter black, putrid blood on the wall behind. The second shot hit the creature right on the nose, and I suppose just enough of the brain was scrambled to do the job, as it moved no more.

We dragged it to the corner of the passageway and used zip cuffs to bind its arms and legs just to be sure. We kept lurking through the darkness. Every sound was thunder and every blinking LED seemed like storm lightning. The ship had the familiar smell of mothballs and a tinge of death. We came to a hatch. It was a large steel door used to keep water from flooding adjoining compartments in the event of an attack or emergency. There was a small circle of thick glass no bigger than the diameter of a coffee can on the door where a peephole would be. I looked through and could see the ship's emergency lighting was on. An eerie red glow filled the small room beyond. I cranked the handle on the door, trying to be as quiet as possible, moving a centimeter at a time. We all winced when the hatch creaked from lack of maintenance. I stopped moving the handle and checked the hole again. I saw movement in the compartment beyond. A loud thud rang through our compartment as something very strong hit the hatch. It nearly opened from the pressure, but fortunately I hadn't fully slid the handle to the open position.

The creature on the other side obscured the red lighting behind. Its face was pressed against the thick glass and it was banging its head in a futile attempt to get to us. Every fiber in my body was telling me to leave and not open the thick steel door. We could still turn back and survive. There were men down there and I knew that every hour they stayed in proximity to the radiated creatures meant they were an hour closer to their death. I told the sergeant that I would slam the latch open, then he would pull the rip cord that I had attached to the door, yanking it open.

As there was no use in being quiet about it anymore, I used no care in forcing the handle to the open position. I slammed it home and Mac yanked the cord. The door flung open and the creature came through. Luckily for us the creature was not accustomed to shipboard life and promptly tripped over the knee knocker, landing flat on its face. Expecting this thing to take its time getting up, I readied my weapon for careful aim. I did not get what I expected. This creature was on its feet fast. This was one of the preserved dead from the New Orleans zone. It lurched toward me and my goggles seemed to crackle like a late-night hometown TV channel that had just finished the national anthem. The last thing I saw was its bony claw reach out before intense light blinded me and I heard the action of Mac's suppressed H&K.

I felt the air move and heard a loud thud as something hit the steel deck. I pulled off my NVGs. As my eyes adjusted to the bright light, I saw Mac's Surefire torch lighting up the compartment. Using two mops from a nearby bucket, Mac and I pushed the creature into a corner and tried as best we could to stack heavy objects on top to incapacitate it like the other creature we had dispatched—again, "just in case." We could not zip cuff the thing, as the radiation was likely at a deadly level. We took no time getting out of this area and through the next. Anywhere this creature had been was probably unsafe. I know it was my imagination, similar to the feeling of your head itching when someone mentions lice, but I could almost feel the heat of radiation on my face and neck.

The next compartment was clear. Only one more steel door separated us from the galley area. We were now facing two problems. First, our NVGs were "snowing out" due to some sort of electromagnetic or radiological interference, and second, the heavy steel door was in fact cracked open slightly. The only real barrier that separated us from the bulk of the undead in the galley was a long, dark corridor and a half-open steel door. I could see their shadows moving through the crack beyond the door. From where we were watching, the door was roughly ten meters away.

The only thing we could do was bust in there and shoot them. No special tactic, no smart way to handle it. I hated this and wished for a better method. We approached the door. I stopped Gunny and Mac and we checked our weapons. No safety, and no inhibitions. We had eighty-seven rounds ready to go between us. More, if we needed to reload, but we all knew if it came to that we were going to die anyway.

We checked our clothing and tried to cover as much skin as possible. As near as I could figure, there were at least ten in there, and at least one of the *special* type. This hatch opened outward, away from us and toward them. I gave the signal and the Gunny kicked it fully open. It slammed against the bulkhead and locked into place. Inside this room were eleven undead corpses. They were all banging on the metal partition and didn't notice us at first until I took a preemptive shot. I killed three before the rest took notice. I had hoped that one of them was the New Orleans creature. We began to shoot, three-round bursts. Limbs, jaws, shoulders and teeth were flying everywhere. I was careful not to aim in the direction of the partition, in case one of the sailors stood near. We were down to three when I heard a loud scream from over my right shoulder. It was Mac. He was bleeding from his face, and one of the creatures was standing behind him attempting to bite him.

I looked again . . . it was the same creature we had shot two compartments back. The one we didn't touch, but tried to incapacitate. It hadn't died. I emptied the rest of my magazine into the creature's head. It fell, most of its head missing. I was almost overrun by the last of them when Gunny took care of them for me as I tended to Mac.

The bite wasn't bad. It was actually not his face, but his ear. The creature had bitten part of his ear off. Mac was breathing heavily and going into what I would have described as shock. I asked Gunny to look after him as I went to check for survivors in the galley. This was no time to screw around. The ship wasn't safe and would need a scrub-down before it could ever be used in a normal capacity again. I rapped on the steel shutter, asking if anyone was alive. I heard a series of mechanical clicking sounds and the door next to the shutter opened up and they started pouring out . . . living. One of them looked pretty bad. It was the one who had the hand-to-hand altercation with one of the New Orleans creatures.

The ship's OIC was present, and I informed him of the situation. He knew it and hated to admit it, but he had no choice but to abandon this ship and hold out on the rig until we could get support from carrier HQ. We got the hell off the ship, with Mac and the sick sailor being first priority. Mac was a dead man. The other man had not been bitten and only needed decontamination treatment. I wasn't certain whether it was too late. On the way out, I stopped off in the one of the ship's heads and ripped the soap dispenser off the wall. I took a roll of paper towels as well. We were finally topside. It was still dark outside. It was only 0300 hrs. Mac and the sailor were in no shape to climb to the platform where the other survivors waited. We rigged a makeshift harness and pulled them up one at a time. I never really knew this Marine, but that doesn't change my sadness. As the acting commander it was my duty to travel to the camp where his wife lived and tell her the news. Although I had no flag to present, it didn't change the need to fulfill my obligation to Mac, as he is and always will be a United States Marine.

Gunny shot Mac in the back of the head two hours after we returned to the rig. He had already passed out from the infection and was not far from turning.

This mission ended the next day, with radio contact being established with the carrier battle group. I relayed a message to command through the radio operator at Hotel 23 and informed them of the situation and location of survivors here. Using salt water from the Gulf and the soap and towels, we attempted to decontaminate Petty Officer Tompost. We left the men with every bit of our food and water and departed the oil rig after making sure a rescue was en route. We also left the sailors a functional radio in the event help didn't show. The only thing we had going for us were a few full cans of diesel and a spot to refuel on our charts. It was a two-day trip back. I brought Mac back home wrapped in canvas strapped to the exterior of LAV number two. I made sure he wouldn't return, but his wife didn't deserve to have his body thrown into the Gulf. He deserved a proper burial.

19 Aug

2350

Day before last I made my trip to the Marine base camp. This is one of the many reasons that I wish I were not the senior man present at the facility. I took four men, including the Gunny, and one LAV. Correction, there were five men. Mac was with us in a pine box, covered by an American flag. The flag wasn't easy to come by, as it took forty rounds of ammunition and ten years of my life terrified away from me to get it. It was the least I could do. Tara asked to come with me to comfort the widow. I told her that it wasn't a good idea, of course. Besides, this world is so full of death and doom. Mrs. Mac wasn't the only one to lose someone, but I still felt for her. There weren't many pre-existing relationships left here in the apocalypse.

I didn't have a formal uniform and the nearest uniform shop was out of business. I knew it really didn't matter. It was a solemn moment when I handed the widow her tattered one-sided flag. I didn't know what to expect. I had never had the honor of doing this. In the movies, the widow always hugs the guy who gives her the flag and they both have a somber moment. All I got was a cold stare and a feeling of hatred. Who am I to blame her? If I can somehow be an outlet for her emotions, then it's fine by me. I do know that I feel bad about what happened. He was a good man.

RIP Staff Sergeant Mac.

Exodus

RTTUZYUW RUHPNQRO234 TTTT-UUUU

ZNY TTTT

1734Z 22 AUG

FM: CDR NADA MISSILE FAC

TO: USS GEORGE WASHINGTON //CNO//

BT

S E C R E T N//002028U

SUBJ://SITREP RELIANCE

RMKS://IAW CMD DIRECTIVES ISSUED
BY RECIPIENT, UNIT DISPATCHED TO
RESCUE OF RELIANCE ON PRE-DET
COORD. CUTTER FOUND OVERRUN BY
UNDEAD W/ O3 RADIATED. ALL UNDEAD
DESTROYED, SHIP SCUTTLED, RESCUE
AUTHORITY CONTACTED. RECOMMEND
RAD UNDEAD NOT BE HELD ON ANY
NAVAL VESSEL DUE TO INAD. FACILITIES.
THIS UNIT DOES NOT ADVISE RAD DEAD
BE HOUSED ONBOARD FLAGSHIP. PLEASE
QSL THIS MESSAGE AND ADVISE.

BT

AR

#N0234

22 Aug

HQ has not responded to my recent communiqué. I have released a radio message preparing the other camp for evacuation. This comes after a thirty-six-hour swell of undead near that area. It will take them two days to transit to this location with women and children. Here at Hotel 23 we are busy finding supplies to expand our safe boundary so that we can house the extra occupants. There is no way we can accommodate them all inside the facility; it simply wasn't built for so many. The other camp has lost eight people since I ordered a contingent to be stationed here. I cannot help but think animosity may exist. Apparently one of the civilian males was allowed to hunt for deer last week and returned with nothing to show for it but a bite from one of the creatures. The man hid the bite for fear of quarantine or summary execution. He turned in his sleep three days later and took the lives of two other civilians—three if you count the young girl who was executed because she was bitten and getting sick. They didn't shoot her like an animal. They gave her a morphine overdose, and after her heart stopped they immediately drilled a small hole in her head above her left ear to destroy any chance of reanimation.

When this type of thing happens, I lose sleep. I know that millions have died in a much worse manner than this over the past months, but it always hurts to see a young child get taken by this sickness. I don't really even know if that is what it is. Some seem to think so.

While monitoring the daily message traffic coming off the archaic dot matrix printer, I saw a message I had been expecting. The ballistic missile submarine that had been submerged since before the plague was forced to surface yesterday. That was the last sanctuary of real death.

The last known place on the planet where men could die in peace . . . until it surfaced.

The man who had died of natural causes and had been stored in the freezer came back after only two hours of exposure. Luckily, they had it strapped to a crate of low-grade beef. The ship's cook discovered it when he went down to the freezer to retrieve the last of the ship's food stores. The cook nearly had a heart attack when he walked by the corpse and noticed its head tracking him across the reefer, gnashing its teeth.

The submarine intends to follow the battle group until it can acquire enough food to stay submerged for a useful amount of time. Its mission now, instead of blowing up large foreign cities, is to scout coastal areas and discourage piracy on the high seas. The status messages that are sent weekly state that most of the nuclear ships won't need to be refueled for twenty-plus years. After that, all bets are off. I doubt there will be enough qualified people to refuel them even in one hundred years.

I'm sending all our LAVs out tomorrow to meet the other survivors at the halfway point and to escort them the rest of the way here. From that point it will take every man, woman and child to expand our safe boundaries. We will have no choice but to make perilous trips to the surrounding interstates to retrieve concrete barriers so that we may better fortify our compound.

Tara and I have been spending more time together than ever since my return from the Gulf. Dean has been dubbed the official teacher of this compound. Of course there are only two children to teach, but soon there will be more. Annabelle is allowed to attend class, on the stipulation she does not bark and disrupt the instruction. I sat in on one of the classes last night. Laura is becoming pretty decent at her multiplication tables. Danny is a little better due to age. She is learning her sevens and Danny is up to division and fractions.

Jan is still the resident nurse and helps out a lot when some of the men come back with bumps, scratches and bruises. John and I have not had much time together lately. I remember in the beginning he was all I had. I suppose I will never forget that. Sometimes when I daydream, I can see John on his roof with his thermos and large rubber yoga band. I can only see it in black and white in my mind, as if it happened ages ago.

I wonder what the response will be from the carrier now that they know we had to destroy the creatures to save the rest of the crew.

<u>05 Sep</u>
2036

Sixty percent. That is the number of survivors we have here from the other Marine outpost. Many are civilians. It was a constant battle to get them here. The chain-link fence surrounding the silo area is packed with makeshift tents and survivors. Hotel 23 is very much over capacity for the interior to handle. After their arrival ten days ago, an accurate muster was taken. We came up with 113 souls. The Marines sent to rendezvous with the other camp at the halfway point met extreme opposition. The convoy was moving slowly to accommodate the civilians who were on foot. Many rode scavenged bicycles to keep up with the armored vehicles in the front and rear of the convoy. The women and children were first to be allowed to ride. The bulk of the casualties came from attacks perpendicular to the formation line.

The undead came out of the thick underbrush and picked off many men with only scrapes and bites. Most men held on and kept contributing to the security of the convoy despite the death sentence dealt to them by the bites. Others simply walked off into the underbrush and committed suicide. The convoy was low on ammunition by the time it pulled into Hotel 23. They were in constant firefights the whole way, pushing back the surge of cold hands reaching over the railings of the vehicles. The convoy did its best to distract the dead away from Hotel 23 before circling back to the compound. The tactic seemed to work, but I have noticed a steady increase in activity since the others arrived. I have been forced to order squads of "fence men" to the chain-link perimeter to kill them. In large numbers, they could buckle the fence. This is the main reason I have organized a team of individuals for missions to the interstate. That gridlocked infinity of concrete barriers holds the key to our temporary survival. We needed the hundreds of concrete barriers present there to reinforce our boundaries to hold the new survivors safely within the fence line.

The most difficult part was getting the equipment needed to transport the barriers. We needed flatbed tractor-trailers and forklifts. Only a few men in the compound were former forklift operators. We were able to acquire four propane-powered forklifts from a lumberyard near the interstate. We have also scavenged and repaired two flatbed tractor-trailers to transport the barriers. Only two truckloads of barriers have arrived since the operation started. The progress is slow but steady. I estimate the fence would hold up to five deep. Any more ghouls than that would force the fence to cave inward, and our new citizens would surely perish. I have given up my living space to the women and children. I have only permitted women who have volunteered to remain topside. Tara insisted that she stay with me. I am okay with this because I cannot let the other women volunteers stay here and discriminate against her.

Last week I transmitted a formal request for a helicopter equipped with antipersonnel weapons and a pilot to be transferred to the compound to help police the perimeter against a large influx of undead. I overjustified the need to ensure that our request be met. We needed some form of air power for both security and reconnaissance in this area. Fixed-wing would be out of the question and more trouble than it's worth due to maintenance and the requirement for five thousand feet of runway. We'll see what happens.

Dragonfly

This morning I received a message indicating authorization of a rotary-wing aircraft, one pilot and one maintenance person to be transferred to Hotel 23. The message did not state what model, but it did state the aircraft was due for arrival tomorrow morning. This aircraft will not only strengthen our perimeter defenses, but will also make it easier to scout for essential supplies. Depending on the range of the aircraft, I plan to fly northward to scout non-radiated cities. I will post a notice in the common area both above and below ground for people to list items of which they are in dire need.

Certain medical prescriptions, eyeglasses or possibly female products come to mind. I'm excited to take to the air again. I have not flown in ages and the Cessna parked at the edge of the field is probably not safe to operate. I know one of the gear brakes is not functioning properly and the engine needs a detailed check-up that it most likely will never receive.

I almost feel as if I'm putting the cart miles before the horse by thinking of ways to use the helicopter. It isn't even here.

John and I played a nice game of chess today in the control room. Dean has a respectable-size class of young men and women now. Including the original two, she now has fourteen students. Annabelle does not fancy all the new children in Dean's class. Dean will have to break up the time spent by age groups as I have noticed that ABCs are a little too elementary for some of the older kids. I stepped in today and heard Mozart flowing through the air.

The children were listening attentively. Who would have

thought? A year ago, the whole room would have been moaning in protest. Considering the terrors these children have witnessed, the beauty of the music was actually making them smile. I thought back to the last time I had listened to Mozart . . . but didn't hang on to the thought long.

Secure space is at a premium inside the compound and Jan has her medical tent set up topside. Only the really sick or injured get to stay down below within the safe steel sanctuary. Not a bad system. Lately, the only thing she has had to deal with is minor cuts and abrasions. I have a standing order to be notified of all injuries reported to the resident medic. I have tasked the *originals* with the duty of drafting a book of rules for Hotel 23. Of course the Uniform Code of Military Justice will be followed, but I feel a need for this compound to have its own bylaws that the people should follow. Seems silly, the need for rules these days. I almost feel like I am rebuilding a government within the compound. Of course any regulation created and imposed will be based strictly on the Constitution of the United States.

08 Sep
1800

Today one MH-60R Seahawk helicopter, along with the allocated personnel, arrived. The pilot, a retired Navy commander by the name of Thomas Baham, was the pilot in command. His maintenance person, an active-duty Navy petty officer, was to be the non-com in charge of keeping the aircraft airworthy until more parts and personnel could be flown in.

My first action was to inquire about the condition of the aircraft, as I planned to execute some airborne recon in the coming weeks. CDR (ret.) Baham was a volunteer. He willingly gave up his safer job with the carrier battle group to relocate to southeastern Texas and work with us at Hotel 23. Although an older man in his late fifties, he still had the fire and drive in his eyes. I had secretly wished he were active duty, and thus would be lawfully in command of Hotel 23 as the senior officer. The Seahawk was a rather large helicopter. The petty officer told me that the range was 380 miles. On the way to the compound they flew by numerous abandoned military airfields that they suspected had at least some JP-5, a common military aircraft fuel.

This type of fuel had its advantages, as it didn't spoil nearly as rapidly as conventional gasoline. It would still be usable if found inside a fuel truck. I had a message drafted to HQ the moment the chopper reported. Although I did thank them for the aircraft, I also requested more parts and personnel to maintain it. Tomorrow I would like to head out with Baham and the flight engineer to survey the surrounding area for useful intelligence.

11 Sep

_2354_

Today marks another anniversary of the day I thought it couldn't get any worse. I suppose times like these make me wish I were back in that time, when the world had no idea what terror was. Undead movement is still growing in the surrounding areas. I feel that there is virtually no chance of survivors in any major city at this point. Of course, the ones that were nuked would be void of survivors. My reasoning is simple. The undead seem to be fanning out away from major areas into mass mobile formations. I am sure the cities that are still intact have a concentration of undead, but they have probably been out of food for a couple of months. This could have prompted them to leave their native areas and search for prey. I could be totally wrong in this theory. Baham has conveyed that the aircraft is ready for recon missions. We have discussed the areas that would be good candidates for survey. Ruling out any areas that have been bombed, we have decided to head north by northeast. Our destination will be Texarkana. This is the safest area to survey while avoiding the undead and radiated cities. According to the charts, Texarkana was not a high-population area and the nearest nuked city to that destination is Dallas, Texas. This gives us roughly 120 miles of safe distance.

Unfortunately, due to the distance, we will need to find fuel. It's 240 nautical miles one way from here to Texarkana.

15 Sep

2219

The aircraft performed well in today's scouting mission. We did not make the long journey north to Texarkana; however, we did find a suitable area to refuel the helicopter. We went north to Shreveport, Louisiana. We had nothing to guide our way sans the inertial navigation system (INS). The INS is a self-contained gyroscopic navigation device that does not rely on any outside information for aircraft navigation. As long as you give the INS a good latitude and longitude before you take off, the INS will keep an accurate gyroscopic position the entire flight. Since the GPS satellites have long failed, it would have been nearly impossible to find Barksdale AFB in Shreveport without the INS. We would have run out of fuel long before we reached our destination. We only had forty-five minutes of fuel left when we were over the base.

The fence was damaged in some areas, but still held. The undead were heavy on the northern side of the base perimeter fence. As we neared the aircraft parking spots, I could see numerous B-52 bombers parked in neat rows outside the hangars. Some of the planes still had bombs sitting on carts underneath. I was not certain, but I had a feeling the bombs that were sitting under those aircraft were not conventional. The pilots just never got the chance to take off and accomplish their assigned bombing package. The aircraft are useless in our current situation. They would require too much fuel and maintenance to be of any survival value. I suppose if we had a qualified or suicidal pilot to fly the bomber we could remove the extra payloads and fly it overseas, but it would be a one-way trip, as I was certain that it would require professional maintenance after such a long flight. I did feel a sting of patriotism as I gazed upon their decadence. I wondered if any of them had flown over the Hanoi Hilton, giving at least some comfort to the guests. We were hovering over a forgotten piece of United States diplomacy. Now the BUFFs were a decaying museum exhibit.

We counted twenty-seven corpses inside the airfield perimeter. There were two fuel trucks, one marked JP-5 and the other marked JP-8, sitting on the median between the runway and taxiway. Since we were on a skeleton crew to conserve fuel we only had the pilot, the flight engineer, the Gunny and myself on board. The Gunny and I had to cover the flight engineer (FE) while he fueled the helicopter. This was an operation that would require the aircraft to remain running. This is not a normal procedure, but no chances can be taken. As we fueled the chopper, a dozen undead approached, attracted to the sound of the rotors spinning.

That sound was extremely loud, and the Gunny and I had to rely solely on sight to detect and eliminate them. I stood aft, a safe distance from the tail rotor, and the Gunny held the forward position. Our shots could barely be heard over the turbine engines and the swinging blades. I was wearing my helmet with the visor down. The helmet served multiple purposes onboard the aircraft and off. It helped shield my ears from the harmful decibels that pierced the immediate area and saved my eyes from flying FOD. Using my weapon, I was able to neutralize most of the undead with only single shots. None of them moved with the same quickness as their radiated counterparts. The Gunny was using the MP5 SD. I hated that weapon for its accuracy and lack of stopping/piercing power, but it was useful because of the silence factor. The only other advantage it had was the ability to interchange ammunition with the Gunny's M-9 pistol.

As I dispatched the last of the undead approaching my end of the aircraft, I moved forward to help out with the increasing numbers there. I had a better killing range with my weapon; I used this advantage to destroy the walkers that were one hundred yards out and closing on our position. The engineer gave us the thumbs-up, indicating that he had successfully refueled the aircraft. I wondered how he got the fuel truck started and later found out that he had carried a portable starter to the truck. He had faced this same situation before and had been prepared.

After the engineer was safely back in the helicopter, I plugged my helmet back into the aircraft's communications system and informed the pilot that the Gunny and I were going to scout the immediate area for any useful items or information. I asked him to keep it hot until we got back for dustoff. The pilot keyed the microphone and told me he and the flight engineer could handle security while we were gone and that they would take off and circle the airfield until bingo fuel if we were not back within one hour.

I secured the side door and waved good-bye as the Gunny and I set out for one of the larger buildings nearest to our position. There were no external markings. It was just another bland government building, lacking any detail that would give away purpose. As we neared the structure, we knew it would be suicide to explore. In nearly all of the windows the shades had been yanked down from the wall, exposing the occupants inside. Some of the windows were spiderwebbed with abuse from the punishment they had received in the past months. There were too many undead inside the building to count.

Since noise wasn't a factor, I readied my weapon and took a potshot at one of them on the top floor. It was banging on the window with both fists until my shot cut through the window. I missed the creature, and it looked at the new hole in the window with the curiousness of a cat looking at a laser pointer. I scoffed at this and the Gunny and I began our return to the chopper. As we turned, I could see and hear the FE taking shots at an approaching group of undead with the side-mounted machine gun. Great for close encounters.

The ride back was uneventful, but any time I could spend in the air was fine by me. I even got some stick time in the copilot's seat. It would take a lot more than this to make me semiproficient at maneuvering this aircraft, as it was the hardest thing I'd ever flown. I looked like an idiot as I tried to hover the beast. Baham had to take over every time.

25 Sep

1900

It finally happened. I won't cheapen the experience by putting it into writing. Last night was a good night, and I feel more human already. Part of me would like to think I cared about her the moment I found her trapped in the broken-down car that day, surrounded by the creatures. Despite her less-than-glamorous living arrangement in the car, she was pretty even then.

The time has been set. Tomorrow morning, I will set out with the Gunny, engineer and CDR (ret.) Baham in the chopper in the direction of Shreveport again. We have decided to survey the area around Barksdale AFB, since the base had an ample supply of helicopter fuel. Texarkana would not be the goal of our expedition this time. John had begged to go with me, as he really wanted to get out of the compound for a couple of days. I had assured him that I really needed him manning the control center and for the basic organization of the civilians. He was not a military man, but the men respected him and appreciated him for his knowledge of the base systems. After dinner he insisted that I memorize a series of code words so that I could transmit my location in the clear using letter and number association.

Annabelle is enjoying herself with all the new children in the compound. The Gunny and I are leaving military command to one of the most senior staff sergeants and civilian leadership to John. There are rules governing who has what authority in the compound and the military men know too well that, constitutionally, their job is still to protect civilians, not run roughshod over them just because they have firepower.

There is also a team of men working on the new perimeter. Trucks come and go daily with new concrete dividers from I-10. Casualties have been zero since the operation officially started. The men have a system for vehicle formation and a certain path that minimizes the undead attraction back to Hotel 23. Most of these men had at least one tour in Iraq or Afghanistan under their belts, but they were the first to admit that convoy operations currently are much more dangerous than they were during the war. The Gunny still insists on the H&K, and I still insist on American metal. We will be traveling light to conserve fuel and are taking a three-day food supply.

Icarus

30 Sep

Time/Location: Unknown

Situation bad . . . surviving twenty-four hours ~~not likely~~ not looking up. Must keep record. The trip going as planned until aft Fading in and out of consc. Head swollen, ear bleeding. Bloody hands.

30 Sep

Making a point to document in the event that I don't make it out. Will write more when better . . . Important.

~~Water should have grabbed more water more are~~

We were overhead Shreveport and decided to take it farther north since we had the fuel and a known fuel source. I was not watching instruments, as Baham was doing the driving. A light came on on the master caution panel. It was the chip light. Baham recycled the light to see if it was simply a short in the panel. It illuminated once again, indicating that there were pieces of metal detected in the aircraft oil reservoir. The normal procedure would be to land the aircraft immediately, but none of us wished to land in the known hostile territory below.

It was not long until we lost useful power to the rotors and Baham began autorotating down to the ground. The altimeter was spinning as if we were coming in for approach. The Gunny and the petty officer were strapped in side by side in the rear of the aircraft. I was strapped in the copilot's seat. The last thing I remembered was an earsplitting noise and the sound of metal tearing and water and dust flying upward over the chopper and across my face.

I don't know how long I was out. I was dreaming . . . it was a nice place. I was with Tara, but not at the compound. I was back in time, in the living world. It felt very real. Then came the light taps on my shoulder . . . then the pulling of my sleeve. Someone was waking me up from this feeling of tranquility. I started to feel my head. Intense pain shot through my temples. Every time my heart beat, I felt the blood surge through my head in spikes of pain. My vision was blurry. I was back in the helicopter, away from my fantasy.

Still blurry . . . I looked to my left in the pilot's seat. I could see Baham looking at me, shaking my shoulder with his right hand, saying something. Why was he pulling on me? I looked back over my shoulder and saw Gunny and the engineer reaching out, as if trying to help me. I seemed to be looking at them through a pool of water. The pain spiked again and my eyes slowly came into focus.

I looked over at Baham. Fear shot through my body as I looked at his chest. A piece of the helicopter's rotor blade was sticking through his breastplate. He wasn't dying . . . he was dead. His taps, nudges and what I thought was him talking were not attempts to wake me, but attempts to kill. He was still stuck in his harness and unable reach me. I sat there stunned for a moment before looking back over my shoulders at the Gunny and flight engineer. I was the only living person on this helicopter. Reaching up to my forehead, I felt a sting. A piece of rotor shrapnel had pierced my flight helmet and was stuck in my head. I didn't know how deep. I just knew that I was still alive and had cognitive function.

I reached down for my carbine so that I could take out the rest of the crew and safely exfiltrate this tomb. When I tried to yank the carbine up to my shoulder, I saw that the barrel had been bent at almost a ninety-degree angle and was caught inside the flight controls at my feet. Cursing, I threw the weapon on the deck and looked around the chopper for anything I could use. The Gunny's MP5 was on the floor behind my seat.

I took out my knife and used it to snag the sling to bring the weapon close enough so that I could grab it. Charging the weapon,

I first aimed at Baham. His snarling teeth and sagging old skin were enhanced by his current health status. He didn't know me anymore; neither did the men in the back. I was going to save the Gunny for last.

I pulled the weapon up and Baham began slapping the suppressor around, as if somehow he knew what was coming. I wasted him. One second later I shot the engineer in the head. His arms went from Frankenstein to limp as if he had never been re-animated. I said some words for all of them and then paid final respects to the Gunny by shooting him in the forehead. I hoped he would have done the same for me. Looking out the window, I could tell that we had been here for at least a couple of hours, as the sun was already nearly at its apex in the day sky. We were in the middle of some sort of waist-deep small pond. A tinge of guilt stabbed me in the heart when I realized Baham had probably thought our best chance of survival was to put it down here. I had paid him back by quick-acting lead poisoning.

It was a good place to crash-land as the portside door was off its rail, exposing the aircraft to the outside world. There were numerous undead curiously circling the pond, somehow repelled by the water. I carefully surveyed the 360-degree area and noticed a gap in them. I grabbed my gear and whatever else I could carry. As I walked to the door to escape the wreck, I ripped the Velcro flag off my left shoulder and slapped it in the Gunny's dead hand.

I made for the door. As I stepped off the chopper, I sank waist deep into the water. This made it difficult to quickly move to the open area for my escape. I was nearly swimming to the shore of the small pond. I made it to dry land and began running. I blacked out shortly after and woke up about four hours ago. I am sitting in a high school football stadium announcer's box at the top of the *home* side . . . I think. It is nightfall and I am hungry and dehydrated. I had to perform minor surgery on myself an hour ago by removing the metal shard from my head with the needlenose on my multitool. Using the mirror from my camouflage paint kit, I stitched myself up with the sewing kit in my bag. The shard went more than an eighth of an inch into my head, above my left temple. I do not know at this time if this injury is life threatening. I have limited food and water but I am conserving as much as possible to prolong survival. This could be the end. I hear footsteps on the metal bleachers below.

01 Oct
Time: Unknown

It's coming back to me in flashes. I vaguely remember fighting three of them. They must have seen me make for the top of the bleachers and followed. When I woke up, I was flat on my back lying in a pool of blood and broken glass in the center of the floor of the press box. As I tried to lift my head up and check the door, I noticed the shatterproof glass. From the looks of it I shot through the glass to kill the things but missed, as the bullet holes are accompanied by larger holes. The edges of the larger holes in the broken glass hold pieces of skin and clothing, indicating they tried to reach inside. There is also a diagonal line of bullet holes starting from the doorknob and trailing down to the bottom left part of the door. After checking my weapon, I figured that I had shot between fifteen and twenty rounds.

Forcing myself to my feet, I stumbled over to the door. Looking through the broken glass, I saw four dead bodies strewn on the bleachers. In the distance I could see another two beyond the goalpost, milling about in search of prey. My memory is still spotty but I remember shooting at least one of them at point-blank range right through the glass, killing it instantly.

02 Oct
Approx. 1600

Woke up this morning to the sound of a dog howling. It could have been a wolf, but with the lack of living humans in North America, I'm certain all the domestic dogs are becoming feral. I'm curious if they would remember me as a living man or attack me on sight as they do the undead. I have seen a canine's resentment of them. Reminds me of how some dogs despise uniforms. Annabelle dislikes the creatures, and the hackles on her back stand up the instant she smells one of them drawing near. I have dried blood all over my face and I continue to inhabit this crow's nest above an overgrown football field. The only evidence that remains that it was ever a playing field is the goalposts and the bleachers on either side.

I am beat up and sore. The crash may have injured me seriously. My kidney area is extremely tender and I find it difficult to stand for very long. In the packs I grabbed from the helicopter, I salvaged three hundred 9mm rounds, five MREs and a collapsed roll of rigging tape. I'm somewhat encouraged by the fact that I had the forethought to grab my pack with my multitool, two gallons of water and NVGs along with other survival odds and ends.

I will try to keep myself to one quart of water per day. If I don't overexert myself, I feel I may have enough water to get healthy enough to move. I also have the equipment that was strapped to my vest under the harness when we crashed (pistol, survival knife, flares, compass). The stitches in my head are very uncomfortable and I wish that I had had something better than sewing thread. A bottle of vodka or any hard alcohol would really help. I have a handheld PRC-90 survival radio that I have been using to try to communicate with Hotel 23 on frequencies 2828 and 243. No joy. Either I am out of range or the radio isn't operating properly. John knew our intended flight path but even if every Marine were dispatched with all vehicles and weapons they wouldn't make it as far north as my location. There are simply too many undead between us. I don't think I'll be making it back at this point.

03 Oct

Approx. 1900

It is time to begin formulating a plan. I'm down to 1.5 gallons of water and the number of undead in and around the field seems to be increasing. I find it difficult to think with the pain I'm experiencing. I keep telling myself to bring it back to basics. I need food, water and shelter. In today's day and age, that isn't enough.

As of this very minute, I can see six of the creatures from my vantage point. They don't seem to know I'm here, and not one of them has made an attempt at the bleachers. With the range and accuracy of the MP-5, I dare not make any attempts to take them out, especially by the grainy green picture provided by my goggles.

The pain in my head is driving me mad. I've thought on a couple of occasions of just leaving the box, going down to the field and killing them all from behind with my knife. Then the pain subsides and I go back to reality and realize what a shit plan that is. When I urinate, I can see small amounts of blood. I figured this out when I accidentally pissed all over my hands today. I must have really socked my kidney when the helicopter autorotated to the ground.

First off, I need to figure out exactly where I am. After I do that, I need to figure out where I can go to get some better gear and try to communicate with Hotel 23. At this point I'm positive they know the aircraft is down. I will rest and recover until I get down to half a gallon of water. I have decided that at that point staying could mean death. It's getting cold here at night, especially when you're only wearing two layers of clothing and have a door with as much unintended ventilation as mine. Damn myself for getting so used to being around others.

My watch is busted, only showing the day under the dead hour and minute hands. I suppose I can just kill one of those things and take its watch. I need to know the exact time of day so that I can monitor sunrise and sunset. It's been about nine months since a watch battery has been manufactured. I'm sure they have a decent shelf life, so I might as well get a digital watch with a timer and chronometer while I can still use one. It's a shame I have to think of shit like this in my condition.

04 Oct

Approx. 0200

Another one of those things found its way up the bleachers at around midnight. I slid on my NVGs, trying to make sure when I turned them on that no green light would spill out around my eyes. I watched the corpse for five minutes as it stood there in front of the door at the top of the bleachers . . . then the batteries on my NVGs slowly started to fade out. I didn't have any more AA batteries in my pack so I was forced to sit there in terror as the thing slid its hand in and around the broken glass.

Every piece of glass that hit the floor sounded like thunder to me. I came very close to turning on my flashlight but kept the urge at bay, knowing that it would attract more of them. It reminded me of the scene from a dinosaur movie when the girl just couldn't bring herself to turn the flashlight off to avoid being eaten by a Tyrannosaur. The only difference was, I was the scared girl who couldn't turn the light on.

Now my species was becoming extinct.

After about thirty minutes of mental torture, the thing slipped and fell backward down the steps and hasn't come back up since. I thought the sound of its falling would bring more, but so far this hasn't happened. I should really pick up some batteries the next time I go shopping. For now, I have a tiny red LED light that I keep attached to my flight suit zipper. Writing this down in red light doesn't seem to affect my night vision and the red light does not attract them. It is such a low-power LED that the creatures have not reacted to it as I sit here writing this.

Approx. 0600

The sun is peeking up above the trees. The glow of the morning is lighting up the area and revealing the undead milling about below around where the fifty-yard line should be. The windsocks on the goalposts are floating on the morning breeze. I didn't get to sleep until about three hours ago and even then I woke up to every sound, every expansion and contraction of the bleachers heated by the morning sun.

This press box is starting to smell very bad. The bucket in the corner is filling up fast and the smell is starting to really fuck me up. I've noticed that the blood in my urine went away. My kidney area is still sore but not as bad as two days ago. I miss home. Was it the smoldering and burning San Antonio? Was it Arkansas? Was it Hotel 23? This is all cloudy to me right now. I just want to go home . . . somewhere happy, somewhere devoid of death and destruction. I wish that I could have good dreams, because that is the only way I can escape this.

Caller

Water is all but gone. I maybe have the bottom eighth of a gallon left. When the chopper went down, we were headed north from Shreveport. I don't know my exact location but after careful consideration I have decided to head southwest back in the general direction of Hotel 23. I need clean water to cleanse my head injury. Pus is seeping out of the open wound and I have to squeeze it every few hours to relieve the pressure. It's also very hot around the laceration. At least I know my body is fighting the infection. I would normally move at night, but my water situation has forced me out into the dead world again. There are about a dozen creatures below and I know they will see or hear me when I leave the press box, as I'm not about to attempt to climb down behind the bleachers and risk a broken leg.

I've been thinking a little more about writing down what has been going on. I think I might ditch this for the time being as I am busy trying to get back, and writing in this situation could prove unhealthy (fatal). I must confess that I tried to stop but it didn't last long. I write when I can and it makes me feel better. It may be sporadic or it may reflect my boredom at times but I stay more sane putting all this shit on paper.

As I write this, I'm trying to remember all my bank pin numbers and email password from before. I've had an account at my credit union for over ten years with the same pin and I can't remember it! I had to really concentrate to remember my email password, the same one I used every day for years until the shit hit the fan.

pin: ~~4609~~ ~~7897~~ 4609

e-mail pword: n@s@1Radi@t0r

I've packed my go bag, loaded the MP5 and put all the frequently needed items at the top of my bag for speed and convenience. Using a collapsed roll of rigging tape, I taped my knife sheath and survival knife to the left shoulder strap of my pack with the handle down. I want easy and quick access to it if I need to get personal with one of those things. I've rested enough that I think I can make it somewhere and maybe with luck hold up for a bit. I'm going to leave in one hour.

Late PM

I went to battle at the football field today. I stepped down out of the press box after gulping down the last bit of water. My pack was full and tight against my body, making my lower back hurt a bit. The first contestant on "The Headshot is Right" was a young male wearing one sneaker and a fucked-up green 7-UP T-shirt. He saw me come out of the box and immediately stumbled up the stairs. I still wasn't sure of myself with this weapon so I let him get pretty close before the action chambered back and the top of his head flipped open like a cookie jar lid. He fell backward, making the bone in his leg snap louder than the bullet that ended him. More witnessed what I had done and came for me.

Again I had to deal with the talented tenth, a very different talented tenth than W. E. B. Du Bois. In my recent travels and travails, I've noticed that about one in ten of these things is either smarter, faster or both than their compatriots. I picked her out immediately. She was more aware and came at me with more coordination than the rest. She stood upright and walked briskly to me, while the others just stumbled. I gave her no quarter and shot her in the neck and head. She went down just as easily as the others, but she probably came from a hot zone. She wasn't as radiated as the horrendous creature on the Coast Guard cutter, but I knew the odd effect radiation had on them. It kept them on a more level playing field with the living—me.

I didn't take care of all of them at the field. I just killed enough of them to keep the threat at a manageable level. My plan was to kill the ones I needed to, fall back to the far side of the field and circle around and retreat. I killed four and kept an eye on the other eight. I tried to get a good look at their wrists because I would be willing to make two passes if on the second pass I could pick up a watch from one of them. I couldn't get a good look and quite frankly I was a little scared to linger on that field.

I made one pass and evacuated the area, heading southwest by compass until I came upon a sign that said "Oil City 10 mi." I was at an intersection of the rural road and a two-lane highway. I walked a ten-yard offset to the road to avoid being seen by anything. In my experience in this world I've noticed the most lethal enemies are not the dead. From my vantage point at the crossroads I could see an old roadblock set up on the southbound side of the highway and a forty-car pileup on the northbound side. A small creek trickled from a drainage pipe near the road. I decided that my need of water temporarily outweighed my need to remain invisible, so I ventured over to the sound of the water.

As I approached the barrel-sized drain, I could swear I saw movement near the distant roadblock. I stood there for a full minute, just to make sure. Whatever it was, it didn't move again. I bent down and drank water until the sound of something caught my attention. I picked up my head so fast I hit the back of it on the top of the drain, temporarily causing me to see stars. I shook it off and kept listening. I made out the sound of an engine, cycling in a rhythmic pitch. It wasn't unlike an electric lawn mower. I tried to look in the direction I thought it was coming from, but I couldn't see it no matter how much I strained my eyes. The sound vanished as quickly as it had come. I sat for a while thinking of what it could be. Motorcycle? No. It didn't seem like that at all. It was something familiar.

I drank until I couldn't anymore, filled up the water reservoir in my pack and moved on, keeping the thirty-foot offset. I saw all sorts of things that a man should never see along the way. Rotting corpses were strewn in and around the roadblock. They seemed to lie in a bed of expended brass, as if an army had attempted to dispatch a horde of them here months ago. There were dead men standing on the highway in a hibernating daze, presumably with nothing to motivate them. I suppose they conserve energy that way. In the distance I could see a pack of dogs running across a field. I was downwind, so I'm pretty sure they didn't know I was near. There were no signs of human life whatsoever.

The sun was getting lower in the sky and it was time for me to find some shelter for the evening so that I could attempt to relax my nerves and collect some thoughts. It must have been two or three miles from the intersection that I noticed a house sitting behind a tree line in the distance. I carefully approached, watching all sides and looking over my shoulder much more than I needed to. It was very quiet, and I was still shaken up from the day's events. My kidney was full of water, and I had to pee. I thought back to playing hide and seek as a child, having to pee at all the wrong times. The house was an old 1950s era two-story. The paint was peeling off it seemingly before my eyes.

I sat and watched it for a very long time. I took notice of the burned-out late-model Chevy sitting a few meters to the side of the house. There were bullet holes in the hood and carriage. The first-floor windows of the home were boarded over, and old human remains were on the ground below the windows. I listened and watched until the fading light forced me to make a decision. The house seemed abandoned. I walked around it, looking for possible entry points. Even the front and back doors were boarded over. The only way in was to climb onto the roof and go in the unboarded upstairs windows.

I mustered all the courage I had and pulled my sore body up the porch pillar and onto the overhang leading to an upstairs window. I never would have made it had I not done pull-ups with the Marines every day back home. I sat up there admiring the view and listened to my surroundings. It was dark behind the window, so dark that I would not want to be in there for anything. The window was raised about six inches, giving airflow to a part of the thin white curtain. It blew in the breeze, or perhaps it was my breathing that was causing the curtain to flutter. I held off for what seemed like hours. I didn't want to go in. I debated sleeping outside but quickly ruled that out due to fear that I would roll off the roof and into the waiting arms of the dead. The sun's light was filtered red through the atmosphere as it said its good-bye with my spirits on the western horizon. I reached into my pack and grabbed my flashlight.

I held my arm out to the window and it felt almost electric as I touched it. I tried to pull it up with one hand, but it had been in that position so long that it wouldn't give. Using both my arms as well as my legs, I was able to get it high enough so that I could crawl in. I parted the curtain and twisted the tail cap on my light. The room appeared as normal as a room in an abandoned home could appear. The door was shut, the bed was made but there were bird droppings and leaves all over the floor.

I poked my head farther into the window to make sure it was clear all around. I was satisfied, so I crawled in. The first thing on my mind was the door and whether it was locked. I slowly walked over to the door, feeling the wood floor creak under my weight. After every sound I made, I stopped in my tracks and listened for any reaction in the hall or downstairs. I heard none. I reached up and checked the lock on the bedroom door—it was already locked from the inside. I then quietly checked the closet and under the bed and everywhere else bogeymen dwell. There was a burned candle and half a box of matches on the dresser.

I debated whether I should light the candle to conserve my flashlight batteries. After some thought, I closed the curtain on the bedroom windows and quietly hung extra blankets from the closet over them. I lit the candle and warmed my hands over its flame. My eyes eventually adjusted to the candlelight and I began to drift off into something . . . not sleep, but something.

I wasn't sure how long I had nodded off, but the sound of thunder startled me awake. I looked down at the candle and noticed that it had not burned down that much. I walked over to the window and pulled the blanket aside, looking out into the field. The lightning struck, revealing a human silhouette off in the distance. I had no idea of the creature's status or intent. I kept gazing out into the void—waiting for the lightning strikes to reveal the night. Eventually the shape went away, and I wondered if I had ever seen it in the first place.

It is still raining now and I've decided to use the bed. No noise has come from the other side of the door but I'll be sleeping with my weapon again tonight and probably every night for the rest of my life.

06 Oct

I awoke this morning to nothing but the sound of the wind outside. I needed to eat. I have three MREs left from the crash. I've only eaten bits and pieces of them since then. I think today is a good day to force more food into my system. My head feels a little better. The stitches itch but I'm trying not to touch. As I look out the window into the distance I can see no sign of the undead. It's dreary outside and it looks like it might storm again.

I started to stretch my body out and get ready for the day when I remembered the most important thing in my life right now—the downstairs portion of this house. I let my mind slip for a second, for the first time in a long time. I forgot where I was. It seemed like I had been in this room for days, but it had only been one night. My mind relayed to my subconscious that the home was safe, that it was mine. Of course this was not the situation. There could very well be a dozen of them down there, standing in a dormant trance, unaware of my presence. They seem to go into some sort of strange hibernation when there is no food or stimulus near. I could imagine a whole family of them standing downstairs in a daze, waiting for the first sign of life to wake them into hunter-killer mode.

I tried not to ponder exploring the house until I had eaten some sponge cake from my pack. After eating, I gulped down some water and started thinking of excuses not to go downstairs and look around. I knew that I had to, because there were things in this house that could keep me alive. It wasn't until the sun had crept through the clouds and was high in the sky that I decided to move on to the bottom floor.

I checked my weapon over and rigged my LED light to the suppressor of the MP5 using the duct tape I had in my pack. I pulled the slide of my Glock back a quarter-inch to make sure I could see brass in the hole. No part of my body was exposed as I reached out with my left hand to unlock the door. It was stuck, probably from being in one position for months. I had to force it open, making a loud clicking sound. I placed my hand on the door, securing it as I listened. If the noise brought them, I would lock it and head for the hills.

I waited for at least five minutes, thinking I heard everything from the undead to a lawn mower to a foghorn. I released my hand from the door and reached down to turn the knob, presumably the first time it had been turned in ages. Twisting the knob, I readied my right hand to kill whatever stood in my way. The taped suppressor of my weapon was the first part of me to make it through the door. The blue tint of LED light lit up the upstairs common area as I panned my weapon around.

I kept wondering whether I had actually checked my magazine or if I had just imagined it. Pushing that thought out of my head, I advanced. I looked back at the bedroom door I had just walked through. There were old bloodstains on the door, as if something had beaten on it until it lost interest. These things know.

Swinging back around, I noticed something odd. There were white spots on the wall where pictures would have been. It's as if the owners of the house made sure to take the pictures with them. I can think of a few hundred more important things than pictures to take. There were dead flies all over the floor, as common as dust. The upstairs floor was covered in layers of both, with no footprints to indicate recent activity. If there was something dead or alive in this house, it had never bothered to wander around up here. This was when I found out why. As I crept to the stairs, almost stepping down, I stopped and looked down at my feet. There were only two steps before they disappeared. Someone had taken them out. Below were the bodies of six undead, all shot through the head. It was starting to make sense. Whoever owned this place had probably taken out the stairs and bugged out to the second floor. They had most likely shot the ghouls and retreated out the bedroom window. That's the best I could figure. That still didn't explain the bloodstains on the door I had come from or how the things got into the house, but I hadn't checked the whole upstairs yet.

I steered clear of the area of the floor near the damaged staircase and slowly made my way to the two closed doors at the other end of the hall. The floor creaked as I walked, but I ignored the sound. I didn't sense anything was here. The first door I came to was an upstairs bathroom. If the power had been on, it would have looked like any bathroom did before the dead came back. Everything was neatly in place, with dust-covered towels draped over the shower rod and a new bar of soap sitting in the soap holder near the sink. I swiped it up and zipped it in my leg pocket. I went over to the toilet and looked around. Nothing out of the ordinary but a weird little plaster mold in the shape of a toilet seat sitting on top of the toilet tank that read: "If you sprinkle when you tinkle, be a sweetie and wipe the seatie!"

For some reason I thought that was funny and chuckled there for a couple of minutes. Before walking out of the bathroom, I checked under the sink and found a plastic container full of various medications. I took a tube full of expired triple antibiotic and a roll of toilet paper and moved on to door number two.

I readied my weapon as I opened the door. It was pitch black inside, with heavy curtains over the windows. I panned my light around the room, revealing its disheveled condition. The bed's mattress was flipped over and dirty clothes and trash littered the floor. Small rat droppings were spread all over the room, adding to the room's "old book" smell. I was letting my imagination go wild before I went into these rooms, half expecting to see something horrible and demented. I was certainly happy not to find an old lady swinging by her neck from a light fixture in a failed attempt to kill herself properly . . . swinging by her purple neck, screeching out in a witch's voice, "Be a sweetie and wipe the seatie!" Not today, thank goodness.

The downstairs remained unexplored, but I didn't like the idea of climbing down there only to get my ass bitten off by a crafty ghoul. I doubt any of them are crafty, but I've seen them do increasingly weird things since they started reanimating. I suppose that alone is weird.

After careful consideration, I decided to take the small hand mirror from the upstairs bathroom and use the rigging tape to attach it to a broom handle from the upstairs closet so that I could get a better view of the downstairs without having to risk my own ass. I was at the top of the destroyed stairs on my stomach for twenty minutes looking around with the broom mirror before I decided it might be safe enough to go down. The only thing that was out of the ordinary were the dead bodies on the floor below and an open door that looked like it could lead down into some sort of basement.

I was so paranoid of falling down into the bodies below that I tied my leg to the sturdy upstairs railing. I'd have hated to find myself facedown on a pile of corpses with more pouring out of the open door and no quick way back upstairs. Using the same dirty sheets I used to tie my leg, I made a makeshift rope ladder for my descent. Feeling more frightened than on my first day of school, I quickly climbed down and immediately sped over to close the open door.

Approaching the door, I noticed that there were definitely stairs leading down into the dark abyss. I didn't care if those stairs led to a cache of M-16s and a year's worth of food, I wasn't going down there, not after what I've been through. I shut the door and scooted a large couch in front of it as quietly as I could. After I was certain that the basement door was secure, I began methodically clearing the bottom floor of any perceived threats. Closet by closet, nook by cranny, I made sure that none of those things were down there with me. I checked everywhere, making sure that not even a severed upper torso could be hiding in wait for me under a table, or in a downstairs shower.

Satisfied that the house was clear enough, I began searching for items that I needed. I went through the drawers in the kitchen, finding waterproof matches and three packs of AA batteries. My NVGs were again serviceable. Further investigation revealed an old box with two large rattraps inside. I took these traps, as I felt they were easily large enough to take a small rabbit or a squirrel when my ready reserve food ran out. In reality, I should have been hunting to preserve my nonperishables, and I may begin to do so as soon as I feel a little stronger.

In a downstairs closet, I found a black and gray hiking pack with "Arc'teryx Bora 95" embroidered on it in gold letters. The pack was clearly of higher quality and more comfortable than the one I was using and looked like it could hold twice as much. I walked over to the bashed staircase, careful not to touch the bodies on the floor. After reaching up to shove the pack onto the second floor, I continued my investigation.

I walked around the lower level of the house, checking out the boarded-over windows and reinforced door. Propped up next to one of the windows to the left of the door was a long mop handle with an ice pick bound to the end. The pick was attached with skill, the twine holding it in place showing intricate knots that formed a pattern, holding the pick very securely to the end. Brown, dried blood covered the metallic end of this homemade spear. It wouldn't be good for hunting an animal, but if you hit one of those things in the eye, or the tender part of the rotting skull, you could bring it down without a shot, saving valuable resources. I took the makeshift weapon and placed it on the kitchen counter. When I went back into the main area where I had made my descent, I heard a creaking sound. I sat still and it happened again. My main fear was that it was coming from the basement area. I walked over to the boarded-up door to take a look outside so that I could make sure I had a clear escape out the front door.

As I brought my eye level to the peephole the outline of a dead man projected into my pupil. I was terrified for a moment, just gazing at it, unable to look away. Its skeletal face was no more than a foot from me on the other side of the door. I wanted badly to shoot the thing through the peephole, but I would probably have missed and complicated things with the noise it would make splintering the wood. I couldn't take my eye off this train wreck. The face was rotted, the milky eyes bugged out and the lips were gone. The thing seemed to stare at me through the door. It didn't move a millimeter the whole time I watched. The creature must have been over six feet tall. Standing on my tiptoes, I tried to look down at an object in the creature's rotten grip. I couldn't quite make out what it was. I waited at the door, only pausing my peek to blink so that my eyes wouldn't dry up. It didn't budge.

My choices were limited . . .

I could either sneak back upstairs (by climbing the sheet) and call it a day or dispatch the creature once and for all at that moment. I chose to quietly look around the house for more supplies that could be of use before going back upstairs. Moving like a cat, I went back into the kitchen to check the cupboard. I caused a slight creak in the floor as I crossed the kitchen's threshold. I paused for a few minutes, listening—creak . . . creak . . . was the sound from just outside the front door. I dismissed the threat, half imagining the creature cocking its head from side to side, trying to decide if it had made the noise or if it was made by some tasty morsel on the inside . . .

Checking the shelves in the cupboard, I found six cans of chili no meat, two cans of vegetable beef stew and various other foods in advanced stages of decomposition. I shoved the cans into my pack and looked under the sink for anything of use. Under the sink sat an old rattrap identical to the two that I had taken earlier. Only the skeletal remains and shriveled tail of the long-ago-tricked rat were present. Satisfied with my find, I grabbed the mop handle with the ice pick and crept back to the improvised rope ladder, fighting back the unnatural urge to peek through the peephole again.

Using the mop handle, I carefully raised my pack to the second floor so that it would be easier for me to climb up. The pack was overfilled and too heavy so I wobbled a bit trying to keep it balanced. A can of chili fell out and hit the floor, making a sound so loud that it might as well have been artillery fire. I cringed as I shoved the pack up onto the second floor next to the larger empty pack. As I bent down to pick up the can of food, a loud banging sound erupted from the front door. The thing must have been hitting the door with something, as it sounded harder and louder than a bare hand. I shoved the can into one of the pockets in my vest and nearly jumped to the second floor.

I lay there on the top floor, using my pack as a pillow and looking at the ceiling as the monster kept the time for me by door whacks. Relentlessly it kept on . . . I heard the door splinter some and decided to use the mirror to watch the door. I jumped and shook a little every time the creature hit the door, making the mirror shake in my grip. A very small beam of sunlight was poking through a hole in the door about two feet above the knob. Blunt objects don't cause damage like that. The door was boarded in three places and I remember it being boarded on the outside as well.

I retreated into the bedroom I had previously commandeered

and locked myself in as the sun dipped to the horizon. It would be dark soon. Using my multitool, I opened a can of chili and pulled out my brown plastic MRE spoon. I sat there counting the thumps downstairs as the sun set. It took me 353 thumps to finish my chili.

Night Run

06 Oct

Late PM

From the sounds below, I can tell that the thing is all but inside. I heard a board hit the floor about half an hour ago. Of course I don't have any idea what half an hour is anymore. In the fear that it may draw more of its own, I've decided to use the night as cover and escape from this place. I spent the evening stuffing the new pack I scavenged from downstairs. I've rearranged everything so that the most needed items will be on top or in a compartment near one of the zippers. There is a lot of extra room in my bag so I'm grabbing a green wool blanket from the closet.

I checked the batteries that I acquired from downstairs. They don't expire for six more years. I put them in the NVGs and turned them on. The green light shining from the optics onto my palm indicated that they were working fine. No use looking through them with the candlelight shining. I also tried my handheld radio again. I didn't hear anything but static. My mind was playing tricks on me as I thought I heard voices on the other end. I transmitted my situation in the blind, but was vague on my location. Maybe when I get farther south I'll use the memorized codes that John insisted I learn. My stitches are itching again so I tried the antibiotic ointment. I hope it will help fight off any infection. In a few more days, I'll be cutting the stitches out.

It's time to blow out the candle.

07 Oct

Early AM

I'm not certain why these things are the way that they are or why they are different . . .

More aggressive and persistent.

When I departed the house last night, I did so from the same window I entered. I made the bed, mostly because it made me feel better to do so but also because it postponed my inevitable departure. After making the bed, I doused the light and put on my NVGs. As I adjusted them my fears became reality when I saw that the noise the creature made downstairs had drawn a dozen more undead to the area. That was just what I could count from one window. By my estimation, there were probably nearly thirty around the house.

As I made my way out onto the roof I could hear the sounds of them moving through tall grass and tripping over branches trying to locate the noise in the dark. Old habits die hard, and I knew I had twenty-nine rounds of ammo in each of my magazines, even though it didn't matter with this weapon. I carefully moved to the edge and looked down. There were two below. Leaning over the edge I popped both of them, missing the head of one. The one I hit fell into the other, giving me another chance. I shot number two and started climbing down the side of the house the same way I had come up. Moving to my best evasion route, I killed three more. Each trigger pull illuminated the surrounding area with a green flash. The NVGs were magnifying the flash from the tip of the suppressor.

I was much too tired to sprint. I walked at a near jog, simply dodging them. I looked back toward the house as I neared the road. One of those things seemed to be nearly running in my direction. For a moment, I thought that it could actually see me in the dark. My fears subsided when it moved off to the side and stopped. It seemingly sniffed the air and slowly turned its head from side to side as if trying to sense me. It held an object of some sort in hand. My gut told me that it was the same creature I had seen through the peephole.

I started to move away from it and turned to the road. I had no idea where I was going. I traveled south for miles along an old paved highway, stepping over cracks so as not to break my mother's back. The signs indicated that I was closing in on Oil City. This road might even take me into Shreveport, a city that I dared not enter. I needed a place to sleep tonight. I walked until I could almost see a bit of light on the horizon, meaning that the sun would be up soon. I could make out a school bus up ahead on the road.

My best guess was that it was about 0430. The cold was getting to me and I needed at least a couple of hours of sleep to face the coming day. I kept heading toward the bus, careful to scan my surroundings. The area seemed clear but there were a lot of unknowns. A few derelict cars and trucks littered the side of the road on the way to the bus. Rotted skeletons were strewn about near the vehicles, picked clean by the dead and the birds.

Approaching the bus, I was happy to see that the door was open, telling me that at least nothing was trapped inside and too dumb to let itself out. Carefully maneuvering to the front, I climbed the bumper and stepped up onto the hood. The bus was slippery from the morning dew. From the hood I looked into the front window down the rows of seats. It was empty. I climbed onto the roof of the bus to get a better 360-degree view of the area. There was no movement except for two small rabbits in the ditch.

I thought about shooting them but it was too dark to risk even that slight noise. I took the wool blanket out of my pack and left the pack on the roof of the bus. I climbed back down the hood and entered the bus door. Throwing the blanket onto the bus driver's seat, I knelt and pointed my SMG under the seats. I could see nothing but an old paper lunch sack. I reached over and closed the bus door with the manual crank lever as slowly as I could, making sure to minimize the noise it made. Sadly, this isn't the first time I've slept in a bus.

With my pack safely on the roof, I could escape out any of the windows and retrieve it if I needed to make a quick departure. If I had kept my pack inside I might not have been able to fit it through the window, losing all my food and supplies if I had to run. I cut strips of vinyl from one of the seats on the bus and very sloppily braided it into a rope. I used this to tie the door handle in place to make sure that nothing could get in to see me without making a lot of noise. Time for sleep, if anyone would call it that.

Late AM

It's about midmorning now and I'm sitting in the fourth seat back on the right side of the bus. I've slept a needed four hours, or so I think. My pack is still on the roof. There is no movement around me and I'll probably climb up, get my things and leave as soon as I'm sure it's safe. The more I think of Hotel 23, the more important it becomes for me to get back there to my family. Even though the thought of my parents' being alive is still inside my head, I know that most likely they are dead. My home is no bunker, and just like every other home built in the United States in the past fifty years, my parents' home was not built to outlast a siege. I wonder how many people might still live if they "made 'em like they used to."

PM.

Still the 7th

As I geared up to get my stuff off the top of the bus this morning, I was confronted with a very grim surprise. The bastard from the house had somehow followed me. I was on the hood of the bus, about to climb to the roof, when I heard the sound of steel on steel. The sound startled me so much I nearly fell off the hood and flat on my back. I jumped forward into the bus window, causing it to crack. Looking over my shoulder I knew instantly that it was the creature, the same apparition that stared at me through the peephole at the old house. How could this dumb thing know anything about following me? An even better question was how did this thing know how to swing a hatchet?

I jumped onto the roof of the bus and just watched the thing work with amazement. It was actually trying to climb up there with me. I wasn't making the same mistake this time. This member of the undead talented tenth had to go. I flipped the indicator on my weapon and blasted the creature in the face, dropping it instantly. The thing made a lot of noise before I killed it, so it was time for me to depart.

Before leaving I checked the creature for anything valuable, and lo and behold it was wearing a beat-up plastic G-Shock wristwatch. I grabbed the watch and looked at the display before stuffing it in my pack along with the hatchet. The digital display read 10-7 and 12:23 P.M.

I kept making my way south and west, passing scene upon scene of decay. How long had it been since I had seen the first of them? I walked and imagined how it would feel to talk to someone again. The feeling of loneliness was setting in. From all my experiences with survival, this was the most serious of all emotions. It is different with everyone, but for me, the emotion attached to being lonely is fear.

I kept pushing the thought of the dead out of my consciousness, but I could not control what I was about to think. The "daymare" brought me to an open field that I was crossing to the wooded area beyond. As if in a scene from a war movie, as I approached the middle of the field an army of radiated dead appeared at the crest of the hill. They immediately ran for me. Right before I could see the rot of their eyes, I snapped out of it and kept walking. There was no sound. Only the slight breath of wind on my face let me know that I was back to this reality.

Caddo Lake

Yesterday I walked until I came upon a lake. The signs leading up to it read "Caddo Lake Boat Landing Ah." The last letters of "Ahead" had been shot off the sign by a shotgun long ago. It was about 1400 when I came to the lake, so I had to start making preparations for somewhere safe to hole up tonight. I carefully approached the boat dock, thinking back to Matagorda Island and how that situation had ended up. Many boats were still docked, and there were a few that had succumbed to the deep and pulled part of a dock down into the water with them. There were two sailboats of decent size docked and still afloat, but one of them did not look serviceable, because the owner had left the sails on deck to endure months of wind and weather. The other twenty-footer most likely had the sails stowed and would probably work. I could see a working anchor and a chain propped up on the rails of the forecastle with a hand-cranked winch.

I was only a hundred feet away from the boat, close enough that I could stand there and observe my surroundings. With the food and water I had on hand, I could pirate the boat, sail it out into the lake and get some real sleep tonight.

My goal was to move south and west back in the direction of Hotel 23. If the lake were shaped to my advantage, I could cover a lot of ground with the safety of water around me. Edging closer to the vessel, I saw no threats near. I wasn't taking any chances, though, and approached the vessel scanning every direction. That dirty fuck with the hatchet got one over on me and I could have been dead or dying right now if my luck had run out on the hood of that yellow bus.

In a moment of nervousness I chambered my weapon again to

make sure I had one in the hole and a 9mm round dropped to the ground. I picked it up and put it in my pocket. I was getting closer to the vessel . . .

Did I chamber my weapon?

I asked myself again. Pushing back the fear and anxiety, I kept moving. I was out in the open, within view of anyone or anything. I was at the boat. She looked derelict, with the nylon lines on the deck covered in mildew and bird crap. The curtains to the belowdecks were closed, allowing me no view of the interior.

I again checked my surroundings and jumped across to the starboard catwalk. Edging to the stern I could see remnants of bloody barefoot prints leading all the way back to the stern. I kept moving aft, making sure to point the dangerous end of my weapon at any blind spot. I followed the prints as they trailed off the stern into the water.

My next task was to make sure that there were no surprises waiting in the cabin below. I twisted on my weapon light and flipped open the door. No smell. Kept walking farther, into the bowels of the sailboat, bending over so as to not hit my head on the fixtures that littered the ceiling. Aside from the familiar *old* smell, the boat was abandoned. I began to inspect the sails, anchor and all the rigging to make sure that she would be safe for my transit across the Caddo.

The sails had some mold, but they were still workable. The motor would probably never work again and I doubted I would even attempt it. It was pulled back and out of the way so it wouldn't matter to me either way. All that really mattered were the sails, anchor and rudder. I checked the pantry of the vessel—nothing but old and rotted beef jerky, two bottles of cloudy water and a pack of bar soap. I checked a small storage locker holding a small CO_2 inflatable lifeboat. Sitting in some storage netting attached to the bulkhead inside the locker was a set of Steiner Marine binoculars. These will really come in handy when I make landfall and when I need to scout ahead on my way south.

After taking one more look out the porthole to make sure nothing was about, I commenced to rig the sails to head out into the lake for some rest and relaxation. Barring being at the summit of Mount Everest or at the International Space Station (poor bastards), this was the safest rest I could hope for in this day and time. It had been awhile since I had taken my sailing lessons, but I still remembered how to swing the boom and raise and lower the sails. The wind was blowing to my advantage, which was the second lucky thing to happen to me in the past forty-eight hours. I'm sure I am due for something else.

Kicking the dock from the bow, I started my travels south and slightly west out of the small inlet toward the expanse of the lake. The sails caught the light wind and pulled me at a speedy three knots toward my destination. This was a happy time for me. I forced my current situation out of my head and imagined I was sailing on Beaver Lake back home before all of this happened. I thought of being home on leave and visiting my family, and of my grandmother's brown beans.

I could see no sign of the undead on the shore but I was a decent clip away from land. I was careful to remain in the center of the small channel as it opened up to the lake. As I approached the mouth of the inlet, I locked the wheel and ran up to lower the sails. I wanted to be far enough away from land to feel safe, but I still wanted to be close enough to swim easily ashore if something were to go wrong with my little floating sanctuary.

The sun was getting low in the sky as the boat drifted to my self-assigned safe zone. I dropped anchor and estimated that the lake was about sixty feet deep. I unpacked all my gear and hung up the wet stuff to dry out. I scavenged the boat once more, checking out the head and galley. There was no usable food but there was a tin mop bucket and an old grill top that had been cleaned before it was stowed long ago. In the head, I found a stack of magazines. I kept some to use as toilet paper when the good stuff ran out.

I had about an hour or so of daylight left so I took the mop bucket and dipped it over the side to get some water. I then took a bar of soap and the grill top and used them as a washing machine to clean up all my dirty gear. Not as good as Maytag but better than nothing. My undergarments and socks were starting to smell pretty bad and I am getting a light rash under my armpits and around my crotch. I spent the rest of my daylight washing and wringing my clothing dry. I used some nylon cord that I found in a trunk at the stern to improvise a drying line below the guardrail in case the wind blew my stuff off the line.

Just as the sun dipped down below the tree line I secured myself belowdecks in the stateroom, wearing only the green wool blanket that I had acquired from the old farmhouse, hoping that I didn't get into a naked gunfight. For the first time in a while I feel safe to sleep and let my guard down so I will do just that.

09 Oct

I slept in until 0830. A light eastern wind kept the boat pointing into the breeze. My head was scratchy around the makeshift stitches. I knew it was time to remove them. Using the mirror from the boat's head and the same needle I had used to stitch my head, I began to remove them one by one. I stopped about five minutes into the procedure and thought it might be a good idea to boil some water to clean the area every few seconds, but changed my mind, realizing that it would be dangerous to make a fire on a boat in the middle of a lake with all my gear spread out. I had visions of a burning beacon signaling the dead and any band of miscreants within twenty miles. After about ten minutes I was done and cleaned up the wound as best I could, rubbing in a small amount of expired triple antibiotic.

My clothing had dried by noon, and I could see that some clouds were forming on the western horizon. Looked like it could possibly rain. I brought my dry clothes down into the cabin, folded them as best I could and repacked them in the order I thought I might need them. Before getting dressed for the day I again dipped the bucket into the lake water and tried to take a modified sponge bath, using one of my clean socks as a washrag. It wasn't a hot shower, but it sure as hell felt better than being dirty. I dried off with the wool blanket and had started to get dressed when I heard them in the distance. The wind carried their cries to my sanctuary and once again reminded me that this was not a camping trip or a pleasure hike down the Appalachian Trail. This was a death game.

I could not tell how far away they were but it didn't matter. Using my new binoculars I scanned the shoreline of the lake. Something was moving along the shore northwest of my position.

From this distance it could have been a deer. I went belowdecks just as it started to rain to check and recheck my gear. There was some motor oil in the sink area so I tried to make good use of it by oiling some critical parts of my weapons. I figured that if it's good enough for an engine it's good enough for a weapon. The guns have seen some use in the past days so I figured that it couldn't hurt.

As I wiped the SMG down, I once again heard a faint buzzing sound. It reminded me of a few days ago at the watering hole. It seemed mechanical in nature. I had enough daylight to sit and think inside the boat and formulate my plan. I knew that Hotel 23 was south/southwest from my position. Just a WAG (wild ass guess) at the distance would be two hundred miles. My general heading in true, not magnetic should be 220 to 230 degrees. At two hundred miles, traveling on foot most of the way, at ten miles per day, I should be in the neighborhood of Hotel 23 in roughly a month. For anyone who finds this, that is/was my plan. I will follow a general heading from Caddo Lake to Nada, Texas until I reach the facility. My first priority is to knock a gas station and grab a road atlas or maybe check for one in abandoned vehicles along the way.

After gaining access to an atlas, I can formulate a better route, going around towns and cities instead of blindly stumbling into them. I'll hunt for food to replace my perishables and try to travel at night when possible. Supply priorities are: water, food, medical supplies, batteries and ammunition. Funny how priorities shift. In the beginning ammunition would have been my first priority.

1623

Sound has strange quality on this lake, like some strange parabolic antenna attracting the sounds of the dead to the mast of this sailboat. I can hear the moans and rasps of them. Terrible things. Thinking of this I pulled out my survival radio and gave it a shot—nothing. Once again I grabbed my binoculars and scanned the distance. I could see them everywhere I could see the shore. They swarmed the shoreline like seagulls. I'm noting any change in trend in their movement at the shore.

western group   50+
          moving north

Sooner rather than later, I'm going to have to make landfall and continue my journey south. I'm not looking forward to making a two-hundred-mile walkabout across dead-infested territory with over sixty pounds of gear. Every now and again I think about this and it still shocks me down to my DNA that this is happening. The suicide rate must have skyrocketed in the past few months among survivors, because not a day goes by that I don't think of ending it here and now. There are no red days on the calendar anymore. I have no days I can rest and let down my guard. Even on this boat I dream of them somehow getting onboard and taking me out. Looks like tonight will be a can of chili, and with my gear safely centralized, some boiled lake water for dinner. All I can do is sit here and enjoy the coming sunset and try to ignore the ominous bellows in the distance.

10 Oct

0630

I feel well rested and recovered enough to start heading south and west on the water. My intention is to triple-check my gear and raise sails for shore. Loneliness is magnified by the solitude of the lake. I remember staying in a hostel in Brisbane, Australia, a couple of years ago. Not wanting my things stolen, I chose a single and stayed there for three days nursing a hangover for the first two. Somehow, in some detached way, that time of solitude in Brisbane reminds me of how I feel now. Maybe it is the fact that I am traveling alone and the only other things that matter to me are my pack and weapons.

2200

After fooling with the sails for an hour or so, I pulled anchor and made very slowly southwest. I know these things can see my sail; I just did not know how the sight of it cruising across the lake would affect their decision to follow. My plan was to run the boat aground to save time. I could not afford the time it would take to properly moor the vessel and tie her up securely. This would be a one-way trip, as after the boat was run aground it would take another motor-powered vessel to pull her back to the lake. Using the binocs I scanned the shoreline for any indications and warning of the dead reacting to my presence.

I tied off a knotted line to the bow so that I would have an easy deboarding when the time came. In between boom swings of the sail, I positioned my three MP5 9mm magazines where I could reach them, with the fourth full at twenty-nine rounds in the weapon chambered. Make no mistake—this was not Normandy beach in the forties but was Caddo beach with potentially more ghouls than German soldiers and one man to push back their numbers.

I wished the vessel had a speed slower than five knots—I wanted to approach more conservatively. After two hours of steering the bow port and starboard, I could finally get a good look at the beachhead that I would be assaulting. On first count I observed a dozen dead at the shore with icy gazes locking to my center mass. Using the compartmentalization techniques that I had learned in the military, I made a poor attempt at pushing the thought of getting torn apart out of my gray matter.

Knowing that this vessel had a draft of at least six feet, I anticipated a respectably violent impact when the sails pushed the vessel and keel into the rocky shore. Nearing land, I tied off the boom and lay flat on my back with my feet braced on the forward railing. Lying on the deck I tried to push the mental image of the dead out of my thoughts by looking up at the mast and clouds in the sky above. Then came the impact . . .

The vessel leaned violently to port while the bow turned starboard and I could hear everything on the shelves below fall and crash to the deck.

Regaining my footing, I shouldered my heavy pack and readied my submachine gun. I estimated that there were twenty of them closing my position with the potential of thousands if I didn't move fast. Aiming as best I could with the short-barreled MP5, I took out five of them so that I would have the time to carefully climb down the knotted rope to the shore. I was down to about nineteen rounds in this magazine as I only had a 50 percent head hit ratio past twenty yards with the SMG. I knew my Glock was loaded and ready as backup as I hit the water at the bottom of the rope. I carefully scanned for any open spots in the group of ten or so that remained and once again played offense as I threaded the needle and ran through them as best I could.

Those ten would turn to a hundred if I didn't lose them, so I decided to run down the shoreline in plain view as fast as I could, prompting them to follow. It was about a mile before jogging became nearly impossible with the pack. I turned ninety degrees right, into the tree line out of my pursuers' sight and then started the system of *walk twenty paces then jog twenty paces* for about an hour. I had successfully lost the dead and was marginally safe in the open plains of what I believed to be Texas. Until I find a reliable map of the area, my plan is to head west until I reach a two-lane highway running north-south and shadow it south until I hit the interstate that runs east-west into Dallas. Of course I will not be visiting Dallas—ever. I will simply shadow the interstate highway system going in the general direction of Hotel 23 using roadway lateral navigation.

As I walked west with the sun at my back I started to feel more energized despite the painful blisters on my feet. What I wouldn't give for some moleskin in my gear. I might try rigging tape. By the late afternoon, I had found a deserted two-lane highway and approached cautiously from the east. I had depleted my water supply down to half the Camelbak bladder so I thought it best to stop at the nearest small bridge over a creek to fill up. It took a mile of paralleling the road before I spotted a steel drainage tube running underneath the road from the field in which I was walking.

The Steiner binocs had already earned their weight in my pack for helping me to find the water supply. As I approached the drain carefully from the northwest, I spotted half a dozen dead cattle—what was left of them. In virtually all of the cattle carcasses the legs were removed and strewn about the field, indicating that they had likely been taken down by the dead. I would have believed that feral dogs or coyotes had done the job if I hadn't seen a long-dead corpse with a hoof mark through its head and a mouth full of cowhide covered in white hair. The beast must have knocked one of them down and taken a lucky step. No matter. The dead had probably swarmed the cattle like Amazonian piranha. I could almost imagine the event in my head, remote-viewing back to the beginning months.

Leaving the field, I moved to the water supply and could hear the trickle of the water as it fell from the drainage pipe under the highway. The pipe was about the diameter of a fifty-five-gallon steel drum. I pulled out the water bladder and had begun to fill it when I heard a shuffling sound inside the pipe. Looking into the darkness I could make out the human shape of what I believed to be one of those things. Using my flashlight I discovered the partially decomposed body of a creature lodged among drainage debris and unable to get out.

The creature's head was caught in such a position that it could not see me. It did, however, know I was there. I poured out my decontaminated water and dried the inside of the plastic water bladder as best I could with a clean set of spare skivvies. Leaving the poor bastard to rot in his steel cylinder tomb, I kept moving, looking for water. Now that I had been forced to give up my entire water supply, I felt even thirstier. I continued to shadow the two-lane highway south. Using my binocs I saw that I was following the direction of Highway 59. I took a few minutes to scratch this down in my journal. I continued to keep a lookout for any of those green signs that gave the mileage to the next city.

HWY 59

The sun was starting to go down by this point so I decided, despite my thirst, that it was best to use the remaining hour of useful light to find a safe place to hole up for the evening. There were houses in the vicinity of the road but I didn't have time to break and enter and properly sweep a house before sunset. I kept moving and scouting with my binocs until I discovered a suitable location to sleep—the top of a relatively easy-to-access roof. I stopped in a field and checked my pack to make sure everything was in place before bolting across the road to the target house. I put the wool blanket I had on the top of my pack for easy reach and extra 9mm ammunition in the zipper pouch on the lid of the pack. I then dropped the magazines from my MP5 and Glock to make sure they were at capacity—fifteen plus one on the Glock and twenty-nine plus one on the MP5. Weapons hot, with the MP5 set to single shot and my pack rearranged, I made for the house of choice, a two-story home on the outskirts of a small neighborhood.

The sun was getting low and the temperature was falling as I sprinted as fast as I could to the fence line. I threw my pack over the three-wire barbed-wire fence and climbed over, being careful not to cut myself. After lifting the pack back on I checked the road in both directions. There was undead movement in the distance on both sides of the road. I crossed the road slowly and deliberately, using the cover of an old car, long abandoned. Standing on the other side of the road, I knelt and scouted ahead with the binocs in the fading light. It seemed relatively clear so I double-timed it to the house. I chose this house because of the ladder that I had spotted four hundred yards earlier. It was leaning against the guardrail of the front porch.

I made it to the house and positioned the ladder so that I could easily climb to the roof and sleep there tonight. Before climbing up, I surveyed the outside of the home, noticing that the front door had been splintered in from the outside and bullet holes peppered the front of the house and the wooden pillars of the porch. Another site of a last stand gone wrong. The whole perimeter of the home was covered in what I call gore marks, places the dead had pummeled for days in an attempt to enter.

Makeshift board barricades were nailed up on the downstairs windows but most of the boards were ripped from the window frames and *all* the windows were busted from the outside. This house would be a terrible choice in which to sleep tonight, but a fairly decent choice to sleep on. Satisfied that this place was condemned and that it was not worth investigating its interior, I carefully climbed the ladder to the roof. Once on the roof of the first-story overhang, I pulled the ladder up with me and then climbed to the second story. I didn't want to take a chance of one of those things breaking through the second-story window and attacking me in my sleep. After making it to the roof of the house I pulled the ladder up with me.

I had a pretty good vantage point with enough light to spare to set up camp on the roof. I pulled out my blanket and strapped my pack to one of the roof exhaust pipes. Using the pack waist strap, I attached the secured pack to my arm so I wouldn't roll off the house in my sleep. I was able to use part of my pack as sort of a pillow. What with being fully clothed, with a thick wool blanket, it is not that bad up here. Good night.

Chain Gang

I awoke this morning to the feeling of cold rain on my face. I glanced at my watch, which indicated 0520, and I could tell my core temperature was falling quickly by the annoying chatter of my teeth. I was dog thirsty and fought through the cold to reach into my bag and pull out an old plastic MRE pouch from days ago. Wrapping the wool blanket around my cold body and tangling my foot into my pack strap, I leaned over the edge of the roof and hung the MRE pouch over the edge where the water was steadily streaming down to the first-story ledge below.

After I filled up I drank the shingle-flavored water until the pouch was empty and then I filled it again. Fighting the chill that nearly shook me off the roof, I kept gathering water until my water bladder was full. I repacked my gear (sans the wool blanket), leaving the bladder drinking tube accessible to the outside of the pack and started to think about moving again. There were no dead in sight from my view on the roof. Using my knife, I cut a slit in the center of the wool blanket so that I could fit my head through and use it as a poncho. It was wool and wet so there was no use packing it away. At least wool keeps its heat even when wet.

I then attempted to position the ladder for my descent to the first-floor overhang of the house. As I lowered the ladder my grip slipped a little and the other end hit the overhang with a loud bang. I put the ladder where I wanted and then put on my pack and started my descent. The rain seemed to be getting worse as I climbed down. When I reached the bottom of the ladder I nearly jumped off the roof in fright, as one of those creatures had its face pressed against the second-story window in response to the noise I had made when dropping the ladder.

I saw it and it saw me. Quickly, I positioned the ladder on the ground so that I could start climbing down. The thing was beating on the window in an attempt to break out and get to me. From the sounds, it did not seem that it had enough strength to break through. I didn't want to think about why, but the visions and memories in my mind when I reached the bottom of the ladder were not of an adult corpse—it was a child.

I left the ladder where it stood and made my way to the road that I had used to find this overnight sleeping arrangement. The rain was making me miserable, and I wanted nothing more than to build a fire somewhere and hang my clothes to dry. I thought back to central heat and air and remembered how dependent we were on electric power to survive as a society. I'll bet we lost thousands of elderly over the summer just because of the heat waves. It had been a bit since I tried my radio so I decided to give it a go and xmit out on the preset distress frequency. After going out three times with no response, I switched the radio into beacon pulse mode and decided to leave it on for a few minutes. The rain continued as I shadowed the road, which I remembered from the day before as Highway 59 South.

As the rain lessened in intensity, I could hear the familiar hum of a distant engine. I had heard this sound on more than one occasion since my helicopter crash miles and lakes behind. Part of me thought it was due to my head injury and the infection that I had endured. I rubbed the area where my stitches had been days before. The soreness and sensitivity were virtually gone. I continued to follow the direction of the road for what seemed like miles. It started to warm up around 0800, and the rain decreased to a light drizzle. The haze was thick and there were patches of fog, largely due to the moisture, combined with the heat of the rising sun. My feet were sinking deep into the mud as I kept my distance from the seemingly empty Highway 59.

After a few hundred yards I had to turn ninety degrees and head to the highway, as I realized that the mud was not related to the rain. I was walking into what appeared to be a swamp. The road started to elevate and just as a patch of fog blew by I could see for an instant that a section of the highway a quarter mile down the road was up on short stilts to raise it above the marsh. It seemed to go on forever that way into the distance. I didn't fancy disease, and I knew that swamp bacteria or hypothermia from walking waist deep in cold mud could kill me just as easily as any of those things. Adding to my fear were the various open wounds I had on my body from being banged up from the crash and on the run from those things. My wounds were scabbed over, but that was nothing that a few hours of submersion in swamp water couldn't fix.

Having no choice, I had to take the road as it departed from ground level and continued into the haze and fog south over the swamp. Visibility was poor and I could see only maybe a hundred yards in front or snapshots of the distance during random breaks in the fog. I walked for twenty minutes and there was no sign of dry land on either side of my position. There it was again . . . the sound of an engine somewhere in the distance, or perhaps over my head. I wasn't sure of the source. My concentration was broken by a metallic sound up ahead. It sounded like chains being pulled across concrete. I tried to listen and separate the sounds of the chains from the mechanical buzzing sounds but could not.

Both sounds became insignificant when I heard one of those things trip over an old bumper that lay rusting on the bridge. It was coming from the same direction I had just walked. I walked over to it and shot it in the back of the head with the SMG. As I looked up beyond the corpse into the distance from where I had come, I noticed more shadowy figures in the fog. It seemed I had some undead stalkers closing on my position. They were still a couple of minutes out. I turned around and continued in the direction of the metallic sounds at a better pace.

Leaving the stalkers behind me, I started my jog ten paces, walk ten paces regimen. Then came the sound of metal on concrete again. I slowed, knowing that the undead behind me were perhaps ten minutes from my position. I had passed abandoned cars up to this point but none of them were occupied and they all showed signs of the *gore marks,* like those on the house I had slept on last night. I crept further. The sound of metal got louder and drove me mad.

It was almost as if the mechanical sound abated to allow for the metallic sound to increase its intensity in a cruel game to send me over the edge. The lack of visibility made it even more torturous. I knew the sound up ahead of me had to be within a few hundred yards, but with the highway up on stilts and the barriers up on either side, the sound could be coming from much farther off.

I tried to drive the thought of the creatures behind me out of my head, impossible as that was, and kept moving forward, squinting as if that would help me see through the fog. The noise was very loud at this point and I could hear the sounds of undead activity up ahead. I now had a choice to make: either turn around and deal with the stalkers behind me or push ahead and deal with the noisy dead in front. The other option was to jump into the cold swamp and hope that the other side was near, and also hope that there were no undead in the swamp waters to greet me as I made my way to land. Since going north was not my objective and getting my ass bitten off was out of the question, I chose to press south on Highway 59 toward the metallic sounds.

The fog remained thick but I could see far enough ahead to know what I had gotten into. I estimated that the stalkers on my tail should be about five to seven minutes behind me, judging from the pace I had used to get here. As I moved forward I could see at least thirty undead dressed in bright orange jumpsuits. On the back of the jumpsuits were reflective letters that said COUNTY. Leg shackles and chains bound most of the creatures.

They consisted of units of three to five inmates per chain gang. It looked like only a few were immobilized. One of them was chained to what was left of a shriveled human leg. It walked around and tugged the leg behind. The things could not see me and I used this five minutes before the others behind caught up to figure out how to get past them. Only around thirty were visible. As I thought of ingenious ways to evade them by jumping on cars or running past, one of the first stalkers appeared from the fog behind me. I shot it in the face, decided that thinking was a dead man's game right now and pushed forward.

As I made my way to the chain gangs, I picked the left side to attempt a breach. The right side seemed to have more of the unhindered variety. My tactic was simple: to shoot the ghouls on both ends of the gang, leaving the middle creatures trapped by the literally dead weight. In all I had to shoot five creatures to accomplish my goal. I used a whole magazine.

I'm not sure whether it was the lack of visibility, or knowing that I was surrounded, or the fact that there were large undead inmates in orange jumpsuits and chains coming at me that made me so nervous. I was freaking out and practically praying and spraying my way out. I had to stuff one of the empty mags in my leg pocket and rack another one as I made my way past the bulk of the gang.

Even though three of the five-man chain gang teams were hindered in movement, they still continued to pursue as the unhindered teams marched past them toward me. The sound of the chains scraping across Highway 59 scared the living shit out of me as I ran from these things. They were not the only threat out there. I passed fifty other undead as I escaped the chain gang. The pack was heavier than ever as I returned to my jog ten, walk ten pattern. Up ahead the fog was beginning to clear . . .

I kept on. Looking back into my new circle of visibility I could see nearly a hundred of them in pursuit less than a quarter of a mile behind. I was starting the undead snowball effect. They were making enough noise to start a chain reaction . . . each pack of wolves howling at the next.

The sound of metal and undead approached as I heard the buzzing again. I couldn't hold this pace forever, and I didn't think that losing a hundred undead could be easily accomplished in one day. As I neared the end of the stilted section of Highway 59 and looked back, I could see much more than a hundred.

I glanced down at my watch; it read 0950. I had been evading for hours. Just as I looked up from my watch I witnessed a huge explosion in the mass of the undead and instinctively cupped my ears and sat down on the ground. Just as my ass hit concrete the overwhelming sound of the explosion hit me like a punch to the chest, rolling me over. I got to my feet and noticed that the explosion had done overwhelming damage to the group that pursued. I didn't question where the explosion came from or why I had encountered a fucking dead chain gang, I just accepted it and got the hell out of it. After a short lunch break sitting under an old propped-up car hood out of the rain, I intend to continue south shadowing the highway again, pending swamps, random high-order explosions or undead chain gangs.

2148

Tonight I have found respite in an old refinery field with sections of high chain-link fence squares spread throughout the area. The oil pumps have long since stopped movement. Most of them are grown over with weeds and are home to nesting birds. The small fenced area was securely locked with a hardened chain and padlock so I was forced to climb over. After throwing my bag over the fence I draped my wool blanket over a section that I thought wouldn't be damaged by my climbing it.

There was no barbed wire at the top, but it was half habit and half safety to have the blanket there to protect against sharp edges. I could not afford to take the chance of getting an infection—there was no place to receive a tetanus shot. After getting inside the perimeter I carefully and slowly walked around the fence looking for holes that wild dogs or undead could squeeze through. Satisfied that there were none, I picked one of the refinery pumps to camp near for the night. It stopped raining down on me around 1500 today, giving me a chance to dry out somewhat before reaching the campsite.

I had some wet gear, so I decided to lay it out to dry on the horizontal metal pipes of the rig. It had been a little cold outside because of the recent rain, but not as bad as it is right now. My thoughts were on today's events and the mysterious explosion that had occurred. I also thought of chain gangs and how I seemed to remember that they were outlawed years before this all went down. I guess when society is failing and you don't have enough police to guard the inmates, chaining them together makes sense. Poor bastards. I can't imagine the horror of it. One of them gets infected and the others are left to fight it, or even worse, four are infected and one is left to fight. No wonder they all eventually turned.

I wondered if the undead child in the house was still banging on that upstairs window trying to get at me, as if I were still within reach. As truly gruesome as the thoughts of the chain gang and child were, the explosion . . . Was it an old weight sensor charge left on the overpass?

In any case I didn't know what to think. As the sun was setting I searched the area for anything of value and found nothing but an old stripped-out Phillips screwdriver half buried in the polluted ground at my feet. I set one of the large rattraps along the fence in an attempt to conserve my nonperishables. With the rest of my remaining daylight I inventoried my ammunition and counted 210 rounds of 9mm. The chain gang fight had depleted thirty rounds of my supplies.

I walked the perimeter once more, careful to avoid the trap, just as the sun dipped below the horizon. There was movement on Highway 59 off in the distance, probably what was left of the group that was tailing me on the swampy overpass. I felt relatively safe here and didn't think that any of them knew where I was. Even so I will still sleep with one eye open and my finger on the trigger and the safety between my ears. Before racking out tonight I intend to slip the NVGs over my head and sleep with them. If I need to investigate something, I won't have to fumble with them and I can just switch them on as needed throughout the night.

Boots

Hours before fully awakening to rain on my face—again—I fell into a daydream phase of consciousness. It was getting cold and my bones had a chill to them that I had not felt since survival school in Rangeley, Maine. My mind wondered back to the POW camp and the stress inoculation.

The cold also made me think of Rudyard Kipling. In my tiny cell they played Kipling's "Boots" poem over and over and over again. The narrator, speaking with a thick Russian accent, said, over and over: *Foot-foot-foot-foot-sloggin' over Africa—Boots-boots-boots-boots-movin' up an' down again.*

After hearing that poem for hours and hours, I had memorized it in detail. Even now I can hear the raspy Russian voice saying it over and over again in an infinite loop in between training sessions. I woke up in the cold rain reciting "Boots" to myself over and over again.

Using the rain dripping off the oil pump, I refilled my water, drank, then refilled it again. I repeated this until I could no longer drink without thinking of vomiting. After a short while, I walked over to where I had set the trap to check on it, as well as to urinate. The trap was empty, indicating that I had to eat some of my valuable nonperishable food. Just as the rain began to subside I decided to build a small fire to heat a can of chili that I had been carrying in my pack for miles.

Using the hatchet, I gathered some dead wood from the other side of the fence and chopped it to a manageable size. I then dug a hole in the ground a safe distance from the oil pump and built a

155

fire using the driest wood I had. I doubt that making a fire will ever be difficult, because of all the things that people have left lying around. Using my multitool I cut some holes in the top of the chili can so that I could hang the can over the fire to heat it. As the chili heated I surveyed the area with my binocs. There was no movement on the highway in the distance or on the other three sides of the fence.

I reached for my survival radio to hail anyone that I could. Since the crash, I have made every effort to conserve its battery power. As I pulled it out to select 282.8 on the handset I noticed that I had inadvertently left the radio in beacon mode from the day before. The battery was dead and I had no spares. I pulled the battery out of the device. The battery appears to be a proprietary type and I doubt I could ever find a replacement. I copied the output voltage and battery type to my journal and threw the battery over the fence to save weight in my pack. Anyone who has gone any distance with a pack knows that every ounce must be justified.

I intend to keep the radio in the event I can rig up power to it in the future. I am now cut off from anyone who could have been monitoring the survival frequencies.

After my morning flashback to survival school I started thinking about the big picture of survival. I knew that some remnants of the U.S. government remained. Aircraft carriers, possibly refugee tank convoys, remote military airstrips as well as Hotel 23. There must be someone out here who can help me get back. Communications with the aircraft carrier had been interrupted before my helicopter crash. Couple that with the stupid idea of researching the radiated dead and bringing them back to the flagship, one might consider that even the carrier could be overrun.

Overhead satellites are likely useless and spinning out of orbit. I know that the GPS satellites have failed already. I have not seen a living person since the crash and I have covered quite a few miles. If the patch of land that I traversed is representative of the rest of my journey, I will be in for serious tribulations. Even if only one percent of the population has survived, I figure I would have seen someone by now. Today I intend to leave a signal indicating my intended direction.

I'll make a large arrow on the ground using rocks or whatever

I have available to signal any surviving airborne assets my direction of travel. The only problem with this is that the aircrew that discovers the signal may decide that it is old news. Either way, I'll take any chance I can get for rescue from this war zone.

The explosion that rocked the overpass is persistently on my mind. At the time I just wrote it off as good luck, but the more I think of what happened the more I realize that the odds of an explosion of old ordnance with that timing is unlikely. The buzzing noise I kept hearing was also present just after the explosion.

There have been some deer running about in the area. Chances are slim that they could elude the dead for any prolonged period. I plan to take one so that I can make my nonperishable food last longer while evading and making my way back south to Hotel 23. The rain has stopped but there is still overcast in the sky today. I am wearing my wool blanket poncho for warmth and I will continue my route south today along 59.

There are a few items that I need to find before I get too far south. I need a road atlas so that I do not find myself critically off track on my trip. Iodine tablets or another way to purify water is also a good idea. Regarding my current route, I have no idea if this road runs right into a medium-sized city or interstate exchange. I have had to reposition my gear so that my binocs are easy to grab. Before heading out in an hour or so, I'll wipe down my weapon with the oil and old rag I salvaged from the sailboat. That seems like forever ago.

There's no discharge in the war! RK—

Deer Hunters

After leaving this morning, I had my gear positioned and straps on my pack adjusted for a long march south. I noticed that my clothes fit rather loosely compared to just a couple of weeks earlier. I know that I feel constantly hungry because of all the walking I am doing. Thank goodness this area of the United States is relatively flat. I think I might have perished if I had had to traverse the Rocky Mountains with so few provisions. After an hour of slowly moving south I saw a buck with my binocs a hundred yards in the distance.

My hunger took over as I went down on one knee and quietly set the pack down next to an old stump that would be easy to find. I stalked the deer in front of me, keeping close to the tree line to avoid detection. One hundred yards would be a near-impossible kill shot with my 9mm submachine gun; I would need to get inside twenty yards to make the shot count. The buck did not detect my presence as I closed on him. I took another look at him with my binocs from fifty yards to make sure he would be a healthy mark. I tried to check him over to verify that he had not been injured by the creatures. I could see no bite marks and he seemed to be relatively healthy. His muscles flexed as he walked and grazed. He did not appear too skinny or too old. I could not count the number of points on his rack because of the foliage around him. I looked back to make sure that I wasn't spotted by the undead and to make sure I could still see my pack next to the old stump. I had stalked closer, to within about one hundred feet, when the ears of the buck perked up, sensing that something was not right. Perhaps it was the smell of a living human or maybe I was not walking as quietly as I intended.

I pulled the weapon up and aimed it at the buck. Using my thumb I checked to make sure the weapon was in single shot, as I didn't deem it necessary to waste ammunition on my mark. It was now or never, as I had a premonition that within a few seconds the animal would get spooked and run away.

I squeezed off two rounds and hit the mark in the neck and behind the head. The animal fell on its side, then got up and started to run. I tracked the animal, cursing half to myself and half out loud over how stupid I was to be so greedy and reckless. I hated killing animals unless absolutely necessary for food, and now I might have killed this animal for no reason, losing it forever. I tracked the blood for what seemed like an hour, carefully gauging my distance from my gear and from the highway to be sure I would not get lost.

The blood drops trailed down into a small valley and behind a finger of terrain. I carelessly ran down and around the finger, thinking only of my growling stomach, and came out of the shrubbery right into a baker's dozen of undead feeding on my mark. They were on their knees over the buck and scratching and biting at the hide of the animal. One of them had already pulled the skin back from where the bullet penetrated. Guilt and anger fell over me as I saw them devour the animal. The poor beast's eyes were open and as I looked through the corpses that were all around it, I felt that the animal was looking at me and thinking, "So this is why you took me?"

I was only ten feet away from the things. I decided to start walking backward to get out of this little valley. One of the creatures looked in my direction with buck blood and flesh dripping from its rotting jaw. It then put its arms out to reach for me. It moaned and then two others looked up and did the same. I turned to run back to my gear and followed the blood trail. I opened the distance between the pursuing dead and myself. I noticed as I ran a dramatically skinny house cat jump from a tree near the buck. It scurried off into the field nearby.

Seeing those things reminded me how close to death I was again. I had thought that I would be desensitized to them after so much exposure. Each one is a Picasso of terror that reminds me that I will be at war until they all rot into the ground whence we all came.

I checked behind me every five seconds and just ran, still cursing under my breath at how stupid I was for even attempting to shoot this animal at that distance with the weapon I had. The *buzzing* had once again returned by the time I was close enough to see the stump where I had cached my gear. I looked all around and concentrated on where the sound could be coming from. The sky was too overcast for me to see anything above the tops of the trees. In a solemn state of concentration I began to hear the snap of twigs in the trees off in the distance. The deer hunters were in pursuit of something new. I grabbed my gear and readjusted the pack straps. I was thankful to be alive but felt deep guilt for sentencing another living thing to be eaten by those fucking abominations. It was almost as if I had scored a goal for the other team. The deer was put on this earth for living things to eat in need, not to be poached by something by the likes of them.

I evaded the creatures by carefully crossing the highway and following the other side. This side did not provide the same amount of cover as the other, as it consisted mostly of a large field for the next few miles, with sparse cover every few hundred yards. I decided to cross back over when the first safe opportunity presented itself.

The rest of my day was spent walking slowly south and attempting to keep my mind off the food in my pack that I needed to conserve. It drizzled most of the day and was generally miserable, but I suspect that in times like these a sunny day would be just as miserable. I had heard the *buzzing* three times total today at random moments and decided to start mentally noting the times of day and duration of the sound.

As I looked at my watch, gauging how much daylight I had left, I began to formulate my strategy for a secure sleeping area. By 1500 I was able to see the outline of a town in the distance. This prompted me to start looking at the highway for signs indicating what I would be walking into. I decided that if the population sign read more than thirty thousand, I'd make no attempt to get near it. After all, I needed some food, a road atlas and maybe some ammunition, but not at the cost of dealing with half a million of those things. Even though all it takes is one of them to do you in, a bite is exponentially easier to evade when dealing with a smaller population. This is not a science, but it makes me feel better to draw my line in the sand.

It would be getting dark in a couple hours. I was getting a little uneasy. Sleeping on the ground was not going to happen in a million years. If I did not find shelter before dark, I was going to stay up all night and keep moving. Originally, following the crash, I had thought that I would limit my movement only to night, but the lack of batteries for my NVGs and the idea of sleeping during the day when those things can see had changed my mind. I know they can't see in the dark, as was evident the other night when I departed the top story of the farmhouse. They responded to sound but could not see me.

My choices were lessening by the minute so I looked to the highway for a place to hang my automatic weapon. There were a few options. There was a Winnebago, but I ruled that out because there would be no escape in the event the RV was surrounded. The next option I came to was a UPS truck turned on its side. Once again I felt that this was too small to use since it could also be easily surrounded. The next option I came to was a large semitruck that had a long feed trailer on the back.

Using my binoculars, I scanned the truck for any sign of death. The windows were rolled up on the tractor-trailer. The truck was high enough off the ground that those things could not climb up on the hood and the rig had a sleeper cabin behind the driver. The words "Boaz Trucking, Inc." were painted on the driver's door. Two of the tires were flat on my side. The rig was leaning a little because of this. I thought it best not to rush into this and just keep an eye on the area to make sure there was no danger. I listened and watched for half an hour before I dropped my pack and headed for the rig. When my foot touched the asphalt I could see clearly in both directions up and down the road.

An ambulance sat derelict in the distance to the north, and to the south I could see a green sign that I thought could indicate the miles to the next town. I made for the running boards to step up to the cab. On the driver's side I noticed the door was locked, but the other side was not. There was no sign of any danger inside the cab. I jumped down and ran around to the other side and opened the door. The old truck smell of fast-food bags stuffed under the seat, and a sun-baked dashboard told me that no one had been in this rig for a very long time.

I climbed inside and looked in the sleeper behind the front seats. The bed was not made but was serviceable. Inside this truck everything seemed normal, other than the faded fast-food bags sitting on the dashboard. I climbed out of the truck, satisfied that it was safe, and went to retrieve my pack. By the time I got back to the truck it was getting too dark to try to read the sign up ahead so I decided it was best to prepare for the night. I placed my pack on the driver's seat and pulled the privacy curtains so that I could not be spotted easily. With the doors locked, I started to inspect the cab for anything of value. I found a disposable lighter and a can of Vienna sausages along with a nice ink pen and a Sharpie marker. I devoured the canned meat. In order to conserve my flashlight batteries, I intend to check the rest of the vehicle over when the sun rises in the morning. The doors are locked and the windows, I suspect, will never come down again.

13 Oct

0822

I slept well last night despite hearing something outside before falling asleep. I was so exhausted. I thought that I would attempt to remain still and quiet and in doing so, I fell hard into deep sleep and didn't wake up until about 0630. The light was shining into the cab through the curtains. I kept them closed as I slid my boots on and laced them up and splashed some water on my face. I climbed over to the passenger seat and peeked past the curtains into the area outside. I thought I could see something moving around far to the south. I reached over and grabbed my binocs and checked it out. There was a single corpse in the distance wandering about the abandoned cars. I could see no sign of any closer threat. Cracking the curtains to let more light in, I began a more thorough search of the cab.

The glove compartment revealed nothing but an insurance card that had expired six months ago and a picture of a man and his family standing in front of the Alamo. My mind drifted back to San Antonio and the fate of the Alamo. The area was nuked and is now a wasteland of radiated undead. I wouldn't go back there even with a thousand AC-130 gunships over my head. The back of the picture was dated December of last year. I looked at the picture and wished that I could go back to that time. I would give many things to have one day of normalcy from before all this happened. Behind the family were others laughing and carrying on. They were oblivious to what the world would be like just thirty days after the tourist photographer depressed the shutter release.

Dead Drop

There is so much information to write and process I do not know where to even begin. After leaving the rig this morning, I kept trekking south and checked the sign that I had discovered the day before. I didn't need to get that close, as the binocs once again saved me some time and energy. The sign read "Marshall 6 mi." I had heard of the town of Marshall, Texas, somewhere before and decided that if I had heard of it then it must be too large to attempt a scavenging operation. As I headed back to my standard highway offset I heard the buzz again. The sky was clear, so I immediately pulled the binocs up to survey the sky above. No joy. I kept walking south and east, offsetting further and further, so that I could go around Marshall instead of through its center. This was going to add some extra miles to my trip. After about an hour the loudest sound I had heard since the explosion commenced.

In the distance I heard the unmistakable noise of the sound decoys. I remember the distinct tone because they were deployed at the start of the undead infestation to draw the things to the nuclear target packages. My mind immediately wandered to the worst-case scenario as I thought to myself, Am I about to glow in the dark?

Obviously this was not the case, or I would not be alive to write this now. The sound was not deafening, because it came from so far away from where I stood. It seemed to come from the east, far in the distance. It was not nearly as loud as the decoy I heard when they dropped the nukes, which leads me to assume that the device

165

was deployed a considerable distance further than the first one I had encountered.

Nervous and confused, I kept my pace south and east until I heard the unmistakable sound of aircraft engines approaching. Looking to the eastern sky I saw the shape of an aircraft flying very low directly to my position. I immediately reached for my pencil flares and launcher but before I could screw the launcher onto the flare to fire, the aircraft pulled up and began a steep climb, shrinking quickly back into the big empty sky. I nearly cried until I was almost killed by a huge pallet falling to the earth attached to a large green parachute. The drop landed twenty feet from where I stood and threw wads of dirt and grass into my face. The chute went horizontal and I quickly ran over to the drop and gathered up the chute before it pulled whatever all this shit was across the field. After disconnecting the chute I haphazardly folded it and placed a big rock on top. This drop was wrapped in very thick layers of plastic wrap and measured about four by four by three feet.

I pulled out my Randall knife and started to cut away the plastic wrap. Spray-painted on some of the plastic layers were the letters "OGA load-out 2b." After removing the plastic, I clicked open the carabiners and pulled off the webbing that held the items in place. On a plastic pallet were numerous hard plastic Pelican cases of various sizes. There was a bright yellow case on top of the others labeled simply with the number 01. I checked the perimeter, reached for the case and flipped the latches open. Opening the lid, the first thing I noticed was a cellular phone. I could tell that this was no normal phone simply by looking at the large antenna folded down the side. The word on the front of the phone read "Iridium." I pulled the phone out of the case and hit the menu button. It came to life, indicated a full charge and gave a notice that stated, "Acquiring Lock." I set the phone aside and inspected the yellow case in more detail. On the lid of the case was a chart that seemed to indicate Iridium satellite orbital paths for this region dated for this month with 80 percent of the satellites out of service. According to the chart, only two hours of satellite coverage per day were available.

The hours were from 1200 to 1400 daily with an error of plus or minus seventeen minutes depending on atmospheric conditions.

There was an asterisk that warned that the availability would shift to the right two minutes and twelve seconds per year with the current satellite configuration. Sitting in the foam below where the phone was fitted was a small solar charger. As I reached for the next case to examine the contents the phone began to ring . . .

I sat in shock for a few seconds before I hit talk and said hello as the noise faded into solid connection from a digital modem shrill. A slow and mechanical voice emanated from the speaker: "This is a remote six recording. Please monitor text screen."

I followed the onscreen text, as instructed.

6 minutes of satellite coverage remaining.
Officer-in-charge reported missing FM Nada launch facility via radio twelve days ago. Since that time this station utilized remaining overhead imagery capability & Global Hawk & Reaper UCAVs to direction find location. Search aborted until distress radio beacon detected. Beacon remained active sufficient time to refine position for Reaper UCAV coverage. Remote Six is one of *garbled* teen facili *garbled* mission as a command and control node for *garbled* . . . gov *garbled.* Maintenance *garbled* dation has mission impacted airborne opera *garbled* on most of air breather aircraft.

Out of the sixty *garbled* Iridium satellites orbiting *garbled* resources and computing power to maintain the orbital paths and data compression algorithms for 2 hr/day coverage.

3 minutes of satellite coverage remaining.
Vast surplus of experimental Reaper UCAV aircraft *garbled* support systems we have resources to provide dedicated overhead coverage for 12 hr/day. Remote Six UCAVs are equipped w/ two 500 lb LGB *garbled* replenished daily w/ full EO/IR optical turret. In C-130 drop you will find device that commands Reaper LGB munitions as well as low-drain beacon. Instructions are included with equipment. To designate target you will *garbled* be inside the Reaper operating time gate, in close prox. to the Reaper and must keep target LAS *garbled* ten seconds. Lasing attempt at less than ten seconds will result

in nonrelease. Deploy low-drain beacon on outside of clothing to
ensure escort. Aircraft will remain angels 10 *garbled* avoid
audible undead detection.

01 minute of satellite coverage remaining.

Utilize text pad on handset to answer the following
question(s):

Do you hear a high pitch sound?

I responded yes.

The SATphone screen went blank. The sound decoy in the distance seemed to get softer until I could barely make out a sound. The sound decoy now seemed to emanate sound all around me . . . just barely audible.

The text screen asked again:

Do you hear a high *static* sound?

Yes.

The sound faded from my detection and the text screen once again asked:

Do you hear a high pitch sound?

I responded no.

Please repeat text.

No.

The text screen immediately scrolled with:

Project Hurricane variable noise suppression activated
on three dimensions. All infected vari *garbled* will flow away
from center eye. You have twen *garbled* hours of variable
suppression battery life remaining. Iridium satellite coverage
degradation immin

Apparently the device that was used to attract the undead to nuclear demise was also designed to make a safe radius by drawing the undead away from the quiet center safe area. Aptly named Project Hurricane, no doubt due to the serene nature of the eye of an actual hurricane when compared to the turbulent hurricane wall. The voice on the phone in the beginning before the data went to text sounded as if it was mechanical, but there is no way this whole operation could have been automated. John must have immediately reported the helicopter missing the instant we were overdue for return.

Many months ago, radios at Hotel 23 intercepted transmissions from a person claiming to be a congressman from the state of Louisiana. Aside from his grim report on the effects of radiation on the undead, he mentioned that he was in limited high-frequency radio communication with a government base equipped with prototype UAVs and a surplus of explosives.

There were numerous boxes on the drop that I needed to inventory and inspect before sunset.

The first case was small and had the symbol for laser engraved on the lid. I unfastened the clasp and opened the case to find a rectangular black device with common pic rail equipment mounts on the bottom. Packed with the device was a one-page sheet of instructions printed on plastic paper and a box of CR123 lithium batteries. The instructions stated what the SATphone comms had referenced. Also inside was a small folder with documents, including a satellite hybrid map of Texas with strange numbered markings indicating various locations. I took a quick second to check the laser device compatibility on the MP5 with no success.

There was a small hex wrench included to adjust the laser beam, but the instructions stated that the device was precalibrated for accuracy within five feet if mounted on the T6 pic rail. Even if I decided to attempt adjustment I would only have about five seconds at a time to do so before a five-hundred-pound LGB detonation wasted something. A very small clear plastic beacon device was pinned to the lid of the case with instructions on how to wear it. The device appeared very similar to the avalanche beacon reflector that I had on my ski jacket, which would have helped rescue personnel find me if a ski trip had gone bad. The Reaper beacon battery life was advertised at six months and the stated purpose was Reaper escort tracking and escort self-destruct avoidance. No boom-boom when accidentally lasing your foot as you trekked cross-country.

On the back of the instructions was a basic capabilities and limitations brief on the Reaper. The satellite text stated that I would have twelve hours of coverage per day during daylight hours. The coverage did not match the advertised endurance of the Reaper, leading me to believe that Remote Six could be more than just a few klicks away. According to the instructions my Reaper would be with me overhead until 1800 tonight and again at 0600 in the morning.

The next case held an M-4 assault rifle with a red dot optic and Surefire LED weapon light with five-hundred rounds of .223 ammunition and five magazines. There was a mount for the laser designator on the side of the weapon opposite the LED light. In the foam below the rifle was a Glock 19 with 250 rounds of 9mm ammunition and three magazines and a screw-on can (suppressor). Two frag grenades were also enclosed in the weapons case. This is the case that was to be a cause for decision on what to leave and what to take.

The next case held vacuum-sealed dried food. There were twenty packets of food with three meal servings in each of varied types. Enclosed with the food was a plastic bottle with one hundred water purification tablets.

I arranged the new food on the ground and the new weapons adjacent to them. Two cases remained. The next case contained a small bottle of gasoline treatment that was marked "experimental" with explicit directions on the back that stated: "1/4 bottle per ten gallons. Wait one hour prior to internal combustion. Exceeding dosage could result in unstable and dangerous combustible liquid." The case also contained a hand siphon pump that was portable enough to think about taking. It seemed the purpose of this part of the drop was to enable me to find and exploit an alternative means of transportation.

The last case contained a compression bag holding a mummy sleeping bag with no brand marking and a very odd camouflage pattern. Digital, but without right angles on the digital print. The bag had a Gore-Tex marking as well as a tag with an NSN number that stated that it was rated for zero degrees C and waterproof.

The bag had snaps instead of a zipper to keep it closed. A canvas pistol holster was sewn flat into the outside of the bag at hip level where one would wear a pistol naturally. This bag was designed to go from sleep to fight in a hurry.

Checking my surroundings to make sure that there were no undead about, I took off my pack and proceeded to unload everything to one side. Now came the time to prioritize items, from items that I absolutely needed to items that were just nice to have. The sun had begun to wane on the horizon when I hit the timer on my watch, setting it to go off in two hours.

Keeping the MP5 was now nearly pointless, with the M-4 as an option and suppressed Glock as the backup. I can't discard the MP5 until I field test the M-4, but I cannot take two rifles cross-country on foot for any extended distance with all the gear I have acquired. I have room to keep my old G-17 as a backup, but the G-19 is the logical choice to wear on my person since it's smaller and has night sights and a detachable can. The magazines from the 17 fit the 19—an added benefit.

The mummy bag is definitely coming with me, replacing the heavy wool blanket that I had modified to wear as a poncho by cutting a hole in its middle and wearing it Villa style. Five hundred rounds of .223 is heavy. I'll think about shooting some tomorrow while I still have the alleged Project Hurricane suppression active. I'll do the shooting right before departure in the morning just to be safe. I had 210 rounds of 9mm left over from the helicopter salvage. Combining this with the 250 rounds from the drop brings the 9mm round count to 460 for the pistols.

I'll be shooting some rounds through the 19 in the morning as well, to ensure its reliability, even though I'll be keeping the 17 as a backup due to its great cost/benefit in weight on my pack. Grenades are a given value, as are the water purification tabs and the dried food. I'll need some new socks very soon and will use the old socks to hold the grenades to ensure the pin does not accidentally get pulled as I transit south.

1610

Sunset Approaching

Working List
* = new gear

Weapons
~~MP5 9mm (4 mags)~~
G-17 9mm (2 mags)
210 9mm rds (combine with new ammo)
*M-4 .223 (5 mags) w/ laser designator, LED light and aim-
point
*500 rds of .223
*G-19 9mm (3 mags) plus suppressor
*250 rds of 9mm (460 total)
*2 frag grenades

Survival Gear
Trekking pack
Combat knife
NVGs w/ spare batteries
Water bladder (100 oz)
Flares/compass
~~Green wool blanket~~
Binoculars
~~PRC-90-2 radio (no batt)~~
Waterproof matches
1 Bic lighter
2 large rattraps
3 packs of AA (NVGs)
1 tube triple antibiotic
1 roll of TP
Hatchet
Digital watch
*Satellite phone w/ solar charger
*Topographical map of Texas
*100 water purification tablets
*Mummy sleeping bag

*Experimental fuel treatment (small bottle)
Heed warning on treatment!
*Small gasoline siphon

Stores
    2 MREs
    3 cans of chili *heavy, eat first
    2 cans veg. beef stew *heavy eat first
    100 oz water
    *20 (3 meals each of dried food)

I've decided it's best to ditch the PRC-90 radio due to not having functioning batteries and the extra weight. The wool blanket and, tentatively, the MP5 are also on the list to discard. I intend to put the weapon and magazine in a safe place and mark it on my new map. I've repacked my gear. The ammunition is the heaviest part of the pack, pushing the overall net weight a few pounds heavier than the original weight. Not having the MP5, wool blanket and radio has offset the increase slightly, but noticeably.

There is a residence not far from my position and now that the gear is packed, I'm moving to a position to sweep it to determine habitability for the evening. The only things I'm leaving behind are the wool blanket, the nearly useless PRC-90 radio and half a parachute. I cut some of the paracord and chute in the event I needed it for shelter. Getting tougher to find military-grade cord these days.

The plan is to sling the M-4 and give the proven (albeit mediocre) MP5 one last patrol before she's cached away and reduced to nothing more than a cryptic mark on a treasure map.

2145

The sun had a little sky left when I shouldered my pack and left the drop. I could tell the pack was a little heavier, as the extra rifle I was carrying accentuated the weight. I walked south and west to the dwelling I had scouted with the binocs earlier. It was a two-story house with the windows still intact. They were not boarded over but they were too high off the ground for someone or some thing to climb into them easily. The sill of the window was about my head height. Curtains were open on some windows and closed on others. It seemed very typical and nonthreatening. I walked the full 360 around the home, checking for any signs of struggle or *gore marks* indicating any previous undead encounter here.

There was no car in the garage. The grass was of course grown up pretty high and the only disturbance in the growth looked like small rabbit trails. I walked up to the front porch and set my gear down. I leaned the M-4 against the wall and made sure the MP5 was fully loaded as I reached out to check the screen door. The screen door was locked, so I pulled out my knife and cut the screen so that I could reach in and flip the switch to unlock the door. As I reached inside and began to unlock the door, something in the window near the door moved. I instantly jerked my hand out of the screen, scratching it as I ran back off the porch and holding back a scream . . .

It was only a curtain that had shifted in the wind, nothing more.

I sat on the porch, concentrating and trying to listen for any reason to force myself to sleep on the roof tonight instead of inside where it would be warmer. There were no sounds from inside the house and no movement outside besides the tall grass in the wind around the house. The sun projected the red-orange glow of the approaching sunset as I made my second attempt. I never knew it would take this much courage every time I did this, every time I needed a place to sleep or reorganize or think.

I walked right up to the flimsy screen door and slid my hand into the screen to open the first barrier to my entry. It took some force to pull the screen door. Some dust and dirt fell on my head as it pulled free, giving me access to the main entry. I reached down to grab the brass doorknob, feeling its cold metal in my hand. I let my hand grasp it for a good while and wondered which way to turn it. Of course, a year ago I would have known this, but the simple, civilized and familiar things get more foreign as time goes on. I slowly turned the knob to the right, and the door swung open with a push from my boot. The room was abandoned, long derelict. No sign of anything for months. It looks as if the people that once lived here left before the outbreak/plague/locusts or whatever.

I kept clearing the bottom level and opening every curtain I saw so that the house could hide no devilry in the shadows. After clearing the bottom level I made my way up what I thought would be the creakiest stairway on planet Earth. I was right. After getting to the top I knew the home was clear, because there was no reaction to the noise I had made on the way up. It didn't matter. I had almost been killed many times before today because I had underestimated the low-gear lethality of those things. I nervously cleared the top floor with the same thoroughness and fear I preserved inside from months before. As I moved from room to room, my mind drifted into darkness and daymares of what I would do if I were to become infected tonight. My first thought was of suicide and how I'd end it with a bullet to my brain. Perhaps I would leave an ominous but witty message, like the young stock boy I had killed what seemed like years ago. How long ago was it?

Snapping out of my morbid thoughts, I kept going room by room, checking in closets and under bathroom sinks to make sure.

What if one of them was under the bed? What if it was a little child?

I had to stop myself. Did I check under all the beds? Obsessive-compulsive, are we? I swept the upstairs again and did the same downstairs before bringing my gear inside and closing and locking every door and window in the house. I noticed four different decorative candles placed in various locations in the living and dining room areas. I brought them upstairs with my gear and picked what I thought was the master bedroom as a base of sleep operations. There were no sheets on the bed and no dead little children under it.

I lit two of the larger decorative candles and placed them on the empty chest of drawers at the foot of the bed. I put my gear near the window that I would use to make my escape if things were to go badly for me tonight. I also shut and locked the bedroom door and pushed another chest of drawers in front of it to buy me some time. I checked the window to ensure that it would open in my second of need. At this point it was dark enough that I could use the NVGs to do a quick 180-degree scan out the window for any sign of them. There were none.

Sitting in the darkness listening to the house creak in the night wind, I began to think of today's events in more detail, and this only brought more confusion.

Why didn't the C-130 cargo plane pick me up at a nearby airfield or cleared strip of land?

Who are Remote Six?

Instead of counting sheep, I count unanswered questions before I drift into a deep sleep, guarded by the flickering light of fortunate candles . . .

Candles used against odds for their intended purpose.

Thread the Needle

I slept solidly last night, with no interruptions. I dreamt of the noise barrage beacons, or perhaps it was the wind shifting just enough for my subconscious brain to actually hear them. The sun is rising in the eastern sky and I have had plenty of time to inspect some of the other documentation that dropped with the gear as well as have a go at some target practice with the M-4 and G19. Enclosed in the documentation is a map of the predicted hurricane noise suppression target set. The three units were deployed to Shreveport, Louisiana, Longview, Texas, and Texarkana, Texas/Arkansas, and they were set to varying intensities, judging by the SATphone transmission.

I'm currently a few miles north of Marshall, meaning that I'll need to split the distance between Longview and Shreveport in half to attain maximum threat avoidance. The noise suppression modeling on the map indicates areas of suppression, with red circles surrounding the target areas that show danger zones. There is a green safe corridor area that depicts a recommended path south between danger areas. The circles are not perfectly round where the suppression devices are located, possibly due to terrain and other factors that limit transmission of sound. This map was obviously modeled via computer. Also of interest are the orange overlay areas over Dallas and New Orleans, with the international symbol for radiation displayed on them. The areas cover a significant radius around the cities, trailing eastward at the small end like a teardrop. Looks like the orange shows the boundary for radiation fallout with winds factored.

The Texarkana noise suppression zone is at least 30 percent larger than the other two for reasons unknown. The recommended evasion path takes me skirting southeast of Marshall, across Highway 80 and twenty more miles south by southeast. The safer green area ends fifteen miles east of Carthage. I do not know what will happen when the batteries run out on the beacons in the three cities. The last time these devices were deployed they were blown to bits by nuclear warheads, taking many of the living as well as the dead with them. My best guess is that when the batteries run out the dead will simply start spreading out again in search of food. I can make fifteen miles in a day at best with this gear on my back. I'll run out of noise cover in about twelve hours, judging from the garbled SATphone transmission.

Also included in the documentation are the estimated infection and casualty rates for North America. Calculations estimate infection and/or casualty rates to be at around 99 percent. The last census I remember had the U.S. population at over three hundred million people. Using some basic math for threat analysis, I think I am outnumbered by more than 297 million undead. That number is undoubtedly growing daily. The undead can afford to make mistakes, they can afford to fall off a cliff or get hit by lightning or get shot in the chest. The living do not have this luxury. Any mistake on the part of the living results in us getting closer to 100 percent infection. My numbers do not include the countless undead I have exterminated or the millions that were instantly disintegrated in the nuclear blasts early this year.

A large folded topographical map of eastern Texas is also included in the documentation. The map is made out of waterproof material and contains illustrations of the common edible plants for the region as well as water-gathering techniques. GPS is gone. This map, coupled with a road atlas that I intend to scavenge, will help me find my way south, back home.

After examining the documents once more I went outside to check the perimeter so that I could test-fire the new weapons. The area was clear, so I locked and loaded and commenced a very short torture test of the M-4. I looked through the optic and immediately noticed how intuitive it was for aiming. I wasn't going to be hammering nails with this, but it was easily accurate enough for a head shot. I was hitting golf-ball-sized rocks fifty yards out with no difficulty, shattering them into dust. After shooting forty rounds through the carbine I broke her down to check the components, then put her back together and shot ten more rounds to make sure everything was running as it should. I was now down to 450 rounds of .223, which made the load a little lighter in the pack.

Before checking the laser designator, I made sure to clip the beacon to my vest over my left shoulder. I then flipped the designator on and hit the pressure switch on the side of the hand guard. As soon as I depressed the switch, I heard a beeping tone that increased in frequency the longer I held down. I quickly released the switch after counting to three Mississippi. I wanted to make sure the thing worked, not drop a bomb near my position. Satisfied with the M-4, I moved on to the Glock and shot thirty rounds with no difficulty. The last ten rounds I used the suppressor to judge how it affected the accuracy of the weapon. No concerns were noted, sans the time it takes to screw on the suppressor. I am not certain I have what it takes to do this quickly at this time and will need practice. The threads seem fine and one must get it right in the beginning to attach the suppressor correctly.

I found some plastic shopping bags under the sink in the kitchen. Saying good-bye to the MP5, I wrapped her up with the empty magazines in plastic bags with a fresh coat of motor oil from the old rag I had salvaged. I checked the refrigerator in the kitchen, but it had been cleaned out a long time ago. It didn't even stink and had not one bite of old food inside. I yanked out the shelves of the fridge and put them in the pantry. After placing the weapon in the fridge barrel up, I marked it on my map and wrote a note that simply said: "Kilroy was here. Check the fridge."

I left the note on the kitchen table weighted down with a candle I had used the night before.

Rearranging the equipment in my bag, I was reminded of the Iridium satellite phone so I decided to turn it on and give it a shot despite the known time gate. I sat and watched it for five minutes as it attempted to search for a satellite lock. No joy. I set the alarm on my watch to remind me of the gate. I want to ensure that I remember to have the phone switched on with clear view of the sky thirty minutes before the comm window.

I plan to leave in a few minutes and shoot the hurricane path between Longview and Shreveport, but not before I eat two cans of food to lessen the weight of this pack. A can of chili and a can of beef stew should give me some energy for the grueling hump I have ahead of me.

1300

The weight of my pack is really taking some getting used to. I estimate that I have covered about six or seven miles since this morning, moving at an average of one and a half miles per hour. I have consumed about half my water, motivated by the fact that the weight is taken off my shoulders and put into my stomach. I have not seen movement since I left the drop zone. Not a bird. The wind is light and variable, causing the lack of *anything* to be even more disturbing. I know that the noise beacons are either dead or very near depletion, causing who knows what kind of result. Every now and again I get frightened and raise my rifle to a phantom target that turns out to be nothing. The last nothing was a shirt left hanging on a long-abandoned backyard clothesline. I thought for sure it was one of them.

Chernobyl . . . I remember something significant from before all of this. I remember reading a news article on Chernobyl and reading an explorer's account of how quiet and spooky it was to her. She carried a radiation measurement device with her and explored the dead city. People had actually booked tours there to see it for themselves. Many requested to leave before the tour's completion due to the quiet. Now most of the continent is dead and will stay that way.

There's no discharge in the war!

I stopped an hour ago to wait on the Iridium comms but there were no texts. I tried to call in to Remote Six by scanning received calls and using the callback function . . . busy tone. I am sitting on top of an old armored car in a ditch with a corpse inside, in the driver's seat. Almost nothing left but bones and a uniform now . . . must have killed himself early. I scan the 360 from here but see nothing around me.

I am feeling sick from the two cans of food eaten earlier this morning and wishing I had already found a safe place to hole up for the rest of the day and night. I plan to keep moving for another two hours before finding a hideout. Sleeping in a vehicle, like the corpse in the seat below me, is not an option. The *gore marks* around this truck tell me that. This poor bastard was probably surrounded for days and maybe weeks before he gave up and killed himself. My map is folded to the area I am in. The map was not printed recently and is therefore not a completely accurate representation of the region, but it is far better than nothing.

Storm clouds are gathering on the western horizon and chances are that it will be a wet night if I end up sleeping under the stars this evening. I feel like I may be catching a cold and I just hope that's as serious as it gets.

2134

Someone is following. After I left my rest area this afternoon the SATphone rang. The time was approximately 1355 and I almost missed the call. The phone was tucked under the top portion of my pack with the antenna sticking out the right side. By the time I took off the heavy pack and unfastened the pack buckles the phone had rung three times. I hit Talk and listened for the familiar sound of digital sequencing as the satellite text data was compressed for downlink.

. . . SITREP follows:
Project Hurricane: Successful. Evasion route acceptably
clear southwest w/ light undead density.

Reaper: Remains FMC w/ two LGBs on rails for
deployment.
Threats: Unidentified armed male trails from north. Thirty
undead w/ two hot located ten mile radius current location via
Reaper sensors . . .

The phone lost synchronization immediately after the last word and I quickly brought out my binoculars and began to scan the area behind me to the north. I saw no sign of an unidentified man following. The phone gave me no chance to ask any questions or direct the text communication. Something isn't right about this relationship between myself and the unit on the other side of the phone. Perhaps there is a problem with the satellite network only enabling remote relay or something of that nature. There must be a data link from the Reaper overhead to a control area where the aircraft is piloted and the screens are monitored. "Thirty undead with two hot." This can only mean one thing—Dallas, Texas. I have seen what these types of undead can do and I will double my efforts to evade contact with any of those things now that I know that there are two of the radioactive creatures in my area.

It is raining right now and I am taking shelter in a farm tractor cab left abandoned in a large field surrounded by a damaged cattle fence. The rear axle of the beast is fouled with meters of barbed wire wrapped around it as a result of running over the fence. Another relic from months ago. Every now and again if I squint my eyes just right I can see something out there. Just enough to scare me into leaving my shelter and running as fast as I can in the dark through the Texas night.

My mind keeps playing tricks on me, making me think I see glowing and radiated undead in the distance—moving quickly. It is cold in here and I have my legs bundled into the mummy bag. It seems to be working well. The tractor is John Deere green. Just like the color I see through my electronic relics every few minutes when paranoia takes over and I must look.

I wonder if the man that might be following feels the same fear. Tomorrow I continue south through the temporary safe area back to my home.

<u>15 Oct</u>

0800

Woke up to the sun peeking over the horizon right into my face and pondered once again the message delivered during yesterday's phone call. Today will be a day of looking over my shoulder as I travel south and west, keeping my foot back just in case. If the situation report from the SATphone proves true, I may be in for some trouble in the near future. The mummy bag that was dropped will be draped around my civilian pack to lessen my visibility to any person who may be following. This man is on foot. Finding a car and getting it running using solar charger, fuel treatment and hand siphon may become my best option for evading the follower. The only drawback to this plan is that using the charger on a car battery would take the entire day for one start attempt, never mind the probability of a hotwire attempt. I'll need to find a car with the keys in it, which most likely means the previous owner will be too.

0900

I have dug a hole in the overgrown farm soil, using the end of one of my large rattraps. Gathering some small firewood I managed to make a semismokeless fire using a sideways stovepipe technique with shrubs and leaves to diffuse the smoke. I heated up a can of chili today and consumed a quarter of my water stores. I know that having less food is never good, but every time I look at my pack I get anxious to eat any and all of the canned food and then the MREs so that all that is left is the dried food. The limit of my anxiousness to get rid of heavy gear ends with ammunition. I will preserve it to the maximum extent in the event I'm forced to defend myself from the dangers that are ever present around me and far in front. It was probably not the best idea to make a fire, in light of recent events, but I need the morale boost of warm food before I depart.

<u>16 Oct</u>

<u>2143</u>

This is evasion. Avoiding the undead follows a set formula. Stay low, quiet, and plan your movements ahead of time. These rules are invalid when evading a human tracker. Staying low and quiet only gives a pursuer time to follow your tracks and catch you if he is following a different set of rules. Careful balance between the two methodologies is all that has kept me out of my alleged pursuer's immediate line of sight. I have received no calls from Remote Six in the past thirty-plus hours. I know now that the fact that there is overhead satellite coverage does not mean that this organization will use it. Despite not seeing my follower, I have the feeling that someone is watching me and I cannot decide if this is paranoia or if I am actually sensing the eyes of a stranger watching from a distance. I have no one to share a night watch. I attempted to remain awake during the long night I have just spent sleeping in the grassy loft of a farmer's barn. Every creak from the wood or flutter from a nocturnal bird's wings brought me to my feet gazing about by the green glow of my relics and looking at the red dot glowing through my optic as I frantically tried to acquire a target that was not there. I never knew fear until tomorrow. I write this because I thought I knew fear the day before, but every day fear takes a new and more voluminous meaning. I had a friend in the military who took a different path in the service than I did. "The only easy day was yesterday" was not his personal motto, but he often referred to it, and it applies more than ever in these times.

My back is sore and I am suffering from fatigue. After last night's torturous experience in the barn, I awoke to the sight of one of them standing in the field facing the loft window where I stood. Pulling out my binocs I watched it look right at me and lurch toward the barn. The thing was one of the originals. It had been dead for a long time and its skeleton showed in numerous places about its body.

I did not wish to let it get to where it could make noise and attract others so I quickly pulled out the pistol and attached the can so that I could make quick and quiet work of this thing. I was happy that there seemed to be only one of them. Once I was sure that I had not misthreaded the suppressor, I chambered a round and started shooting. It took two shots to bring the thing down, the first shot hitting the neck and the second hitting the bridge of the nose. The thing fell and I examined it from the safety of the loft window to determine if it might have anything of value. It had nothing left but a leather belt holding up rotting pants, and I decided that whatever the thing had in its pockets it could keep. While eating my last can of chili cold in the loft of the barn, I noticed that I had only one item of canned food left (beef stew). I think I might save it for a couple of nights.

Canned food was getting old, and I despised it cold, but eating it was giving me the excuse to listen to my surroundings before climbing down the loft ladder. I didn't want it to seem like I was doing that for my own sanity. I sat and dined and nonchalantly listened for any sound that would keep me in the loft any longer.

I set out this morning knowing that the Project Hurricane coverage must be abating, as evidenced by the fact that I was now seeing the things in close proximity. This really put me in a bad mood as I began moving and forced my mind to wander to my most recent good memory of hot chili. I suppose a good meal is the only thing I have to look forward to and the one guaranteed motivator I have to get home. I remember deploying to the desert all those times. I remember the war and how much I missed home and how much I always had something to get me through. The thought of camping with my family or the thought of purchasing that new rifle with the tax-free money I had earned from the tour I was on or the idea that I'll actually get a weekend off someday if I just keep my head down and get the job done.

I'm reduced to thinking about warm food. That is my pick-me-up for today. Tomorrow perhaps it will be that I can lament the fact that the helicopter I crashed in had substandard maintenance and was built by the lowest bidder with no living certified mechanic for hundreds, possibly thousands of miles. Chip light. I was forced down in nearly uninhabitable territory because a flake of metal in the engine casing caused a catastrophic failure in the aircraft's ability to remain in the air. Any landing is a good landing if you can walk away from it, unless you walk away from it dead.

Tonight I found shelter in an abandoned gas station, the type of oasis that was out of business long before the fall. No sign of life but the remnants of rats from months or years before. The place was cleaned out. Looked to be decades old and had probably been a profitable place back in the day. The pumps were analog readout and there were no security cameras installed above them on the roof. Under the old wood counter inside the store was what looked like an old shotgun rack from days gone by when that was perfectly acceptable.

Like today.

There was an old used set of snow chains that worked well to secure the entry points. They would slow a human assailant and downright stop one or two undead. I set up shop in an area with visibility to both access doors. From either heavy door I could see fifty feet to the tree line. The grass was very tall beyond the old, cracked blacktop parking spots but afforded enough visibility. The wind is howling and I hear an old piece of tin barely flapping on the gas pump roof. It is getting colder and I think that this winter will be a challenge if I make it that long.

17 Oct
0800

I slept poorly after waking up to a series of disturbing dreams. I dreamt of hundreds of different things but could only remember two. It seems like the ones I really wanted to remember escaped my grasp. I was on the top of a hill looking down on millions of undead. There were several 20mm gun emplacements manned by what looked like U.S. military personnel in various different types of uniforms. I looked at myself as if I was a third-person spectator and looked into my own eyes as I gave the order to fire. The undead were still a mile in the distance but the 20mm barrels were spitting shells downrange so fast that a moat appeared below the feet of the disintegrated ghouls. I saw AC-130 gunships flying low and taking out thousands with their guns. Old F-4s and A-4s flew low and dropped napalm, decimating the enemy, but they still moved forward. I flashed to the next dream, inside Hotel 23 with Tara. She was alone in the environmental room crying as she looked through a box of my belongings. As the tears slowly dropped from her cheek I heard her say, "Where is it?" and I faded from my subconscious back into the reality of the situation. I had tried my best not to think of her since the crash. It only complicates my situation.

Waking up, I was reminded that I was down to only one can of vegetable beef stew, which in a way is good news as that is the last of the heavy food besides the two MREs that I have broken down, throwing out the heavy cardboard to lighten the weight. I lit the candle once again to cook the can of beef stew. I didn't feel well this morning and I could not decide if it was the broken sleep or the onset of a cold that made me feel weak and aching all over. I drank half my supply of water and consumed the entire can of food before repacking my pack for the day's travails.

1200

I have made good time today despite my apparent weakening condition. I'd love to drink a gallon of orange juice right now, as that always seemed to help in a less fucked-up world. About two hours into my hike this morning I spotted a glint behind me from the direction I had come, just a subtle reflection. Pulling out my binocs I could see nothing. The wind was blowing colder by the day and off in the distance at around a thousand yards there was no sign of movement besides the swaying foliage. In case there is a call, I have the phone hooked into the solar charger hanging from my pack as I make my way toward the bottom of the map. I've accepted that they are not daily occurrences.

I spotted random pockets of undead in the past two hours and observed them in the various fields and areas around me. None seem aware that I am in their vicinity. I keep scouting ahead, readjusting my course to maintain safe distance from the enemy. Anything closer than a hundred yards would most likely result in contact with them, depending on the wind and their level of decomposition. I have the pistol and suppressor at the ready, strapped to the outside of my pack, in the event I need to neutralize one of them. I can't take the chance of making noise if I am being followed or tracked.

1600

No call today. I feel that my paranoia has cost me some time, as I kept looking over my shoulder to see if I could catch a glimpse of my alleged follower. I could see no sign. I feel as if I am being watched, but it is difficult to tell if the feeling comes from the warning or if it's a bona fide sixth sense. Hell, it could be both. Tonight I take refuge in an old tavern right off the road. I took shelter early, as I feel I am about to be stricken very weak by this bug I have caught. I cannot eat but I am forcing myself to drink the rest of my water. I hear thunder on the horizon and the feeling of approaching rain is in the air. Numerous bottles of alcohol remain on the shelves, never looted. I picked out a dusty bottle of Maker's and unsealed it, drinking directly from it. It stung but soothed my throat and made me feel warmer than I actually was. I sat in a corner booth in this old hole-in-the-wall tavern known only as River City Liquor and Eats. Some people preferred a booth when going to eat out. I suppose I'm a corner-booth man.

I know all these bottles of alcohol have medical value for disinfection and pain killing. I wish I had the room to take more than a small fifth of whiskey. The wind is kicking up and the rain should follow, not long after this sentence.

18 OCT

0900

I was able to refill my water supply three times last night due to the heavy rain. Checking the drawers of the manager's office, I discovered a bottle of prenatal vitamins. I checked the back label to make sure they wouldn't make me grow breasts and popped the top and took a double dose. They were about to expire, meaning they were probably weak in effect. I needed vitamin C in my current condition. My appetite was down but I kept forcing water into my system (two-hundred ounces since last night). It seemed like I was at the tavern door with my rifle in one hand and my gun in the other taking a leak every fifteen minutes. I feel it prudent to make River City Tavern my home for one more night so I can regain some strength.

1500

I was outside, weary and shaking, waiting on the call that never came. Leaning against an old derelict vehicle in a ditch just up the road from the tavern I spotted one of those things. It spotted me too and started shuffling quickly toward me. I had no time to pull out the suppressed pistol. I leveled my rifle on the thing and put the red dot on its forehead and squeezed the trigger. That was that, only it was very loud and no doubt would draw them to my location. After the satellite window came and went I quietly made my way back to the tavern to think this through. It was becoming more difficult to think as time went on. I felt my fever go up by the hour. I noticed when I got back to the tavern that a propane tank in the shape of a huge aspirin sat in the back. It was possible that this place had the resources for cooking and such. All that was left in my pack was the dried food and MREs.

2200

The propane system in the tavern works. Using rainwater and an old skillet, I made some of the dehydrated food and forced it down. It tasted pretty good despite my body telling me that I was not hungry. It was dark outside, so I decided to get more practice with the M-4 optic using NVGs. I dialed the red dot to the first setting and it seemed to work just fine with the NVGs. It would be fine for a limited engagement, but the muzzle flash would give me away after one shot, maybe two, depending on the observer's distance. At least I have the capability to use it at night if necessary. As I was peeping through the optic with the NVGs I saw movement out the window. It was pitch black inside so I knew that the things could not see me. I kept my weapon trained, focusing on the dot, making sure that any threat could be neutralized. Then I saw them . . . ten to fifteen of them. They were moving about on the road seemingly aimless. I held my breath and watched them and talked myself out of checking the action on my weapon at least thirty times. I might not survive if they find out that I'm in here. I was weak from a cold, and a night engagement in these small confines would give them the advantage. Too many ways to die here tonight. Remaining low and quiet and unfortunately awake.

19 Oct

0645

The morning looks as if it will develop into a clear day. The creatures left the immediate area around 0200. I didn't force myself to sleep until 0300. I am operating off of three hours of sleep and I feel like I have a hangover. I continue to drink water and I even found some old sealed-up coffee. Not the best thing in my condition but I need the caffeine this morning. I will not stay here another night. I move today or I may not be moving anywhere again. Where there is one there are two and where there are fifteen there are a hundred. I'll attempt to do ten miles today.

1200

I'm resting at the military crest of a ridge, with rocks covering my back. I have made a somewhat gruesome discovery. There is what looks like an old grain mill about a klick down into the valley. I would have missed the structure if it were not for the smoke rising from what appears to be living quarters near the mill. There is a separate building that looks to hold livestock or possibly prisoners. I have set up a nest here with the sleeping bag as my hideaway. My gear is safe in the waterproof pack, covered by some branches, and I am observing the area closely, deciding what to do.

There are people walking about, perhaps roving guards. I need to monitor their movements and document their patterns.

Guard 1 (crossbow man): Observed leaving living quarters randomly between 1030 and 1130.

Guard 2 (fat woman): Observed patrolling grain grinder every fifteen minutes between the hours of 1030 and 1130.

Guard 3 (AK-47): Observed standing guard fifty yards from structures, seems attentive. Did not leave guard shack.

1300

Situation: Close observation over time revealed that an armed hostile party is holding captive at least one civilian. Grain mill has been modified to utilize human power. They are using creatures to turn the mill. Not certain if the mill is for grain or for pumping water. Creatures are secured to the mill with harnesses. No mouth restraints, but they are fitted with some modified form of horse blinders. They are stimulated to walk forward by the fat woman, who comes every fifteen minutes.

1330

Observed an uncovered military troop transport truck approaching the compound with only two individuals in the back and one driver in front. They seemed to be part of the staff here at the compound. In my binocs, I could see the fat woman's mouth open up to a shrill scream at the men after they offloaded what looked like a body (really dead).

1400

So much for making ten miles today. I am going to take the diplomatic approach with a five-hundred-pound LGB (laser-guided bomb). I decided this after I observed them attach a living person to the grain mill wheel to further entice the undead to move forward. Stick and carrot. I plan to find a place to hole up for tonight, then observe their daybreak routine and execute preemptive attack. It seems as if they are trying to keep a one-to-one ratio of living to dead on the wheel. They are tied so close to the dead that I thought I could make out one of the ghouls actually touching the back of the living person in front of it with its bony fingertips as they made their rotation in perpetual circles.

Part of me wants to drop high ordnance on them right now, but if I don't find a place to hole up for the night, I will become even more ill or could succumb to undead attack in my sack here on the high ridge ground. I'll take out the one in the guard shack first with my rifle. He's the only threat to me at this range, from what I can see, and one person is not worth the bomb. After taking out the guard, I'll lase the structure that I deem hostile and try not to cause collateral damage to the wheel containing the assumed friendlies and scattered undead. It's only a plan at this point. At one point today I witnessed a flash on the opposite ridge but could not spot movement with my binocs.

Another morbid but beneficial aspect of all this is that I can test the functionality of the Reaper flying overhead on an actual target worthy of an LGB. If all goes well I can take out the bad guys without getting within four-hundred yards of the structure. It's raining and I continue to feel ill and continue to refill my water and drink it to the point of wanting to puke. I have no choice, as there are probably no sterile IVs or saline within a hundred miles not guarded by a thousand undead. No call today, but I did attempt to trickle charge the SATphone with the solar charger while I continued to observe the compound below.

2000

Left some gear at my hiding spot near the mill and found a hiding place for the night in an abandoned unlocked car sitting on a hill. It was a stick eighties Volkswagen Bug. I picked this vehicle because it was off on a side road at the top of a hill. I got inside and checked for keys—there were none. I released the emergency brake and the car quickly started to roll. I only let it go for two feet before I put the brake back on. I could safely sleep inside the vehicle and if I were attacked by the undead in the night I could simply release the brake and roll down the hill. If the car were not a V Bug, I'd attempt to hotwire. The decade is right for the job, but I don't know where the essential parts are located, as the engine is in the trunk. Last time I did this it was Detroit steel. Wish I had that Buick Regal right now. Sleeping with one hand on the e-brake tonight.

20 OCT

0800

Up early this morning planning the attack and analyzing Reaper documentation. Double-checked the beacon and double-checked the Reaper coverage times. Would have attacked at night if I had the coverage. I slept relatively well with no unwanted interruption besides the local wildlife. An old owl kept me awake for a bit. What I would give to be able to fly right now like that wise old owl.

Change of plans: If I shoot the man in the shack and then the Reaper doesn't work as advertised, I could be a dead man. I wish I could remember how many inches a 5.56 round dropped at five-hundred yards from a sixteen-inch M-4 barrel.

The Reaper should be on station already or shortly. I tested the laser and heard the beeps resonate. Batteries check good. Aim-point checks good too—1× magnification will do no good so I'll need to get to about four-hundred yards to increase my chance of a hit on the guard. No way his AK-47 is more accurate at that range, so I'll take the chance. Found an old Chevrolet station wagon (bonus cool points for the wood paneling) not far from the V Bug. Checking my surroundings, I popped the hood to check the belts and hoses. Some were cracked but overall serviceable. No keys but I could work with this. Using the same technique I had used months before I should be able to get this old battle horse running all the way to Wally World. I had the phone and charger with me, but I had left the fuel treatment at my observation area just below the ridge line. I needed to scavenge some wire. Disconnecting the battery using my knife I pulled it out of the car and carried it to a clearing just out of sight of any foot traffic. I unfolded the charger so that the cells would get full exposure to the sun. The instructions to charge the phone were to only expose one cell. This was a big battery. The solar cell unit had no name brand markings, which I thought was odd.

I covered the battery with a plastic shopping bag scavenged from the back of the wagon, leaving only the unfolded charger exposed to the elements and the partly cloudy morning sky. I'm taking off in a few "mikes" to do more reconnaissance and possibly bring the pain down if need be.

Sniper

Enemy structure is leveled and on fire. I arrived on site this morning at 0850 hrs and prepped for my incursion inside five hundred yards to the target. The manpower situation was the same as was observed yesterday. I saw the fat female slice the back of one of the living slaves tied to the wheel, probably in an effort to entice the thing behind him and turn the wheel faster. The wheel only had one living being. Looked to be a middle-aged man. There were scratch marks on his back from the fingernails of the creature behind him. There was no doubt in my mind that the man was already dying from infection at this point. I carefully watched the wheel to confirm that he was the only living creature walking in a circle.

At about 0930 hrs I lased a spot of ground between the wheel and the living quarters of the people that were running this place. After approximately six seconds I got a steady tone on the device. I kept the device true on target as the LGB impacted . . .

I was flat on the ground but the blast still blew my hair back and popped my ears. The structure shattered into oblivion and the grain wheel flew into the air like a Frisbee at least a hundred feet from where it originally stood. Obviously the infected male was now dead. The blast blew the guard shack over like an old outhouse, leaving the guard dazed and confused. He eventually got to his feet and started running around shooting in all directions.

After wasting five rounds I eventually brought him down to the ground. I have been waiting here for any sign of movement for thirty minutes now. It's probably best to let anything alive bleed out. I'm about to go scout the area for survivors and make sure everything that is dead stays dead. In a slight hurry, since the blast was loud and pretty difficult to miss no matter what your heart-beat status.

1350

As I walked to the only structure that didn't get destroyed or heavily damaged I noticed bodies on fire that still walked. Bringing the M-4 up to my shoulder I waited until within fifty yards before taking them out. Killing seven in all, I approached the building and unlatched the door. The structure was slightly damaged and leaned a little to one side. Jerking the door open, I felt a swift wind of flies blowing past my head. It was at this moment that the SAT-phone went off while fifteen ghouls started to flow out the door. I sprinted back the way I came with the things in tow. Right hand held the M-4 and the left hand on the phone . . .

Shooting as best I could, I tried to fight and read the screen. I suppose this was the end-of-the-world version of driving down the freeway with a cell phone and coffee while you shave.

All I saw on the other end was: "SITREP: Unidentified male closing your posit. Armed. Reaper LGB battle assessment: Thermal indicates only two living bipeds in area. Project Hurricane Ex . . ."

The rest was garbled.

I danced with the ghouls for a good bit and had to change magazines and run in circles like an idiot to keep them a safe distance away. That's when it happened: I put the red dot on the forehead of one of those things and its head exploded before I pulled the trigger. Then a shot rang out. As I watched the creature in front fall, I didn't notice the one behind. It was almost close enough to put its teeth around my neck. In the corner of my eye I caught its head explode and decayed pieces of bone hit me in the shoulder as the shot rang out in delay once again. There was only one left, so I waited and kept my distance, trying to find some cover.

I hid behind a moldy hay bale and watched another head explode, then another. The report came less than a second after the head was impacted, not totally destroying the head, but taking a good-sized piece off. I reached for my binocs and scanned the area all around. Nothing. No sign of the shooter. I crawled until

I couldn't stand it anymore and ran as fast as I could to my gear cache up on the ridge.

To my surprise I did not get shot in the back of the head on the way up. The smell of smoke and bad beef jerky was in the air, making me even more nausated than I already was from being down with a cold. I sat up on the ridge line scanning all around the valley floor and surrounding areas. After about forty-five minutes of this I caught a glint of something. I could barely make out the outline of a torso at least five to six hundred yards away on the opposite side of the valley. The person was holding a small reflective mirror or piece of glass of some sort. Then he started walking and I could see that the man was wearing some serious camouflage on his legs and was carrying the top part of the ensemble in the hand opposite his rifle. Every now and again he'd signal, then check my area with binoculars and signal again to indicate spotting me.

After a few minutes of this, I decided that if the man had wanted to kill me he would have done so already. I kept my gear hidden and walked down to the valley floor with only my M-4 and sidearm. At two hundred yards we dispensed with the binoculars and closed the gap. At pistol range we stopped and squared off. He was wearing a light burlap ghillie suit and had dark skin and dark black hair and a beard. The man put his weapon and signal mirror down on the ground in front of him and stepped back a few paces. My pistol was tucked in my pants behind my back so I felt safe enough to lay the M-4 down and step back.

He yelled over to me in a heavy Middle Eastern accent and said: "My name is Saien; I mean you no harm. I have been tracking you for days."

I noticed that the weapon in front of the man was an AR-type sniper rifle.

I asked him why he had been following.

"I'm trying to get to San Antonio and you were going in the same direction."

I informed Saien that under no circumstances was I headed to San Antonio for at least a few hundred years. He frowned at this but understood as he replied: "Are you sure?"

I said that I was and that I had escaped the city in January right before they dropped the nuke. He began to reason his way out of that by stating that he had heard that some of the cities listed were not destroyed. I had to flat-out tell him that I saw the blast from the airport tower I was hiding in at a safe distance east of the city.

"Have you seen the special ones? The ones that move faster?"

"I saw one of them for sure. On a ship in the Gulf of Mexico. They are lethal and need to be avoided."

"I agree, my friend. From my apartment one hundred miles south of Chicago I witnessed them do things that I did not imagine were possible. Later down the road as I was leaving Chicago, I saw them open unlocked car doors and even sprint . . . but not far or long. They came out of Chicago, I'm certain. I saw the blast out my window last January. Two weeks later they came south. They chilled me—is that the right word?"

I chanced a half smile and told him that it was, I supposed.

"I saw those things go door to door, or so it seemed. One of them even rang the doorbell and turned the knob. More dead birds fell from the sky around the time they arrived. The dead were dumb animals, to be sure, but some memory remained. Do you know why?"

I responded with one word . . .

Radiation.

"I heard the same on the AM radio from someone in Canada working from an AM relay. I observed one of them standing at a door for a month before it moved. It just stood there barely moving, almost sleeping . . . until a raccoon happened upon the porch. The thing fell on top of it and devoured the animal, leaving nothing."

I asked the man what he wanted in San Antonio, and he replied that he had many brothers there. I saw him reach behind and touch a blanket that was strapped to his back. He saw that I had noticed and withdrew his hand. As I stared at him, his response was: "Allah has left this place. Many days since the fall of man I have questioned my belief and lost him. I no longer believe."

In my heart I felt that Saien was genuine and did not wish to harm me, at least today. It was another level of surreal, talking to a living human besides myself.

I inquired, "Do you have more gear?"

"Of course I do, it's hidden, just like your gear is hidden in the hill behind you."

He then said: "Sir, I have tracked and watched you before you found this foul place . . . I do not understand how you placed the explosives on the buildings. I never saw you infiltrate. Did you go at night?"

"I brought the explosives in early this morning."

It technically was not a lie. Trust is to be earned over time, never given.

My turn to ask the pointed questions, and I inquired where he learned to make head shots from a thousand yards.

"Afghanistan."

"Fair enough. What brought you here?"

"I was a freedom fighter, or I thought that I was. I came to Illinois to help my brothers. Before I could do this, the dead began their dance."

I decided to probe no further, as it was a good trade for discussing the origin of the explosion or any detail regarding Remote Six.

I suggested that we check out the rubble for anything of use and he agreed. We walked over to the building where Saien had saved my ass from the creatures. Some of those things were hanging on meat hooks with random limbs missing. A large cooking pot (like a witch's caldron) was in the center of the room. This was fucked up to the fifth power, but it appeared these people were eating the dead. The creatures gazed at us and snapped their jaws. I saw nothing of use in this building, so Saien and I set the place on fire and went to gather our gear.

I asked if he had any wire, as I needed it to secure transportation. Confused, he replied that he did not, but he was sure that we could find some in the abandoned cars. He was right, but something about leaning under the hood scared me to death. I thought of the monster with the hatchet that nearly cleaved me up the middle. We gathered our gear and made for the solar charger. Walking with Saien had reinforced the need for diligence. He seemed to stop every ten steps, listen, and sweep the distance out front with his scope. This is probably the reason he is still alive. I noticed that Saien had an oversized M-16. I asked where he got it.

As he handed it over so that I could check it out, he told me that he liberated it from an abandoned FEMA camp tower on his way south from Chicago. Upon closer inspection, I noticed the rifle was chambered in .308 with a bull barrel, an SR-25. The scope had a small holo sight mounted on it. He told me that the glass was no good at much less than a hundred yards. The holo sight was for the closer encounters. The weapon was extremely heavy compared to my M-4. The ground where we are standing is a long way from Chicago, and I can't even fathom how he made the journey. I've almost been killed ten times since I crashed less than a hundred miles from here.

We walked and listened all the way back to the area where the wagon sat in derelict condition, as it had for months. I enjoyed the light movement without my gear and strained at the weight of my pack as we returned. Saien and I quickly split up the duties. He disconnected the battery as I went hunting for wire. Here was the problem. We could not add the fuel treatment without first knowing if there was gas in the tank. It would be a waste of the solution. We had to connect the battery and get power to the dash, then check the manual to calculate how much fuel was in the tank so that I can put the proper mixture inside. Too much public math.

I left our base of operations just as Saien was lugging the battery back to the wagon. I had a multitool and my suppressed pistol. I made for the V Bug to cut her guts out so that I could start making time south. The explosions and gunshots worried me. Since January, I've never seen noise fail to draw the attentions of those creatures in some way. There was always cause and effect. Approaching the Bug I observed one of them on the road facing the other direction beyond the car. The day was cloudy and it looked like I was in for a nagging drizzle. Miserable morale sapping weather.

The creature stood there in the center of the road facing away from me. I arrived at the V Bug just as a loud clap of thunder rang out. The creature stirred and looked about, as if looking for the thing that had created the noise. Foolish thing.

I popped the trunk to get at the wiring around the engine compartment. I used more thunder to disguise my work as I cut enough wire to perform the wagon's starter bypass. It felt like I looked up every five seconds to make sure the creature was still unaware of my presence. It started to walk up the main highway to where Saien and the wagon were. Yanking the last bit of wire from the Bug and stuffing it in my pocket, I drew the pistol and started walking quickly to intercept the creature. I was on a side road off the highway. I then heard Saien scream out, "My friend, you need to hurry!"

The creature broke into a trot in the direction of Saien. I had to run to catch the creature. It was moving faster than any of them I had seen. Not sprinting pace, but fast enough to *chill me,* as Saien would say. It was now that I found out how difficult it was to sprint and shoot accurately with a pistol. The creature kept a stiff-legged pseudo-jog going until the suppressed round I fired hit the thing in the shoulder, knocking it down. I took advantage of this and kept up the chase so I could close the gap and get the head shot. Despite the shattered shoulder, the thing was on its feet as quickly as any sacked quarterback would be. It snarled and started a stiff-legged jog in my direction. I aimed my weapon and emptied three rounds into its head before it fell to the ground twitching.

I sprinted for Saien and was so out of breath by the time I reached him that I was seeing stars. He pointed down the road and handed me his rifle. It was damn heavy, which reinforced my respect for Saien's constitution. He was obviously a tough son of a bitch to carry this thing a thousand miles. I braced the over-sized .308 AR on its bipod on the hood of the wagon and peered downrange through the looking glass over a mile in the distance. Past the reticle, I could clearly see battalions of those creatures moving along the highway in our direction. The scope was power-ful enough to let me know that we would have a lot of company soon. I asked Saien how far they were. He said "two thousand me-ters." This gave us thirty to forty minutes at best. Saien looked nervous so I didn't think it would do any good to tell him that one of the radiated dead had been about to run up and bite his ass five minutes earlier. In the back of my mind, I knew I had one five-hundred-pound laser-guided bomb left on the Reaper orbiting over my head. I was thinking that there were at least fifty of those creatures in that group. I asked Saien what he thought.

He laughed in my face and said: "No, what you see before you is well into one hundred infidels approaching."

Working quickly, I explained to Saien what I was doing, ". . . plug wires to the coil wire . . . attach the wire to the . . ."

Saien interrupted with, "Yes, yes, my friend, I know . . . positive end to the positive side of the coil. We must move faster."

Saien alternated between helping me with the bypass and judging the range of the *infidels* approaching.

"Eighteen hundred meters."

"Roger."

I told Saien to run to my pack and pull the treatment out of the side pocket. Now that power was to the dash, I could see the fuel gauge. I quickly turned off the headlights and the heater to save power. I checked the dash. Half a tank. I then disconnected the circuit to save power. I pulled out the owner's manual and determined that the wagon had about nine gallons of fuel remaining in the tank. Doing the quickest math I could, I calculated that the amount of treatment to add to the tank would be less than one-quarter of the bottle. The gas had been sitting in this tank for at least nine months and was probably nearing a year old. I didn't guess it to be too far gone, so I decided to put one-eighth of the bottle in the tank. I quickly did this and shook the vehicle back and forth to slosh the solution into the gasoline as best as I could.

Just as I read "must wait one hour prior to combustion" on the bottle, Saien called out:

"Fifteen hundred meters."

We didn't have an hour left. Saien didn't respond when I asked him how it looked. He just shook his head and kept one eye glued to the optic. I was able to see them with my naked eye. It had drizzled and they were still kicking up debris from this distance. Judging from the time it took the creatures to transit three hundred meters, I estimated that we had thirty minutes of useful time before the first wave was on us. I quickly reconnected the solar panels to the battery and laid the panels out on the roof of the wagon. Thirty minutes may not do much but it was better than nothing.

I located the starter solenoid just as Saien called out:

"Twelve hundred meters."

Everything was set and it all depended on the battery charge and the gasoline treatment. I frantically packed my things to be ready to go in the event the vehicle failed to start. I had everything prepositioned except for the solar panels on the roof of the wagon. If the vehicle didn't start I would use my remaining minutes to shoulder my pack and move as quickly as possible out of the area. Saien would be of little defensive use with his sniper rifle. With a nineteen-round magazine and a twenty-four-inch barrel, the .308 isn't nimble enough for what was headed our way. Nothing really was, short of a GAU cannon.

I started to gather Saien's things together to place them in the rear of the vehicle for easy access when he told me to leave his bag at his feet and that he would take care of it.

"One thousand meters."

The creatures were well inside a mile and moving directly toward us on the highway. I felt a strange energy in the air and thought I could hear them crushing debris and moving forward like an undead tank division, hell-bent on destroying everything. I reached into my pack, pulled out my binoculars and hung them around my neck. Cleaning the body grease and dirt from the lens with my T-shirt, I peered through them and saw the fifth dimension of hell.

The creatures were moving forward at comparatively high speed and zigzagging back and forth across the highway as they moved forward as if sweeping and searching for something. Obviously this was not the case but the creatures were moving with a purpose. I dropped the binocs to hang around my neck, disconnected the solar panels and reconnected the dashboard circuit. I then completed the connection between the starter and the juice and the car turned over a couple times but didn't start.

It had only been twenty-plus minutes since I administered the additive. I disconnected power and reconnected the solar panels to at least get back some of what I had just lost in the start attempt.

"Seven hundred fifty meters."

His voice was louder and displayed a bit more nervousness than last time. I raised my binocs and had another look. The creatures appeared to be in similar stages of decomposition, but this stage was not nearly as bad as it should be. They looked relatively fresh, not like something that had been dead for nine or ten months. This fact, combined with the fact that they were moving faster than the undead I had experienced in the past, led me to believe that the radiated *scout* (so to speak) I had neutralized earlier was only the beginning trickle. A river of lethal undead was approaching.

I checked and double-checked my M-4 three times and tested the laser device for beeps just as Saien called out, "Five hundred meters."

I could hear them. Wailing moans and unearthly sounds were getting louder on the air. I could not keep from looking. Through the lenses I could see them scan an abandoned car for any signs of food and move to the next. The car down the road shook from side to side as the army bumped by. Saien reached down for his pack and began to open the top so that he could get at something inside. I didn't have time to wonder what he was doing but I knew that he couldn't hold off the undead with the weapon he was using.

He then started shooting.

I screamed at him, asking him what the fuck he was doing.

"Taking out the fast ones."

I told him to fucking stop and that he would just let them know for sure we were here. I think I was right, as the sound in the air modulated to a different tone after the report of his last shot stopped echoing.

"Three hundred fifty meters!"

I shook the vehicle, ramming it with my shoulder, thinking somehow it would help the treatment work faster in the tank if I kept it sloshing inside. The creatures were getting close enough that I could hit them with my rifle. I made the decision to deploy the Reaper. It was our only chance to buy some time for the treatment to take effect. Using my binocs to judge the range, and bouncing my estimate off Saien, I lowered the optic down to the creatures. As I peered through the glass I could see that Saien's estimate of the number of creatures that were headed our way was better than mine.

I activated the laser device . . .

Beep . . . beep . . . beep . . .

. . . a constant tone. Drizzle and sweat was running down my forehead and into my eye, causing it to sting as I kept the device steady on a piece of ground fifty meters behind the front mass of the creatures.

I thought I saw the warhead for an instant on a ballistic trajectory straight down into the mass of creatures. The explosion rocked the ground two hundred meters in front of our wagon, and most of the creatures hit the dirt in the blast.

I screamed out to Saien that I would explain later, and he nodded and checked his pack again. He kept looking through his sniperscope as I once again made an attempt to start the car. I checked the crowd and estimated that at least fifty creatures were getting to their feet and once again lurching forward in our direction. I ran through the hotwire procedure again, checking to make sure that all wires and points were connected.

"One hundred fifty meters! Hurry!"

Saien was getting very nervous, and this raw emotion was being transmitted to me. My hands started to shake as I checked the wires and began to connect power to the dash. Saien threw his rifle into the backseat and reached into his pack and pulled out a suppressed MP5.

He then said in his Middle Eastern accent: "Get the car started, Kilroy!"

I connected the power to the dash and turned the car over again, probably using every bit of energy the battery had left. The car jacked over once, twice, and on the third time the engine came to life—the sweetest sound I had ever heard. I slammed down the pedal to get the juices flowing in the engine, thinking that it might speed the battery-charging process. I jumped out of the car, grabbed the solar panels and chucked them in the back on top of Saien's gear.

Just as I got settled into the driver's seat, Saien opened fire on the approaching undead. I had my pistol in my lap with extra mags ready. Slamming the vehicle into reverse, I started to back up and told Saien to fall back and get into the car.

He acted like he did not hear me as he kept firing at the undead, taking out the fastest one so that another fast mover could replace it. The creatures were very close. We would be overrun in seconds if he did not get into the car. I screamed at him as loudly as I could and threatened to leave him if he didn't stop.

He finally snapped out of it, fired one last round into a fast mover less than fifty feet in front of our car and jumped in, riding shotgun. I slammed on the gas, driving by rearview mirror, increasing the distance between the creatures and us. Nearly in shock, I made a comment to Saien about how fast those creatures moved.

He replied callously with only, *"That* is not fast, my friend."

He didn't elaborate, and I really did not want him to.

I flipped the car around, put her into drive and put the pedal down to escape the advancing mob. The sun was getting low in the sky by this time and we needed to find a place to park the vehicle. As we drove Saien told me of how he saw the C-130 drop and how he observed me moving the equipment around and entering the abandoned house where I reorganized my gear. He had been tracking me for quite some time. Saien was vague about his survival and also about his time in Afghanistan. The Reaper UCAV bombing I triggered with the laser never came up in the conversation, but the man seemed intelligent enough not to miss something of that magnitude. I kept scanning the engine and fuel gauges to ensure that this old wagon would hold up during our journey south.

It seemed that every five to ten miles we had to stop to assess a roadblock. Some of the wreckage was easy to navigate around and some of it nearly stopped our progress altogether. Optimally we'd need a larger truck with a winch or good towing chain to pull debris off the road. The third and fourth roadblocks we came to in our search for shelter were obviously intentional, a throwback to bandits and highwaymen long dead. Large-caliber bullet holes riddled the vehicles, and skeletal remains occupied the defending side of the wreckage. Two rusted AK-47 rifles lay decaying on the ground. We had to stop the vehicle anyway to assess how we would get around the wreckage so I hopped out and picked up the salvageable AK (the other was all but destroyed). The only damage to the weapon was a bullet hole through the wooden stock and rust all over the metal components of the weapon. I couldn't get the bolt back, so I slammed it against the wrecked car. After two attempts the bolt flew back and a round ejected from the weapon. I walked over to a wrecked motorcycle, smashed the oil indicator viewer on the side of the engine and flipped it over to spill out the motor oil. Reaching down, I filled my hand with oil and liberally splashed it on the bolt assembly of the AK-47.

I took out the mag and jacked the slide back about ten times. I put the ejected round back into the mag and threw the weapon in the back of the wagon. The mag was full. I salvaged the mag from the wrecked AK and tossed it into the back with the other. I'll take the extra weight, since I'm not humping it. Just as I closed the back door, Saien came around the wreckage and told me that we could make it around with no trouble. As I got back into the vehicle, in the back of my mind I was thinking of how the sun was getting low and that my Reaper UCAV was now empty and probably returning to base. As we weaved slowly down the road we continued to pass remnants of last stands. Some cars contained the caked leftovers of undead corpses still moving inside their clear caskets even though sun-baked and rotting.

As we drove along the side of the road we came to a new-car dealership. The cars still sat in neat rows along the road. Before the world fucked itself up, car lots seemed to have a uniform look with vehicles lined up in perfect rows. A car lot had held a very neat and clean appearance. Fast-forward to now and many of the cars have flat tires and the once-even rows now look like a staggered collection of cars in a junkyard. Hail damage and the rest of the elements have taken their toll. It was going to be dark in about half an hour. Saien and I made preparations to park the wagon in the showroom of the dealership so that we could sleep in relative safety and still be able to drive out of the building with assumed lower risk if we were swarmed as we had been before on the road. Using my hatchet and some of Saien's tape, we were able to unlock the sliding door to the showroom floor. We set up the ramps and swept the showroom for danger. Saien had my abandoned MP5, and we began to systematically go room to room through the sales offices. There was no sign of anyone in the entire dealership. We secured the back doors by placing office debris (old boxes full of paper, and so forth) against the doors so that nothing could find its way inside while we slept.

The main back door had a place for a two-by-four as a barricade for after hours. Before setting the plank I opened the door to see what was back behind the showroom. The maintenance area was housed behind but we didn't have the daylight left to properly clear it. I shut the door and put the plank in the slot, securing the door against anything short of a battering ram. I backed the wagon onto the showroom floor and shut and locked the large sliding glass doors, cutting Saien and me off from the rest of the world for the night. Before retiring for the evening I will ensure the solar charger is connected to the phone in anticipation of the morning sun and tomorrow's possible contact.

I rounded up some paracord from the drop and, using tape, I made some magazine pulls so that I can easily pull the M-4 magazines from stowage in the event that I'm running and gunning my way out of somewhere. Tomorrow Saien and I will need to visit the garage so that we can acquire the raw materials we'll need to get the wagon prepared. I've noticed that there are road atlases in a stack in the corner. They were probably gifts for the new-car customers here. They are dated for last year but something tells me that there has not been a huge number of roads constructed since they were last printed.

In my spare time in the dealership I checked out some of the maps that were in the drop. They were overlaid with a military grid. The map was laser jet printed and some obscure machine language was present. There was a legend on the back and I found myself flipping the map over and over. Then something clicked and suddenly a light bulb went on in my head.

The area where the supply drop occurred was marked with an S, presumably for supply. The letter S had a diagonal line through it, probably signifying that the drop had already occurred. There were other places on the map with an S that seemed to follow a logical path south to Hotel 23 (within twenty miles either side of a straight line). They did not have the diagonal line through them, which could indicate drops we would find ahead of us. There were areas marked with a radiation symbol. Dallas was one area marked, as were random other areas along our path that probably gave off enough radiation to trip national sensors. It could in theory be anything large and dense, such as a crane or a fire truck that had absorbed enough radiation to hold and emit a residual amount. It could also be a large group of those things, like those we had seen today, although I doubt the relatively outdated (in real-time terms) map would be useful in pinpointing the location of a mass like that.

Random items of concern: Charge the phone, rewire the wagon, garage, reorganize gear and distribute sixty 9mm rounds to Saien.

Sticker Price

As my eyes gained focus on the light reflecting off the dusty show-room floor, I saw Saien lying belly down on his drag bag with his rifle scanning the area in front of the dealership. It would be ab-surd to attempt a head shot through the thick glass, so I wrote this off as him just making sure that things were kosher in the area. The man remained alive, despite traveling hundreds of miles through an apocalyptic wasteland to where he is today. I'm not qualified to question his methods, and even if I were, I am too jaded to care.

I cleared my throat to get Saien's attention. It took him a few seconds, and then he whispered over his shoulder, asking, "What do you want, Kilroy?"

I didn't want to argue that Kilroy was not my name, nor did I wish to give Saien an American history lesson, which would be about as valuable as a lesson on the Mayan civilization.

I said, "Saien, we need to clear the garage area and scavenge some wire so that we can reliably wire the wagon for the journey."

Saien looked at me as if I were an idiot and asked, "Why do we not charge the battery and treat the fuel on one of the new vehicles on the lot?"

Fighting off embarrassment, I had to admit that his sugges-tion made more sense than spending an entire day wiring an old wagon. Using a factory ignition method would be more reliable, and using a new vehicle could save us a potential breakdown in no-man's-land.

Despite what he said, we would still need to charge the battery on the vehicle that we would liberate from the dealership. There was a selection of hybrid vehicles on the lot but they were mostly smaller in size.

"Another question, Kilroy: Why do you write in that book? What is so important that I see your nose buried in it when we stop? You are going to die writing in that, you know."

I wasn't sure how to answer. I just told him, "It helps." I think he understood what that meant.

Saien and I debated about vehicles and decided that although the hybrid vehicle would save us from scavenging gas by the order of half, we would need an SUV with a towing package and tow chain to get around all the cars and debris blocking our way from here to our destination. During our discussion I noticed that the sleeping rug that he had rolled and attached to his pack was very ornate. It appeared to be an oriental carpet. I didn't know Saien, so my first assumption was that he was Muslim and this was his prayer carpet. He has seemed troubled since the action died down and I could see conflict in his eyes.

I suggested that we pick out a vehicle so that we could start the charging/fueling process, and he agreed. Before finding our ride we decided to check out the garage and maintenance office area of the dealership for any threats that might lurk there. Saien put a fresh mag in the MP5, and I was at the ready as we opened the door. Nothing was out there but the apocalyptic silence that still tortured my nerves. The back end of the dealership was fenced off with chain-link. Saien and I walked around the perimeter and saw nothing outside the maintenance area but the corpse of a canine that hadn't been able to get out of the fenced area to keep himself alive. For some reason this caused me more grief than I had felt for some time. I imagined the poor animal thirsty and unable to eat or drink and just dying on the ground in misery.

With this on my mind I didn't notice the creature approaching on the other side of the fence. The screeching sound of the creature's reaction broke me from my thoughts, and I instinctively raised my weapon and put the red dot on the thing's forehead. Of course, there was no reaction from the creature, and it just advanced into the fence, striking it and falling straight back to the ground. I lowered my weapon, let it hang down on my sling and asked Saien to pop the creature with the MP5 to avoid the noise that my M-4 would create. Right before he carried out my request, I told him to wait. I wanted some more practice with my Glock. I attached the suppressor and gave the creature two to the chest and one to the head, Mozambique style. There was no particular reason I wasted the first two rounds; I just felt I needed the practice. One of the rounds that I aimed at the creature's chest damaged the fence but still had enough energy to penetrate the creature's ribs.

I kept my carbine slung and walked the perimeter with the pistol at the ready. There were no other creatures in the immediate area. I did look farther down the field adjacent to the dealership with my binocs. I saw two of the creatures, but they were walking away from my position. If we practice vigilant noise discipline we should be fine—unless we get swarmed like before.

The door leading to the administration portion of the garage building was locked. Saien and I both peeked through the window and stayed there making sure nothing was moving about. My head was planted to the window so long that the glass fogged over, making standing there useless. If there was anything in there it was not moving or was really dead. Saien pulled a small rectangular leather zipper case from his pack and out came a lockpick and tension wrench. Through his clenched teeth, holding another shaped lockpick rake, he asked me to cover him while he worked. Within a few seconds he had the door unlocked and his gear put away. We readied our arms and went inside. I called out quietly, asking if anyone was inside. Of course, I knew that no living thing would be here, but if there was a functioning dead thing inside it would no doubt react to my voice, giving away its own location.

Dust, mold, and a corkboard were the main showpieces of the office. On the corkboard were handwritten notes and messages dated the first week in January. One of the handwritten notes stated, "The End Is Here" and "The time to repent has come and gone." There were internet printouts of the major headlines broadcast when the world started to crumble. They ranged from, "How Will the Dead Affect the Economy?" to "If Anyone Is Left, This Is It."

The latter article, printed from the *Wall Street Journal* homepage, I saw fit to read, and I attach it here:

J.L. Bourne

If Anyone Is Left, This Is It

Hello everyone, I'm . . . well, who cares who I am . . . with the *Wall Street Journal*. I'm not a columnist or a writer or a newsman of any kind. I'm the *Wall Street Journal* system administrator. Our generators are at 37 percent fuel capacity and I feel that if I do not get this out the story will never be told. We lost power in the New York metropolitan area early on in the epidemic. Our grid is so fragile it's a wonder it was working before this happened but I must digress.

Why am I still here? Great question. I was told by corporate that the situation was under control in the building and that I would be receiving a nice promotion for tending the server farms and network issues during the crisis. My family would be taken care of and the company was sending armed security personnel to my home to assist. By the time I figured out that no one was really in control, it was too late to leave.

My family is no doubt dead, as is the rest of the city. I'm safely locked in the server farm here and I can honestly say that I'm very happy that we have thick steel doors as a server physical security precaution, because they would be destroyed by now if they were anything but thick steel. I'm slowly going mad because of their methodical (debatable) and relentless pounding. I ran out of water yesterday and had to bring one of my water-cooled servers down so that I could scavenge the water from the coolant tubes. They hold exactly 1.25 gallons of closed-circuit H_2O. It tasted bad but has kept me alive. I'm currently devising a way to evaporate my urine using the generator heat to create water for drinking. With one of the telephoto lenses and a digital camera that I acquired before I locked myself in here, I can see through my window down into the streets of New Zoo York.

I have spotted nothing living down there in a week. The last living thing I saw down there was a police officer running. I snapped a picture of him with my camera as a souvenir of the last living thing in the streets of New York City.

On the overseas news wire I am reading interpreted stories of Europe being actually worse off than the United States, if you can believe that is possible. The U.K. is no different. Apparently their decision to disarm their citizens decades ago did not pay dividends when the anomaly occurred. Of course I am compelled to be unbiased and apolitical in my writing here, but I would love the feel of a rifle in my hands at this very moment. If any of you reading this are safe anywhere with your weapons and prepared, I envy you. I do not think I'll make it from this ivory tower. There are dozens of floors below me that I'd have to traverse before reaching the street, and for what? The second I hit the street I'd have to start running, but to where?

Did the government information czars cover up any news? Hell, yes, they did. I am an eyewitness to that. We had gag orders as early as January 3 not to report on the anomaly overseas or the situation on the Eastern Seaboard. We had our own "man in black" here in the building personally screening every piece of news that went out with his black Sharpie marker cutting up the First Amendment as if it were a Scrabble rule.

That's old news, and the average family sitting at home knew the writing on the wall. You can censor the news but you can't effectively censor the internet. Video and social websites were buzzing with mobile phone footage and photos of the real story. I have archived as much of it as possible on server NYT2 located off-site at our mirror server farm in Wichita, Kansas. That server is solid-state and should protect the data long after the lights go out in the Midwest. There were pictures taken that still jump out at me. I remember America complaining about gas prices before all this. One cell phone image of a gas station sign I saw had gas sitting at twelve dollars per gallon. A week later reports of it going for a hundred dollars per gallon were rumored. A woman sitting in a news van in Chicago uploaded her last days to the net via her phone. She was surrounded and overrun and one of the windows to the van was smashed and three of those things were stuck in the window trying to get in. They were eating the driver as the reporter cried and said her last words before opening the back door and jumping into the crowd in an attempt to escape.

I am all that is left alive on my floor. There is no way down and no escape. Good luck to all of you out there. If any of you see this and are in the area, please stop by for a visit and end it.

Staying alive,
G.R., System Administrator,
Wall Street Journal IT Department.

Saien and I checked every nook of the maintenance office area and moved on to the maintenance bays. After checking the maintenance bays and scavenging some small items that were light and could be of use, we made for the dealership's key locker to pick out our next ride. After assessing the pros and cons of the various vehicles, Saien and I decided on an extended cab diesel pick-up truck. It was new-looking and seemed in decent working order, other than the tire on the right front being a little low. The compressor in the garage obviously wouldn't work without electricity, so we will have to find one of those cheap car lighter compressors at some point along the way or we'll have to jack the truck and use a bicycle pump.

Amazingly, there are no jumper cables anywhere in the area and even if there were, jumping another vehicle would be too decibel-costly. Saien stood watch as I pulled the battery on the Ford and set up a charging station. I wanted to siphon the gas from the wagon but it would have no use on the diesel. Looks like we may be stuck here for at least a day while this battery charges in the sun. I placed the solar charger on top of the truck and put one of my dirty pairs of skivvies underneath to tilt it south. After a full, uninterrupted charge the battery should be suitable to start. I really wish I had access and skill to weld some bullshit over the windshield *Mad Max* style so that Saien and I could have something durable for our trip and something we could shoot out of without worrying too much. I continued to check the vehicle over where I could. The oil seemed fine and at the proper level and the key from the key box fit the ignition with no problem. The spare underneath the truck bed was full-sized and was full of air. I kept checking my watch. I didn't want to miss any possible communications during the satellite phone window today. Since the solar charger is being used for the truck battery, I'm forced to keep the SATphone turned off to conserve the battery until the window.

An air of strangeness surrounds Remote Six. Nothing checks out in my head. The odd gas treatment, the Reaper beacon technology and the remarkable solar panel that seemed to charge batteries faster than my commercially bought home panels ever could.

The sticker price on the truck was $44,995. The sticker also stated that this rig got 17mpg on the highway. The owner's manual said the tank would hold 26.2 gallons of diesel fuel. Using mental math, I calculated that that was over four hundred miles per tank. Hotel 23 was over two hundred miles from here. A full tank of diesel would get me home.

I studied the owner's manual, specifically on the tire change. Sometimes manufacturers used some ignorant proprietary means of loosening the spare tire or something else. Sure enough, this truck required the owner to assemble some device to crank the tire from the bed frame through the back end of the truck. I saw no value in this and knew that it could mean that we would be in for some trouble if we had to pull a NASCAR pit stop on a road somewhere. I detached the spare and threw it in the bed of the truck, as there was plenty of room. I also took some time to verify the jack lift points. I found a towing chain in the garage and threw that in the back end of the truck to make it easier to clear roadblocks. I also spotted a coffee can full of old spark plugs and asked Saien to gather as much of the ceramic from the plugs as he could and to try to keep the pieces as large as possible. The ceramic pieces could prove useful later for a little B&E.

In a fleeting thought, I disconnected the charged battery from the wagon and took it over to the truck. They were not the same model battery, but I thought I'd give it a try anyway. Saien was using vise grips to crush the ceramic from the old spark plugs while I tried my science experiment. Before I got too involved in this, I walked the perimeter once more to ensure that we were not in any immediate danger of being overrun. Back at the truck I set the wagon's battery in the spot where the dead battery was. I haphazardly connected the vehicle wires to the battery and went to the driver's side to see what I could see. I flipped the ignition to power the dash so that I could see the fuel level. I was very lucky to see nearly a full tank in the truck. Diesel was not as refined as gasoline, meaning a longer shelf life, so I decided to see if I could get the truck started without fuel treatment.

I told Saien what I intended to do so that we could discuss the pros and cons of starting up a vehicle out here and possibly drawing attention. It was around eleven when we loaded up the back of the truck to attempt to start it up. Our thinking was that if no undead came to the noise, we'd stay a little longer to make sure our gear was packed properly and that everything else was in order.

I keyed the ignition and the truck sputtered for about five seconds before turning over. I then had a thought about the battery. With gloves, I reconnected the factory-new battery to the truck while it ran so that the alternator could do its job instead of the panels. The vehicle alternator would charge the dead battery much faster than the sun, no matter how efficient the panel.

After reconnecting the truck battery and quietly shutting the hood, I walked the perimeter once more. I saw no sign of activity in any direction around the car dealership. Checking my maps, I estimated about 230 miles or so until we'd reach H23. We should be in radio contact before that time, depending on the transmitter we used. John would be monitoring the aviation distress frequency, so that would be the best way of reaching H23 at the soonest possible time. The trouble would be finding a serviceable VHF radio to make the transmission. It would take about thirty to forty-five minutes to get a decent charge on the battery, so I thought I'd double it to at least an hour to make sure. I opened the door and took in the new-car smell that still lingered despite months of abandonment. Flipping on the heater, I enjoyed the feel of artificial warmth flowing over my hand. It had been a while. With our gear stored in the back, it would be possible to catch some sleep in this vehicle if we picked good spots to hide during the night. On another truck we discovered a bed cover that could easily be transferred to this truck. That seemed useful to keep our gear dry and any undead stowaways out of the back. The next order of business was to take the bulbs out of the taillights and remove all the reflectors from the truck. The only lights I wanted were the headlights if I needed them. The undead were not the only enemy. I covered all the exposed areas with duct tape to avoid any chance of an electrical short. The truck would never be road-ready without a professional welder's help, but it would have to do for our trip. I flipped on the radio and scanned both AM and FM bands.

Nothing.

Nothing to mark the existence of what once was a bustling medium of information flow.

Consulting the overhead maps, Saien and I plotted our next leg southwest. We are not far from Carthage, maybe fifteen miles. It looks like we need to keep it that way. We would need to head down Highway 79 and veer south to intercept 59. The priority will be to stay on county roads as much as possible and dip into larger roads only when necessary. When I estimated 230 miles, it was a straight-line estimate. Looking at the road schematics overlaid on the imagery, I saw that this could add some time and distance to the trip. We must also consider that we will not be able to maintain the speed limits of a year ago with all the debris and other dangers that lay waiting for us along the way. My cousin James hit a buck in his truck a couple of years ago, totaling the vehicle. That deer couldn't have weighed more than 150 pounds. Hitting a two-hundred-pound corpse could end our day quickly. Corpses do not try to get out of your way. They are like bugs to a zapper. They don't care what is between them and the light, they just go.

With the imagery I had received from the drop was a transparent sheet of plastic with two oblong orange circles, another asymmetrical orange shape and a radiation symbol in the bottom right corner. I then realized the purpose. I put the transparent sheet over the map of the region and it showed the fallout areas covering Dallas, San Antonio and New Orleans. The Dallas and San Antonio areas showed extensive damage, but the New Orleans fallout areas indicated a decimated area covering southeastern Louisiana, southern Mississippi, part of southern Alabama and the tip of the Florida Panhandle. After a minute of my jaw hanging slack

Saien asked what was wrong. I told him I had friends in all these areas and that I was taken aback to see proof that they were most likely dead. He said he was sorry for my loss and took the overlay from the map, prompting me to move on with the planning. I was confident we could make the outskirts of Carthage in a day if we worked together.

As we sat there discussing our plan, I kept catching Saien glancing down at my rifle. I knew that he wanted to know how I caused the explosion from the day we met as well as the explosion on the advancing undead when we were getting the wagon running. I finally broke down and told him a sanitized version of what I knew. I told him that the drop was from the government and that I had been in previous contact with what was left of them. I explained to him that there was a Reaper UCAV orbiting overhead watching our every move and waiting for me to lase my target with the device mounted to my rifle. I saw no reason to inform him of the beacon device or the fail-safe associated countermeasure.

I showed him the iridium phone and told him that the only time it would be usable would be between the hours of 1200 and 1400 due to the degraded satellite orbit. He asked me who was on the other end, and I informed him that it was always a mechanical-sounding recording with a text situation report (SITREP) and that he knew as much as I did on that subject. I told him that I was headed to a place in the vicinity of Nada, Texas, and that he was welcome to help me get there if he so desired. As San Antonio had been destroyed and that had been his original destination, his silence told me that he had no other place to go. It being late October, we decided to build a fire in the maintenance courtyard for warmth. The October chill was definitely in the air, and last night I was very uncomfortable as I tried to get my few hours of sleep.

Before all of this I loved my eight hours of rest per night. Now I am lucky if I get five hours. I only take what I need as the thought of sleeping away what little life I have left disturbs me. The SATphone is on and I'm just waiting for the call.

2100

A message arrived today at 1350 instructing me to proceed to the next drop point marked on the chart, southwest of my current position, and that the drop will occur tomorrow at 1500 hrs. No mention of Saien or anything else in the message. I checked the chart and circled the next point along our path southwest with the letter S designating the location. The imagery I had in my hands indicated that the area was over a small airport. The drop was located east of Carthage just off highway 79. We have made preparations to leave in the A.M. to increase our chances of finding the drop point. I am not sure how I am expected to pinpoint and navigate to the area on the map with so little detail about exact area/coordinates at which the drop is to occur.

A few hours ago Saien and I decided that we should start a fire to fend off the late October cold. I gathered firewood from outside the fence just as the sun began to set. We stacked the wood and Saien tore a page from a book he was carrying in his pack. I noticed the title, *Milestones*. The cover was simple, and it appeared that this was not the first page he had torn from the book to make fire. The book looked as if it was missing about half of the original pages. We cooked some of the last remaining heavy foods and filled our stomachs for the long day ahead tomorrow.

"There you go again, writing in your book."

"At least I'm not tearing pages out of it."

"Goodnight, Kilroy."

"Same to you, Saien . . . one eye open, man."

"Both eyes, my friend."

Buggy

We have been on the road since 0700 weaving in and out of wrecks. We've had to get out of the truck half a dozen times to tow cars out of our path. Half of those times we've had to kill undead. Most notable was the corpse that still lay waist-strapped to its gurney in the back of an ambulance unbeknownst to me. It posed no threat, but it severely freaked me out when I tried to attach the towing chain to the back of the ambulance and the damn thing sat up in its bed like Dracula and reached for me, mouth agape. I had no idea that it was inside. It was of course hideous and decaying and will be one of hundreds of horrible snapshots I'll carry in my brain until I die.

I pulled my sidearm, punched a hole in its head and shut the ambulance doors before its back hit the bed. After hearing the suppressed shot, Saien ran over to the ambulance and asked what happened. I told him not to worry about it and to be glad he wasn't on chain duty for this round of roadblock fun.

We have taken a break in an open field on top of a hill. Saien is on watch while I calculate our current location and how far we are from the airfield. Highway 79 is the shortest route, but a smaller county road may be our fastest considering the volume of cars that have been left abandoned on the highway. As I tuned through the AM and FM bands to see if I could hear anything from the high ground, I cleaned up the salvageable AK-47 as best I could. Using some oil and sandpaper taken from the maintenance bay of the dealership, I dismantled the weapon and removed the rust from it. I must say that it really does look like baling wire on the internals of the weapon. I took my knife and cut the jagged wooden edges where the bullet passed through the stock and sanded it down as best I could. The hole wasn't in a bad spot and the weapon didn't have a sling, so I used some of the paracord from my knife sheath and fashioned a makeshift sling for the weapon through the hole of the stock. It was now fully serviceable, with approximately forty-five rounds loaded between two magazines. I again coated the exterior liberally with oil and threw it in the back of the truck with a round in the chamber and safety engaged.

I scanned the area with my binoculars and saw no immediate threat from any direction. The morning sun was beating down but it didn't quit cut through the chill of the fall. For some reason it felt considerably colder than past Octobers I remembered. After catching the supply drop east of Carthage, the next high-density areas will be Nacogdoches, Lufkin and then Houston. Even in the helicopter, Baham didn't dare fly over downtown Houston. It's the nearest megacity that didn't get the nuclear treatment and could still have human survivors as well as potentially millions of undead. There is no doubt that I would be either dead or undead if we had crash-landed inside the Houston city limits.

1900

I'm on the roof of the airport administration building at the south end of the runway with Saien. My thoughts drift back to the tower with John months ago, but there is no tower at this airport. The drop occurred just as planned today at 1500, with one complication. The aircraft lost control and crashed at the north end of the runway a little less than a mile from where we are. Just after the gear left the cargo door, the aircraft seemed to have trouble stabilizing its center of gravity and went nose-down toward the runway.

I could see the nose start to pull up but it was too late to recover from the stall. The aircraft hit hard and started skidding down the runway until one of the wing tips snapped off and fuel started spraying everywhere. This caused the aircraft to wobble as it skidded, making the other wing dig into the concrete and cause the airframe to spin around like a top. By the time the aircraft came to rest it had lost both wing tips and two engines had been thrown about a thousand feet back our direction.

Disregarding the gear that had just been dropped near our position, Saien and I made for the wreckage. I found it remarkable that the aircraft was not in flames and thought at the time that whoever was piloting the aircraft was a lucky bastard. That was until I made it to the front of the aircraft. There were no windows on the plane. The aircraft resembled a porcupine, as its spine was covered in antennas but there were no windows anywhere on the aircraft. The back cargo release door was still open where the aircraft had just dropped its payload. I asked Saien to boost me up so that I could peek inside. After getting inside the cargo bay and fanning away the fumes from the aircraft fuel, which will stick to my clothing for at least three days, I made my way to the front of the plane. On the way I noticed that the standard C-130 open bay toilet (with curtain) was not present, another indicator of what was going on with this aircraft.

I was over the center of the fuselage now. It was difficult to walk with the intense fumes and the fact that the aircraft was canted to one side, resulting in a funhouse affect. There was no door to the cockpit, only an olive drab curtain. I felt as if I were about to meet the Wizard of Oz as I swept the curtain aside, only to find what I had suspected since viewing the exterior of the plane—no pilots.

This aircraft was not an air breather, it was a modified C-130 UAV not unlike the Reaper orbiting over my head at this moment. The aircraft controls were still present, but there were no seats and no windows to the outside. There was a rack of computers with a fiber-optic connection leading into the avionics. No manufacturer markings were present on any of the equipment in this aircraft. There was no cabin pressure indicator on the instrument suite, and I saw no auxiliary oxygen tanks. This aircraft seems to have been stripped down to minimize weight for maximum unmanned endurance. Assuming this aircraft burned about four thousand pounds per hour at optimum burn bagged out with full fuel, it could have come from anywhere in the United States. The exterior had no unit markings or BUNO/BORT-type tail number. It was painted in a dark-blue urban camouflage color scheme and appeared well maintained.

I went back to get Saien to see what he made of the aircraft and the situation. We both went forward to check out the cockpit again. Saien agreed that fiber-optic connection to aircraft avionics was not something he had ever read or heard about. The fumes were starting to get to me at this point, causing me to forget cause and effect once again. It was very dark in the interior of the aircraft, with only red lighting, probably so that the recovering maintenance crew could see the interior to accomplish a proper postflight checklist after landing.

Using the cargo webbing left over in the bay, I fashioned a quick ladder so that I could get out of the half-closed cargo door without twisting an ankle or worse. As I climbed down the ladder, the fresh afternoon air hit me and my brain started to recover from the fumes that were in the aircraft.

I watched in a relative daze as Saien climbed down.

I thought about the crash, and then I realized that it had made considerable noise and there was no doubt we'd have company by nightfall at this location. We hopped in the truck and got the chance to hit a hundred miles per hour on the runway with no obstructions in front of us for over four thousand feet. As we cruised back toward the supply drop we discussed again the unmanned aircraft and the implications of the crash. We got to the crash site and immediately noticed two pallets—one small and one large.

The large pallet had a vehicle sitting on it wrapped in plastic. The only marking on this drop were the letters DARPA engraved into the metal portions. Saien and I pulled out our knives and began cutting the plastic wrap and gathering the spare paracord and webbing and other parachute materials.

The vehicle was a desert sand buggy with a heavy roll cage and thick metal screen welded over the passenger/driver area. There was a place to stand on the back above the engine with a harness-type mast structure welded on the frame to keep the rider from falling. There was also what appeared to be two machine-gun mounting points. The vehicle could hold three people, with minimal gear, if any. There was a cylindrical "beer keg" tank on the back above the engine and heavy off-road tires all around. I entered the vehicle and started it up with no trouble, then drove it over behind the airport administration building near the roof access ladder and jogged back over to the smaller drop. Saien was already cutting into the cargo by the time I arrived, very much out of breath. I didn't think we had much time before more of the dead started to trickle in. The crash was much louder than a gunshot even from nearly a mile away and the engines that the aircraft threw are still popping and cracking somewhere in the distance.

The smaller pallet contained two large black Pelican cases that required a two-man lift and a heavy crate marked *Auto G Rounds*. There was also a smaller case in with the other cases. The large cases were stenciled *Auto Gatling A* and *Auto Gatling B* respectively. We heaved the cases into the back of the truck and hauled ass back to where I parked the buggy so we could think of our plan for the evening. I brought the case marked *Auto Gatling A* up to the roof with Saien's help, leaving case B in the back of the truck. Instead of parking the truck near the buggy, we parked it a hundred yards on the backside of the building in the event the undead swarmed the ladder area. We'd at least have two chances at an escape from the confines of the roof. The smaller case contained what was described by enclosed documentation as a long-range Geiger counter, enabling remote Geiger measurements.

The buggy is parked right under the ladder in plain view of the road, but the truck (with most of our gear) is parked in a less obvious position. After getting our essentials to the rooftop (food, water, shelter, weapons), we opened up the Pelican case to determine if it was worth the weight and trouble. Inside was a weapon that I had never seen before. It appeared that Remote Six was going to great expense to give me what I needed to stay alive. This weapon was a miniature baffled Gatling gun that fired small-caliber linked rounds. The instructions that came with the unit were similar to the Reaper lasing device instructions—they got the point across but that's it.

The unit included a low probability of intercept (LPI) radar that worked inclusively with a thermal-imaging sensor to act as an undead deterrent. The thing was built to last, and the diagram indicated several deployment options. The instructions stressed that the gun was not suppressed, only baffled (whatever that means).

Option one was to simply open the case and face it in the directions indicated by the arrows and flip the on switch, similar to claymore instructions. Anything moving below the temperature of ninety degrees Fahrenheit would be designated hostile and neutralized immediately at the rate of four thousand rounds per minute but preset to one-hundred-millisecond bursts. The on-board radar used a very low-power emitter (less than half a watt) and was stated effective for target acquisition out to two hundred yards.

The second mode of operation was buggy-mounted. The instructions were to loosen the twist screws and lift the unit out of the case (radar, fire computer, battery and weapon were attached to one steel bar that fit onto the buggy mount). The third mode of operation used the magnetic and suction trimounts included in the case. A diagram showed a schematic of the units mounted in tandem on top of a semi-truck trailer facing opposite directions in figure one of the manual and a schematic of the units using the mounts as tripods in front of a building in figure two.

The specifications claimed sustained operation for one hour between charges if under continuous firing conditions and twelve hours if in radar and thermal scan operating condition only. The manual went on to list vague limitations of the system.

The system was said to have a known issue of shooting at moving water, windblown tree branches and flying birds. The last was due to the thermal sensor's inability to pick out the avian heat signature due to size and the radar cross-section limitation of the system. There was a warning next to this section stating that use of the system when ambient air temperature reaches ninety-four degrees Fahrenheit is not recommended. No reasons were given for this warning in the documentation. The sun was about to go down at this point, so Saien headed down the ladder (with me covering) to fetch some ammunition for this weapon so we could see how option one works out tonight. If this thing uses radar coupled with thermal for target acquisition the night will have no effect on its operation. One final warning stood out ominously:

> WARNING! The Automated Gatling system is a prototype weapon and shall not be relied upon for primary defense.

After reading the manual and putting it back into the case (loading instructions were printed and affixed to the lid), Saien returned with two cases of ammunition from the crate and we loaded the weapon, pointing it in the direction most likely to see undead incursion—the road.

I flipped the toggle to the on position and listened to the gun calibrate to its surroundings with a whir. The LPI radar made a sound similar to a camera click, probably acquiring an initial 3D map picture for ranging and elevation, and the system immediately went dormant. The only indication of activity was a dim glowing green LED on the rear of the gun.

The sun was nearly down and it was time to build a small fire in a coffee can to warm up some water for our dry food. Saien tore another page from *Milestones* and started the fire in the coffee can. I slid on my NVGs and walked opposite the fire looking over the edge of the roof out to the road. I did see movement in the distance. The movement was at the very edge of the capabilities of the goggles, but it was present. I could also see infrared indications of a small fire, probably where one of the aircraft engines landed after the crash. It was not visible without night vision and was probably contained to the internals of the engine. I whispered to Saien to angle the weapon left a few degrees to better engage the area I thought the threat would flow from. The radar recalibrated immediately after Saien stopped moving the system and the gun did one full gyro check before going dormant again. I kept my eye on what I thought would be the threat and saw nothing.

Saien poured some water into my canteen cup and I made my dinner for the night sitting Indian style with my NVGs pulled up above my eyes.

Saien asked again, "What does this writing do for you, how does it help? I'm sorry to ask again."

"No trouble, Saien. I don't mind. Much better than talking to myself."

I didn't really know what to say or how to answer his question, so I started at the beginning and told him the whole story of my vantage point and how it began for me. I told him that it was a resolution of mine to keep a documentation of my life because I felt that life was quickly passing me by, even though I was still relatively young in years. The last time I ever spoke to my grand-mother was last year during vacation. She was old beyond her years and I loved talking to her and listening to her stories. She told me that the older people get the more they lose track of time, so a person should do everything he can to slow it down.

"Time here is finite, Junior," she said.

She was getting old and I thought in the back of my mind that this could be the last time I would see her. We ended our discussion with my memories of my great-grandmother, her mother. I told my grandma of how I remembered that great-grandmother was still sharp in her eighties and told me stories of how she crossed the mountains between Fort Smith and Fayetteville on a covered wagon and remembered when men rode horses to town and carried guns on their hips. She died the summer after she told me of the old frontier Arkansas.

Saien saw more now, I think. He understood that my grand-mother was trying to get me to slow down and be aware of life and living. I suppose documenting all this is my only link to what I was and to what she was. He said that what he missed most was his sister. The last time he spoke to his sister was via email a month before all of this. She was living in Pakistan with her husband and was having a baby. Saien was going to be an uncle. He smiled as he said this and I kept my morbid, defeatist thoughts to myself as I wanted him to cherish his memory of his family. Saien drifted off to sleep after dinner and I hoped his mind was with his loved ones.

Lights Out

The rooftop is littered with spent casings. I was so exhausted last night I thought the ripping sound I heard was a dream. It was not until Saien was slapping the NVGs off my head that I woke to the sound of the mini–Gatling guns blazing away and hot casings hitting my face and neck. Saien put on the goggles and just stood there watching in the darkness. It was approximately 0300 hrs. After about five minutes of random gun bursts the radar recalibrated the weapon gyros and the system went silent once again. I asked Saien for the optics so I could see the battle damage. I checked out the roof first and noticed hundreds of rounds (not even a dent in the ammo supply) scattered all over the roof. Walking closer to the edge I could see scores of creatures on the ground. One of the creatures was still writhing on the ground but seemed to move without purpose or logic. Gun B seemed to jitter in response to the random movement on the ground so I decided to pull my sidearm and attempt a suppressed shot to prevent the gun's gyros from burning out. It took three shots to fully neutralize the creature. This was a small group of undead, but the sentries had made short work of them.

It seems that these devices could be worth their weight. After trying to go back to sleep for the final morning hours, Saien and I thought it a good idea to discuss how we would logistically handle our new gear. I told him that I thought it to be smart for the buggy to run point, followed by the truck. We both agreed it was sound to deploy an automated Gatling on top of the buggy until I thought of the operating limitations of the weapon. What if I turn on the weapon and it tracks Saien's truck? The truck is moving and would therefore be targeted by the thermal/radar sensors. If we rolled in a convoy we could not deploy the buggy while moving. We could not risk getting taken out. We'll also need to charge the batteries in the device using either the jumper cables and the truck or the solar panels. It was decided after discussion that I would drive the buggy and run about a quarter mile ahead of Saien to scout any potential bottlenecks in the highway. Saien would have the MP5 and AK loaded and ready in the event I got stuck or broke down in front. It was very cold in the mornings so I had no choice but to bundle up if I was going to go riding down the highway in basically a steel cage with four wheels. We'll wait until sunup before we pack our gear so that we can see if the guns missed any targets before they have a chance to get up and return the favor.

27 Oct

0630

We have been on the road for a few days since we acquired the buggy and automated weapons. There has been no contact via SATphone. The going has been very slow due to wreckage and the typical mayhem of undead corpses moving about on the highway. When either Saien or I clear wreckage, the other must cover the area with full attention. We have saved each other from attack numerous times recently. Days ago (or was it just yesterday?) we came upon an old hulk of a semi-truck jackknifed on the road. The trailer was riddled with high-caliber bullet holes and shrapnel marks, which piqued my curiosity. After establishing a moving perimeter in a circle around the wreck we moved in. We checked all possible angles and upon closer inspection discovered that this was a feed truck. The feed inside was long ago ruined by water damage and summer heat. Saien covered me as I jumped up on the running board and peered into the cab. Abandoned. No sign of trouble inside and no sleeper cab to hold surprises. This rig was meant for short haul. The owner probably lived not more than a hundred miles from where he abandoned his rig long ago. This unknown blue-collar contributor to the dinosaur that was the U.S.

economy could still be holding out somewhere, his back to a barricaded door.

Inside I noticed a CB radio. What caught my eye was that it appeared to be installed on a whim, wires still hanging out under the dash and around the gearshift. Following the antenna wire outside the cab I noticed that the antenna wasn't very tight either. I headed back to the truck bed to find the tin of spark plug chips so I could get inside the cab and see about salvaging the CB radio.

As I approached the truck, Saien whistled and pointed behind me. One of the creatures methodically approached, eyes locked on us like a lion stalking prey. Its hands were slightly bent and it walked in a half crouch, carefully moving forward. When I drew my sidearm the creature snapped into offensive mode and moved forward more quickly. I slowly squeezed my trigger and took its right cheek off. It kept coming, causing me to step backward until my retreat was stopped by a minivan. I kept squeezing off rounds until the creature fell not more than a foot from my boots. It still twitched for a few seconds, the last bit of evil seeping from its miserable frame.

I shook this off and went at the semi. With a small handful of spark plug ceramic I gave the driver's window a slow overhand pitch. The window shattered with very little sound. Most of the sound was a result of the broken glass hitting the running board and tank. The truck smelled very old inside. Months of mold and sun-bleached fabric particles whirled around the air inside the cab. I picked up the pieces of ceramic that I could find and went to work on the CB radio with my multitool. I checked to make sure I was being covered while I worked, as I had no choice but to keep the door open so I could get under the dash to remove the wires. This process took about fifteen minutes, as I wanted to avoid damaging the radio or the wires. As I removed the radio I noticed another radio under the seat, wrapped in its original wiring. The trucker's original CB must have given out, forcing him to purchase another and perform a truck-stop install.

I took the radio out of the semi and put it in the backseat of the pickup along with the antenna. Grabbing my binocs I went back to the truck and climbed up on top of the trailer. Scouting in all directions, I noticed that it seemed there were more undead about than in the days before. I yelled down the situation to Saien and we traded spots. Saien agreed that there seemed to be more undead in our area. Saien covered as I attempted to wire the CB radio to the truck. Salvaging parts from the surrounding vehicles, I was able to install the radio better than it had been installed on the rig. Finally, I checked the rig's fuel tank and determined that there was enough fuel inside to top off the truck. Saien and I worked to do this as we continually checked our surroundings for danger. After siphoning the diesel, we attempted to test the radio. The receiver worked, but we didn't know how effective our transmission was because there was no reply to our broadcast sent out in the blind.

I had the CB set to channel 18 so Saien could hear any transmission that might occur while we are on our convoy. Later in the day we came upon a small town, the same type of town you see in a Norman Rockwell painting. Although no living testament to Americana was present as we made our way down Main Street, there was an air of tension, and I felt that something watched from the windows. Something wicked. I kept scanning the second-story windows as I idled through. Since the outbreak occurred in the winter, the windows were closed. All but one—a second-story window above a flower shop. I stopped the buggy, jumped out and signaled Saien to cover while I secured the immediate area. A light breeze blew the thin curtain of the open window. Upon closer inspection of the area I noticed that the cars looked as if they were victims of a vicious hailstorm. Huge dents pocked the horizontal surfaces and the windows were all cracked from a great force. It didn't register logically in my brain, so I kept looking and noticed that the faces of the buildings were all damaged as if someone had pulled a great anchor chain along the side of them.

The place had been swarmed. It appears as if the huge mass that swarmed the streets of this small town had long since moved on, bringing the original townie ghouls with them in all the noise and commotion. I estimated that thousands had moved through here, so many, in fact, that they were climbing on cars and grinding the building fronts to get through.

Thinking of the radiated undead, I stayed clear of any dense metallic objects to avoid unnecessary exposure. There appeared to be a makeshift roadblock consisting of midsized cars at the other end of Main Street. Amazingly, the fronts of the cars had been pushed outward, away from where I was standing. Whatever size this swarm was, it had moved in the same direction Saien and I were headed. I can only hope it was months ago. Saien and I agreed that there was no advantage to checking out the second-floor room above the dead flower shop. We drove off toward the old roadblock and saw remnants of corpses with half their torsos in the street storm drain, and half out . . . just waiting to rot enough to fit down the drain and be washed away forever.

28 Oct

2100

We found shelter in an old power plant west of Nacogdoches, Texas. My maps give telltale indications that Nacogdoches was once a moderately populated area. The plant was completely surrounded by a tall chain-link fence, excluding the front and rear parts of the structure. In these areas a swing gate stood, designed to stop vehicles from entering without authorization. The gates looked newer than the rest of the plant and were probably a result of post-9/11 security measures. Saien and I had not seen a need to deploy the automated Gatling guns since our night on the airport rooftop. We had spent most of the nights since then sleeping on top of linked railroad cars, parking one vehicle near our position and one vehicle a few hundred yards farther down the track as a backup means of escape. This was how we found the power plant. The rain was coming down as my watch alarm went off, warning me it was two hours until sunset. Just as we were about to give up on finding a set of rail cars to provide shelter for the night, we came upon "Anaconda." Saien and I had been staying sane by playing stupid games like naming the trains after snakes, depending on color and how many rail cars were linked together. The past few nights were black snake and garter snake. We also tried to find as many states as we could represented on the license plates of abandoned vehicles. Approaching Anaconda, we could verify it was a very long train. Most of the green hopper cars were filled with heaps of coal for what seemed like miles.

We drove alongside the tracks counting cars. The ground under the cars was stained black from the months of rain seeping through the coal and hitting the ground. Nearing the end of the line, we saw the massive mountain of coal near the power plant and the rusting hulks of bulldozers used to move the black rock. One bulldozer was overturned and the rest were parked in a row. We counted 115 rail cars, not including the propulsion locomotive. Fog was rolling in as we neared the front access gate. I pulled the buggy inside and Saien followed in the truck. I got out and pulled the gate closed behind us, latching it into the hole in the ground with the T-hook. Saien was already doing what I was thinking. He pulled out the Gatling and we set it up at the access point. Setup took three minutes. I parked the buggy in a spot that would facilitate a quick getaway, and Saien and I drove to the back of the plant to set the second Gatling. It was raining and miserable and I was happy that these prototype devices depended on radar and thermal for target discrimination, because I couldn't really see that far in this mess.

As the sun moved lower behind the dark clouds I thought the same thought as I did many nights before. The Reaper UCAV overhead would soon be headed home along with my two five-hundred-pound laser-guided bombs. Finding a secure room with two exits didn't take long. We didn't have time to clear the area before night fell so we had to make the best of it. I've not heard a peep from the Gatlings and I like it that way.

29 Oct

1200

Saien woke me up this morning for no good reason—just to take a piss. Although I was annoyed by this, we had already agreed that neither of us should go anywhere without the other person in visual range. Grudgingly, I stepped outside behind him in the cold October morning. The sun was out and I realized that I needed to answer nature's call too. Saien faced the forward gate and I faced the aft gate as I helped to fill up a mud puddle from last night's rain. Looking out into the distance toward the cannon, I noticed that it was canted to the left. When I left it yesterday evening it was calibrated facing straight forward toward the access road. Putting away my gun and shouldering my rifle I stepped toward the gate. I walked for a few seconds before I heard Saien's steps behind me. As I got close enough I noticed the wind rolling the spent casings around at the base of the system. Only a few. Looking out into the street I could see two dead birds. I ran over to them and saw that they were ducks. It was then I realized I had walked into the field of fire of the Gatling and yelled for Saien to turn off the weapon. I picked up the two ducks by their necks and we rushed to get them ready to eat. No need to waste this golden opportunity for fresh meat.

I lopped off their heads with my knife as Saien ran off to get some coal from the massive black mountain. After forty-five minutes or so of preparation they were good enough to cook. We set up a campfire with the coal and kindling and had some duck for brunch. After eating most of the duck we began clearing the power plant and looking for anything of use in the area. I was getting sleepy with such a full stomach but I had no choice. I didn't want to waste the meat. As we attempted to add method to our area-clearing we came upon the stairs leading to the main control room on the second floor. At the top of the stairs was a corpse. It was so long dead that it looked like a sea bag full of bones. It was dark, forcing me to turn on my weapon light and use my muzzle to flip the remains of the corpse. I could barely make out the embroidery on the coveralls, but the man's name was Bill and he was a lead boiler mechanic. Walking up the stairs with Saien covering I could see *gore marks* on the heavy steel door. The door was locked. Saien asked me to cover him as he pulled out his pick set. Under his breath he complained that a rake would not work for this lock. He'd need to pick it pin by pin. After ten minutes he had the door unlocked and his foot planted to keep it closed if something was inside that wanted to come out. I knocked on the door and then put the muzzle of my rifle inside. No reaction. Saien swung the door open and our bright lights penetrated the darkness of the defunct control room, cutting through the floating dust. There was a wall of windows that offered a view down into the generator level below. It was so dark that I could see only the rounded generator tops. They looked like large round steel bales of hay in a field. After shining my light into the abyss I could see movement below. There were creatures on the generator floor. Number unknown. All observed were in coveralls.

We were relatively safe here above the mess below. A thick layer of dust covered the computers and switches and various mechanisms of the room. A large green logbook was sitting at the main desk in the center of the room with an ashtray, desk lamp and pen. I opened the book. It started with the date January 1985. After a few weeks of entries in 1985 the last 1985 entry read, "Log being decommissioned due to new computer logging system installation implementation, Signed, Terry Owens, Plant Manager."

The book was decommissioned in 1985 with only a couple dozen pages filled in. The next entry read:

> Log recommissioned by Bill. End of the world. Computer systems unreliable. —Bill
>
> January 15—We have sixty days of coal remaining and a train on the way to the plant.
>
> January 16—Coal train arrived. No conductor aboard. Parking brake set.
>
> January 17—We are down to 50 percent crew. The Department of Energy has authorized shutting down infested grids. We will be receiving the list soon.
>
> January 18—List of deactivations received.
>
> January 20—Using only 15 percent previous consumption.
>
> January 21—We have one bulldozer operator remaining. Without her, we will be unable to feed the burners and generate juice. We have hired a walk-in to sit with her and shoot the things that keep trying to climb on the dozer.

January 31—Government announced city destruction plans. *Cities match January 18 DOE list.*

February 1—We're still here.

February 5—Plenty of coal, not much to do with it.

February 6—We are down to one burner and generating power for the plant only.

February 20—They are at the door. Getting out through vent below control panel. Shutting plant down. Only one left.

Lights out. —Bill

---

30 Oct

0700

The automated weapons have been going off all night. We have heard strange noises outside in the darkness that can only mean an undead posse in the vicinity of the front of the plant. We are packed and about to recon the area now that the sun is up.

0900

Automated weapons are spent and knocked over. Through Saien's scope we can see that the ammunition has been depleted and dozens of bodies lie around the emplacements. Some of the creatures still thrash about, their brains damaged enough by the Gatling to render them useless but not completely neutralized. We decided to hide the technology so that raiders with bad intent cannot salvage it. Leaving the plant soon.

Bridge of No Return

After countless hours and countless trials since the coal plant, Saien and I had one more major obstacle between the last stretch to Hotel 23 and us. Upon surveying our maps carefully, we only really had two options:

1. We could trek north and perhaps find a way across the river that lay ahead.
2. We could take the Livingston Bridge.

Most likely the bridge on our charts would be two lanes wide, based upon the highway it served for crossing.

Going north could put us close to a larger city as we attempt to go around the lake. The only drawback to option two was the unknown material condition of the bridge. After discussing various pros and cons we decided the bridge option made the most sense. Yesterday in the A.M. we adjusted our course south and a little west to rendezvous the bridge. I was taking the lead with the buggy as Saien trailed not far behind. The landscape was so monotonous that it barely warrants description ... abandoned wrecks, packed SUVs, scattered emergency vehicles and of course the dead. Many times I have caught myself canceling them out like an expensive noise-canceling headset—a dangerous habit.

When the sun reached its highest point in the sky, I signaled from the buggy that it was time to pull over. I picked a spot at an abandoned group of rail cars. This system of shelter had not let us down to date, causing Saien and me to rely on it when possible. We attempted to warm up as we sat in the sun on top of a boxcar marked "Northern Railroad." The exterior of the car was decorated with much precollapse graffiti. Gang signs and cryptic hobo signals made up the bulk of the markings. After I finished inspecting one side of the car and started on the other, Saien called for me to come up. As I climbed the ladder to the car and looked up over the top I spotted Saien lying on his drag bag staring out to the east. I came over and asked him what was up.

He extended his bipod legs, rested the butt of the rifle on his jacket and said: "Look."

Peering through the powerfully magnified Japanese glass, I could see the reason for Saien's concern. Out to the horizon I could see a great cloud of dust swirling about. Without looking through the optic of Saien's rifle, one could mistake the dust cloud for a small rain cloud surging on the horizon. It seemed that we were seeing firsthand a possible undead swarm. It would be nothing like what we had encountered the day I met Saien. The mere presence of a swarm roughly ten miles in the distance did not mean they were headed directly to our position. It would be prudent to assume that they would be moving southwest in our general direction and upon contact with the river's edge would move either up- or downstream. The river could cause them to funnel in our direction or they could move upstream as a collective. We spent the rest of our shortened lunch attempting to verify the direction and speed of the mass, without success.

Later//

We made the best time we could to the ingress point. Stopping short of the bridge on a high knoll we conducted some reconnaissance. A rusting Abrams tank was pulled crossways in the road right in front of the bridge. The paint still held, but rust marks streaked down the thick armored steel portions. Shooting a reading with the Geiger revealed that the tank was emitting medium amounts of radiation. It was nothing immediately deadly, but I would not want to spend a few nights inside. There were *gore marks* all over the tank and civilian vehicles in the vicinity were heavily damaged, much like to the old town Main Street we had passed through days before.

Before heading down the hill to the bridge we surveyed the dust cloud. The cloud was visibly growing and there were very faint sounds on the wind that unsettled me to the point that I had to make a conscious effort to remain in the game. Moving down the hill, I was demoralized by the size of the bridge. It was so long that the vehicles on the other side looked like specks in the distance.

Nearing the rusting Abrams's hulk I could see that the hatch was barely open. I jumped onto the tank and strong-armed the hatch. Geiger readings remained constant. I shined my light inside, causing a bird to fly out of the opening, scaring the hell out of me. The tank was clear.

There was no way to get our vehicles past the tank without moving it. Towing the tank was a nonstarter. Its weight was many times that of the truck. There were operating manuals tucked into a storage cabinet near the controls. I followed the instructions and was able to start the turbine after three attempts. The tank was still operational, but it seemed that the jet fuel inside was contaminated, as I never got the turbine speed up to optimal operating temperature as indicated in the manual. This caused all movements to be delayed and sluggish. The controls on the tank were like bicycle bars with a hatch open light, master caution, panel dim, reset and master warning light mounted above the steering controls. Right below the handlebar was a small lever with R, N, D and L transmission settings.

After a short warm-up period I put the tank in D and activated the throttles, causing the tank to lurch forward. The smell of burning jet fuel permeated the tank and everything inside it. After stopping the tank I was able to leave it running so that I could help Saien get the vehicles onto the bridge.

After getting the buggy and truck safely on, I ran back to the tank to repark the beast. As I approached I noticed that someone had spray-painted the word "TROLL" on the side of the turret. I climbed back in and attempted to put the tank back. I destroyed the guardrails on both sides of the bridge and nearly drove off into the water before giving up and accepting a 90 percent solution.

There was a gap large enough for a motorcycle to squeeze through on one side. Before leaving the tank, I flipped on the radio and put on the headset. Every frequency I tuned in on the SINCARS radio returned with static not unlike a jamming-type signal. I could hear RF energy but nothing was being relayed. I sent out a distress call on 282.8 MHz and 243.0 MHz to Hotel 23, letting them know my situation and position. If this area was being jammed it did not mean H23 was also. For jamming to be effective, the jamming emitter must be directed at the receiver, as jamming the transmitter would do nothing on the receiving end.

I repeated my transmission three times before shutting down the gas turbine and heading back to the vehicles. The dust cloud was still present on the horizon. I thought of the tank and how useless it would prove as its lack of fuel economy, coupled with its crushing weight, rendered it a hindrance. I doubted the bridge could take the weight. We were halfway across the bridge when we first made visual contact with the swarm. The sound billowed like great tubas reverberating in my chest.

In a stroke of merciful luck they broke into view two miles upstream. On Matagorda Island during my stint at the docks, I observed the creatures standing at the water's edge, hesitant to enter. I know that when they hit the shoreline they will follow it until they come to a crossing point. Saien and I kept clearing the bridge roadblocks, fitting the wrecks where we could on the left or the right. It was like the old sliding puzzle game where you tried to fit fifteen tiles in chronological order with only one empty space with which to rearrange the numbers.

When we were three-quarters of the way over the bridge the creatures hit the water's edge. The wails and moans jabbed at the front of my brain and nearly knocked me off my feet. There were thousands. Later I would discover via SATphone text message that over five hundred thousand undead were part of Swarm T-5.1 as designated in a cryptic Remote Six message text.

As the head of this long, terrible viper hit the water in the distance upstream, I could see the wake of white water, and the wails of frustration and primal hate intensified. Saien and I kept working, careful not to make too much noise. Using my multitool, I disabled the horn on the truck so that it could not be accidentally pushed during our clearing operation, as has happened before.

An armored car with four heavily damaged run-flat tires was giving us trouble because of its weight. We worked the problem for nearly thirty minutes as the legion of undead built up on the shore upstream. Their radius was growing so large that I could make out individual creatures in the distance. While attaching a tow chain to the old Ford next to the armored car, I heard a familiar shrill and instinctively reached for the M-4 slung across my chest. Checking the clear plastic viewport on the polymer mag I knew I was as ready as I could be.

I scanned the area around the vehicles and heard the undead moans loud and overlapping. Some of them sounded like gurgling. I stepped to the guardrail of the bridge and peered over. In the deep-flowing, chilly water below I could see dozens of creatures thrashing and moaning. Water had freely seeped into their dead lungs, causing their sounds to be even more frightening. Looking upstream I could see the waterway heavily dotted and clumped with the creatures flowing downstream from the mass and under the bridge where I stood.

A handful of the creatures drifting at the whim of the river current caught sight of me standing above them. Their clawed hands reached skyward as they passed below the bridge. Despite our best efforts we were unable to budge the Ford, as the armored car was wedged too far into the other lane. The cars that we had repositioned behind us gave room to retreat but there were too many undead to consider that option. The number and size of the swarm less than two miles upstream was growing in our direction and soon we would no doubt be in detection range, if we weren't already. I made the decision and instructed Saien to put the vehicles in a line in front of the repositioned cars, giving me a clear shot to the armored car. If we could not make it over the bridge without our vehicles the undead would pace us indefinitely and eventually get us.

With only my M-4 and extra mags I sprinted back to the other side of the bridge. Leaving the hatch open I jumped into the tank and started the massive turbine engine. A Christmas tree of fault lights illuminated: "Low Turbine Temp. Hatch Open." Pushing the throttle, I steered away from the bridge, impacting the metal guardrail. The screeching of metal was deafening even over noise from the undead.

The sound caused an audible retort from the creatures below and I forced myself not to waste valuable time looking at the physical reaction of the mass. I took the gamble and rolled the tank onto the bridge, pushing the throttles forward to gain momentum. I could feel the bridge shake below the treads as the vehicle's speed reached 30mph. I clipped one of the cars as I sped past Saien on a collision course with the armored car.

Throttling back to 10mph to avoid injury, I was reminded of physics and the mass differential between the puny paperweight of the armored car and the behemoth tank. Like brothers at a poolside cookout, the war machine easily pushed the car over the guardrail and into the river.

I made every attempt to throttle back to idle but the spin-down time of the turbines was not responsive like that of a car or truck engine. What I thought were the brakes only complicated my problem by yawing the tank at an awkward angle.

The tank followed the armored car into the deep below.

Time slowed to a crawl as the steel brick of a vehicle rolled over the guardrail, tipping like a seesaw. As the tank free-fell ten feet to the water's surface, I tried to leap through the hatch. I was halfway out as the cold water rushed inside, holding me in place, taking me into the green murky abyss of the river.

After the water flow equalized and the immediate shock of the cold water abated, I swam to the surface, following the air bubbles. I could make out the bodies in the water, their legs moving as if they were trying to walk as they floated down river. My rifle slapped my back and head as I sidestroked to the surface. When I hit the air I wiped the water out of my eyes, brought my rifle above the water and took shots at the undead around me. After killing three I noticed the river was taking me under the bridge. I screamed for Saien to move the vehicles off the bridge as I made for the shore, kicking and brushing past the corpses that I had just shot.

After I hit the beach I could see the horde approaching the bridge. The tank crash, the gunshots and the truck noises obviously had had a hand in making them crazy. Saien had parked the truck and was making for the buggy to get it across. There was no time. Whistling loudly, I signaled him to fall back and cover me. The buggy would be an acceptable combat loss.

Taking cover behind a deadfall on the bank, I surveyed the bridge. Carefully picking a spot between support pillars on the undead side, I lased the target. Forcing my body to stop trembling from the cold water, I held the dot on the bridge as the tone increased in frequency until it was steady. Four seconds later a five-hundred-pound bomb rocked the bridge, collapsing a section of it forever. I was sitting there surveying the damage when I was startled by a corpse hitting the rocks ten feet behind me, a half-second before I heard Saien's shot. Saien waved and signaled me to come toward him up the bank.

The river seemed to be full of bodies as I ran up the bank to the truck. Through my binocs I witnessed numerous joggers on the opposite bank, many with severe radiation burns to their exterior, verified by Geiger.

Rally

Today marks the first contact with Hotel 23 personnel in over forty five days. A week has passed since our departure from the bridge, and we are currently sitting northwest of Houston, Texas. We started monitoring the CB radio at night after noticing that there was less static present. Last night Saien and I found a telephone company utility building surrounded by a high chain-link fence. After picking the padlock (with a tire tool) we spent the night inside the perimeter sleeping in the truck, listening to the fading static. At about 0100 hrs we heard the signal key but no voice. We instantly keyed back with a distress response. There was no intelligible reply for an hour but we kept transmitting.

The signal faded in at about 0215 with: ". . . this is Gator Two on search and rescue in Sunny Side Texas over . . ."

I replied with the Dragonfly call sign and was greeted by Corporal Ramirez, United States Marine Corps.

"Sir, good to hear your voice. We picked up your distress signal on the ninth and departed the following day in the direction of the coordinates you relayed. Movement has been slow due to the large groups of those things we have encountered and road wreckage. What's your position?"

After I gave my position to Ramirez he gave me instructions to sit tight while he planned a route for the two-vehicle convoy to meet. I asked for an update over the radio of the situation at Hotel 23. The corporal replied by telling me that it was not a good idea to give the update over the radio and that there were some things happening that he needed to tell me about in person.

After some radio silence, Corporal Ramirez came back up on the CB.

"Sir, time for payback. I get to save an officer's ass, just like before the world went to shit. The rally point I recommend is San Felipe, not far from your position. I propose we meet at the north end of town at the 1458 before the bridge. There is a field three hundred meters southeast of the bridge. The town is small and there should be a minimal hostile footprint."

I consulted my maps and agreed to the rally point, in a nonjoking manner, on the radio.

1200

We rallied to Corporal Ramirez at 1000 hrs. After a short firefight with a dozen or so of those things, we set up a small perimeter and debriefed for a bit in the safety provided by the LAV. While the gunner manned the crew-served weapon, Ramirez told me of the oddities going on back home. From the armored vehicle, he took out a small binder of written reports and a few photographs. I recognized John's handwriting. Ramirez stated that a few weeks back an aircraft started appearing in the skies above Hotel 23. I immediately identified the aircraft as a Global Hawk UAV. The picture was marked as having been taken with a handheld digital camera with an 18-200mm lens and I could just make out something large mounted under the fuselage. The picture was not clear enough for me to identify the payload, and I didn't remember the Global Hawk being weaponized.

We continued to generally debrief and I introduced all the Marines to Saien and told them the stories of how he had saved my life more than once since we had met. The Marines seemed to be very friendly toward Saien, but he was visibly nervous around them for reasons that I could not waste time trying to discover. I also warned the Marines that there was an undead mass unlike any they had ever seen about eighty miles northeast of where we were now. We had destroyed a section of the bridge and tried to line cars up in roadblocks behind us along the roads we traveled when possible. This would slow them down but not stop them. I told them of the C-130 drop plane, dead drops and the unusual equipment that I had attained from a group known only cryptically as Remote Six.

This prompted everyone into action, and we decided to roadblock the 1458 bridge with abandoned cars before we did anything else. Using the LAV, we put four cars into position and smashed them together. This would slow any oncoming mass of undead and increase the gap between us. This bridge was too close to Hotel 23 to destroy, as it may prove logistically valuable in the future. I saw a billboard a few hundred yards away, threw Saien my binocs and asked him to climb the board and check out the area. One of the Marines went with him for backup.

I asked everyone to pull back from the bridge a few hundred yards south. After Saien returned he told me of a dust cloud at the very edge of his visibility to the north. We decided that this could mean the mass of undead or it could simply be weather. We were roughly fifteen miles from Eagle Lake Airfield, according to the map in the LAV. Incidentally, we were also close to Interstate 10. Before nightfall we'll attempt to cross the I-10 threshold and head south a few more miles to add a safety buffer from the interstate.

2100

It had been seven months since I had been on foot in this area of Eagle Lake. Not much has changed. The moon illuminated the road and abandoned cars and airport tower and also the more frightening things in the dark. Earlier today when we caught sight of the I-10 overpass in the distance, we sped up, weaving to avoid the wrecks. The LAV was moving at 60mph in front of us and we were keeping up. As we roared under the overpass I heard a thump hit the truck and looked back. One of those creatures had walked off the overpass, hit the closed tailgate of the truck and tumbled behind into the ditch. As I kept driving more of them fell from the overpass. Some got to their feet and some didn't.

After we put I-10 far behind us, things got a little easier. We stayed on county road 3013 until we were on the outskirts of Eagle Lake, very near the airfield. I consulted the notes I had on the area and we decided to convoy into the airfield complex, set up a perimeter for a couple of hours and then plan the rest of the short trip back home. Upon arrival at the airfield and exploration of the hangar, I saw the dark smudges of the remains of the creatures I had killed months ago still under a blue tarp in the corner. The summer heat had really done a number on the remains. Using my flashlight, I could see the deformed copper-jacketed bullets that I had fired sitting in the rotting liquid goo of the dead.

I was reminded by my journal that I should also be watchful for any living human enemies that may be present in this area. I remembered the large crosses I had discovered, months ago, on my last trip en route to this area, with creatures crucified upon them. We sat under the illumination of a red-filtered M-4 light and planned our route home.

Home

We've traveled to Hotel 23 from Eagle Lake under cover of darkness. The place looks dramatically different, with the concrete barrier complete around the perimeter. The civilians and military have succeeded in working together and salvaged enough of the concrete highway barriers to form a formidable wall. I doubt that even the tank I sent to the bottom of the river could get through this wall without getting stuck. More to follow after I have fully debriefed John and especially Tara.

17 Nov

0500

My sleep schedule is ruined because of the change in my surroundings. Tara is sleeping next to me. I'm ashamed to have blocked her out of my thoughts for so long during my period of mechanically induced exile. This is something that only a veteran can really understand. Sometimes before and during deployments you seem to detach yourself from the ones you love just to make things hurt a little less.

Using the notes in my journal I spent the entire day resting, rehydrating and debriefing John, the Marines, Tara and anyone else who wanted to listen. Saien quietly listened, and I could tell he was absorbing my debriefing. John had not sat idle in my absence and had penetrated several different networks on the military mainframe. He also confirmed what the Marines had hinted at when we

253

met at the rally point. Despite only getting the Cliff Notes version from Ramirez, I still discovered that someone had been jamming my receiver. John said he could hear my transmissions and did in fact pick up my distress beacon coming in loud and clear on October 11 as well as the distress call made on November 9.

I'm still in shell shock and can't overstate how great it was to see everyone. Laura asked how my vacation went, and I told her that it went very well and thanked her for asking. She asked me if I brought her a souvenir and I told her that it was not a fun vacation but more of a working vacation. She understood what had happened to me—I could see the intelligence in her eyes. Her parents did a good deed by shielding her, but she knew. Danny walked up, punched me in the arm and said: "Good to see you!" He then proceeded to give me a hug. Little Annabelle even gave me a bark and a lick on the nose to signify that she had missed me or at least noticed my return. Dean immediately tried to feed me and had noticed that I had dropped quite a few pounds since she last saw me. I suppose it was true. The man I saw in the mirror looked like one of those guys from a reality survival television show after a couple of weeks in the wild. Multiply that by ten and that was about where I was—wild-eyed and hairy.

1100

After a shower and a shave (my first real cleansing in over a month) I felt much better. I had a horrible rash on my waist and legs from sleeping in my clothing for so long. I suppose the last wash for my clothes had been on the sailboat millennia ago. Tara said that she needed to talk to me later today after I was finished debriefing John. Something wasn't right. Something I didn't notice until this morning. Dean found me this morning around 0630 and forced me into a haircut. I now felt fairly presentable, with the only visible evidence of my absence being minor cuts, scars, bruises, weight loss and the slight limp I have incurred from my severe shin splints.

This morning was spent with John, Saien and the senior enlisted Marines. I flipped back and forth in my journal and went over key incidents during my time away. I showed everyone to the best of my knowledge where the original crash site was as well as Saien's and my rough route back to Hotel 23.

We then went into discussions about Remote Six. I passed around all the hardware I had obtained since being exposed to this organization as well as the provided documentation that I had retained. The materials passed around were: the maps of eastern Texas with the drop locations and other symbology, the M-4 with attachments, the automated Gatling manuals, iridium SATphone, experimental fuel treatment and a few other odds and ends. We deliberated the entire morning over the materials, the documents and the notes I took on all communications with Remote Six via the SATphone.

One of the ideas we came up with was that Remote Six was some sort of secondary government, previously established in case the main government was knocked out. The term "Fifth Column" was also discussed as it relates to the data at hand. John pulled up the computer screen on one of the flat-panel displays in the secure compartmented information facility (SCIF) in which we were located. He pulled up a network file system that he had cracked not long ago, and this referenced many government facilities on a map that indicated "status GREEN." The only location out of the many on the list of active facilities that I recognized was the pulsing green dot sitting just outside Las Vegas, Nevada.

An hour into the meeting I was concentrating on the discussion when I felt a hand on my shoulder from behind. I jumped out of my seat and slapped my chest to reach for my sidearm. I wasn't wearing my load-bearing vest.

It was Tara. My open hand shook uncontrollably and I had no way to explain what I was experiencing. My mind was still out there in the void. Lost. I couldn't hold a pistol steady in my hand if I tried. Tara brought down some coffee for the group. I apologized to her and explained that I was still a little jumpy from my extended stay outside the wire. Of course she nodded and said that she understood and kissed me on the cheek and walked out.

I quickly summed up the major points of the meeting and went after her. I caught up to her in the passageway and she embraced me quickly.

"I honestly thought you were gone."

"So did I. There were times that . . ."

"Don't talk about it. Let's just enjoy the time we have now. The time we have been given."

"I think you are right. Let's try."

At this point John rounded the corner with a "one more thing" comment and Tara just laughed and told John he could borrow me but he had to return me in one piece.

John laughed and told her that he'd do his best.

John had found a networked program that was embedded in the overhead imagery system previously discovered. Although many of the satellites were not functional and have probably re-entered the atmosphere, some of the multimission satellites were still working. The radiation sensors seemed to still be operational, and the satellite broadcast indicated hot zones overlaid on a United States map. This system was able to finally give us the locations of most if not all of the fallout areas as well as intermittent hits on probable locations of undead swarms if they had been radiated or had come from areas that were.

John had spent the last few weeks cataloging areas and track-ing movements of any hits that seemed to be mobile. He kept his documentation on paper in the event the system failed, as so many have before. The system name was "Wasteland." It was probably named by a cynical USSTRATCOM/NORTHCOM/DHS program-mer before all of this happened, as a casualty assessment tool. John noted that this system had not been working for the past two days.

We were all concerned about the Reaper that was probably orbiting over the complex. I expressed that there was really noth-ing we could do about it as we had no offensive capability against airborne targets and the Reaper was never directed against me or Saien. I had little doubt that the aircraft was data-linked back to some command center and that it was receiving real-time video feeds of Hotel 23. John commented that the aircraft carrier had suffered an accident resulting in loss of SATcom radios, which is why we lost contact with them for a short period a couple of months ago. The SITREP was sent out over a secure network via the existing WAN between our two units that were set up via the working overhead Inmarsat network. We had acquired a few of these phones on a scavenging mission a long time ago and set up a communications network with the carrier in the event the main system went down.

The SITREP message reason for comm loss was: "SATcom system damaged due to failure of radiated undead containment measures." I cursed so loud it made everyone jump.

I said rhetorically to the group: "Didn't we warn those idiots about this?"

I asked John when the last time we received a SITREP from the carrier was. He told me that he had been unable to establish a good Inmarsat connection since my return. After he said this it was as if everyone got the same idea at the same time and the light bulb above our heads got bright.

The jamming signal was following me and had been since Remote Six located me. Now the whole compound seemed to be cut off from the outside world with no early warning systems or network access.

18 Nov

0500

We received a transmission on the SATphone yesterday. Since my arrival I had had a guard stationed topside with the phone from 1200 to 1400 in the event contact was attempted. It was the same mechanical voice instructing the recipient to look at the text screen. The text gave instructions to log into the network using my common access card (CAC) and initiate launch in accordance with Executive Directive 51. Sets of coordinates were given for the launch as well as the physical location of auxiliary control. John and I discussed this after the phone lost connection and spent the rest of yesterday investigating and analyzing the information.

By 1900 we had made a startling discovery. John, Will and I had originally thought that this compound held only one nuclear intercontinental ballistic missile. After going through the instructions and initiating the subroutines we found that there were two more nuclear missiles at the ready in silos a thousand yards to the west of the compound awaiting launch sequence. Apparently, the only way to launch the warheads is to initiate the proper coding sequence while my CAC card is in the card slot reader. There is a small chip on the card with encryption that acts like the keys to the system. I remember that my card was recoded months before during one of the carrier supply drops. We were given launch codes and coordinates via the Iridium, so in theory it would be possible to launch the warheads.

John wasted no time plotting the coordinates given on a chart. They coincided to a location within six miles of the flagship carrier's position of intended movement as indicated on their last situation report. They were operating in a location in the Gulf of Mexico west of Florida and conducting replenishment operations. Remote Six was seemingly trying to destroy the carrier battle group, for reasons unknown. I did not refuse to comply during the text session and the screen continued to provide instructions on a loop with the final text question: "Have you initiated?"

The loop flashed four times until I finally ended the call. We then went searching for auxiliary control. The Marines found the door to the second control node first.

The doorway resembled an old cellar bulkhead. Heavy foliage and deception netting concealed the entryway. The door was made of steel and required a cutting torch to get inside. I saw no need to stay while the Marines secured auxiliary control and left them to the task of ensuring that no former residents of Hotel 23 remained inside.

18 Nov
1900

The text repeated again yesterday and today ordering the launch sequence to be initiated. The only difference was that the coordinates given varied by a couple of dozen nautical miles. They were adjusting for the movement of the carrier fleet. I asked the communications officer to send a message in the blind to the carrier to attempt to warn them again. He will be repeating the message every hour until I rescind the order.

The team sent to AUXCON breached the door and discovered that it was just a carbon copy of Hotel 23's main control center, living quarters and all. The only problem was that no subterranean tunnel connected the two control centers. There was a passageway reported in AUXCON that indicated an egress tunnel similar to the main control center layout. It was not yet known where the AUXCON egress tunnel let out in relation to the main egress tunnel. I was briefed that there were a few items of interest in AUXCON that I needed to see and that it was safe and clear for visitors.

Jan passed me in the hallway and asked how I was doing. I told her that I was fine and that I needed to talk to her about the status of medical care at Hotel 23. We sat down for a bit discussing the new (to me) military personnel she was working with and I found that they were very well trained and had seen a lot of battle in the past few months. She had learned a few things from the enlisted medics and they had learned a few things from her.

They had successfully conducted a few scavenging trips to secluded hospitals (both human and animal) in the area. She described one particular supply run, to a small-animal hospital a few miles away. Being the resident doctor, she had volunteered to go on the medical raids with the convoy to help identify useful items. The marines had cleared out the Happy Paws clinic minutes before Jan entered with Will. He insisted he go with her, and what husband would not? The stench was of course of dead flesh, which put the operators on high alert. They held their suppressed SMGs tight to their shoulders with flashlight on full one-hundred-lumen setting. One operator was positioned in front of Jan and Will and one behind, in pincer formation. That is how it is done. They entered the kennel area, and to their horror found cages with dogs long dead inside.

Some people take it really bad when seeing the evidence of an animal's suffering. I am no different. Hearing her story wrung my gut, and hers too, as she told it. Her eyes strained as if peering off into infinite space as she told of the cages with rotting dog corpses and the broken teeth and bloody claws from the dogs' using their last bit of strength in a vain attempt to bite and scratch their way out of the metal cages. The kennel was not full, only about 40 percent. The charts on the sides and floors near the cages showed the same story. Owner on vacation and will return at so and so time. All the dates were January. In her description I could see the animals lying in their cages with eternal snarls of agony penetrating the wire metal doors.

Hurricane

We were attacked.

It is very dark outside now. We sent the word out to the battle group in the blind over radio warning them of the intentions given to us on the SATphone. We had no way of knowing whether the ship had received our communiqué. The radio-jamming signal continued throughout that morning, as it had since my return and before.

We lost dozens the morning the device was dropped on us. Retribution for not launching? Even if we had launched, they would have likely hit us anyway. What would be the point in leaving us alive? Nothing makes any sense.

The now-deaf topside observers wrote on a whiteboard what they had witnessed. A whistling sound—getting higher in pitch—was the last sound they heard until the javelinlike Hurricane beacon slammed down into the ground, splitting one of the civilians in half from shoulder to hip.

The device immediately started transmitting its deadly payload, a sound so unimaginably loud that it immediately caused deafness in anyone who was above when it hit.

The device was reminiscent of a huge bee stinger—the magnified view of the top of the stinger pulsating, pumping poison into the arm, the ground. The device was stuck deep into the earth, slightly canted to one side, and was louder than words can describe.

We could clearly hear the barrage of noise and feel the vibrations through the thick steel and concrete from inside the bowels of Hotel 23. John immediately turned his available turret cameras onto the device and the other cameras to the perimeter areas overlooking the visible horizon. It was only a matter of seconds, maybe minutes until the sound reached the hardened internal ear canal hairs of the dead hundreds of miles away, turning their attention to this location.

They would geolocate the compound like a fleet of FCC vans hunting a pirate radio station. John transmitted an emergency message in the blind requesting help and a brief situation report on what had happened.

All available men and women in a position of leadership met and discussed alternatives. No one was allowed topside without good reason and double hearing protection. Even with the added hearing protection the sound was louder than standing next to the speakers at a rock concert. Watching the video surveillance, I could see that the sound disrupted and tilled the ground. The intense sonic energy moved the lighter civilian vehicles parked near it, not unlike a cell phone vibrating around on a coffee table. The device must have lodged itself twenty feet or more into the ground on impact.

All attempts to destroy the noise mechanism ended in failure. It seemed to be constructed from thick case-hardened steel or some other alloy. The internals at the top of the javelin were sealed. An already deaf Marine volunteered to try to destroy it by climbing to the top with a tool bag and a grenade. He didn't make it off the ground when he attempted to bear hug his way up. The device vibrated at such a resonance that every part of bare skin that touched it was sheared off in layers. Shots were wasted at full auto attempting to penetrate the top of the device. LAVs were systematically rammed into it.

Nothing worked.

I was in one of the LAVs. The beacon sound was barely dampened by the thick armor. The sound was so intense that it seemed to steal every breath. We established a perimeter with backs to the device, waiting for the undead to appear on the horizon. There were no indications at first. I peered through the thick-layered glass of the armored vehicle just as another object slammed into the ground two hundred yards from my position, nearly hitting one of the other LAVs. Shortly after the crash, I heard the distinct sound of supersonics overhead and caught the wing flash of an F/A-18 Super Hornet. After the small explosion subsided and the fire died down I could see by the wreckage what the craft had been—a Reaper UCAV, probably the same aircraft that had shadowed me for all that time after my crash and until my return to Hotel 23.

Immediately, the radio light flashed inside the vehicle, indicating a valid signal. Putting the headset on I could hear a voice speak clearly and concisely, warning repeatedly that there were A-10 Thunderbolts rolling in on our position from Scholes International in Galveston. The "Hawgs" were targeting the barrage beacon with 30mm cannons and they were asking all friendlies to rally east of the target so as to minimize fratricide.

Time to on top: twenty-one minutes.

After the Hawg controller finished transmitting, I could hear a faint signal and a voice identifying itself as the carrier air boss. He was ordering a division of F-18s to drop dumb iron bomb payloads on our position to complement the more precise optically aimed Warthog 30mm cannon strikes. With the jamming signal apparently destroyed along with the Reaper UCAV, I transmitted back to John and the others on a discreet channel what I had heard and that we were going to rally east a few hundred yards. The command center tuned in to the action on the radio as we started the engines and rolled east. We sat on a knoll overlooking the compound. There were dozens of undead already drawn to the beacon from the front of the compound area near the large steel double doors.

From our vantage point we saw iron hell rain down all around the compound via a division of F-18s dropping iron bombs onto pockets of undead. One F-18 used its airframe as an offensive weapon by going supersonic a foot over groups of undead to rip them apart or disable them with concussion. Explosive forces violently shook our vehicles as John reported in via radio below that the lights were flashing underground. After ten minutes of bombardment I overheard the codeword "winchester" on the radio, signifying that the fighters were out of ordnance and returning to mother. The sonic beacon had survived the bombing runs with no damage. The cursed device continued to transmit our position for all the dead to hear for miles around. Of course, the fighter super-sonics didn't help our cause much either.

The LAVs remained in formation east of the beacon as the first of the Hawgs rolled in hot, conducting a first pass before slamming the beacon with a mix of tungsten and depleted uranium 30mm rounds. Gaping up at the A-10s I could not help but wonder how they could fly so slowly.

The vulcan cannons began to grunt loudly, causing something that I had not expected . . .

The Hawgs cut through the sonic beacon javelin device as if it was paper. It was utterly disintegrated into shards, except for a few feet of alloy nub sticking out of the ground. The immediate silence shocked my system more than the overhead air strikes. I flung open the hatch, yanked the brass out of my ears and watched the rest of the strike from the top of the LAV. I could see Saien doing the same thing a few dozen meters to my right. He had his rifle sitting on the turret and I could see him scanning to the distance in the direction of what was quickly becoming a vast dust storm on the horizon.

Getting back down inside the LAV, I turned the vehicle optics to my face and looked out to the horizon. The dust plumes looked identical to the cloud surrounding the horde that Saien and I had encountered previously. There would be no stopping them. Not with a thousand A-10s loaded for bear. I immediately radioed down to John and the rest to prepare for evacuation from the facility immediately.

There were hundreds who needed evac. The carrier was steaming at full speed to rendezvous the coast to conserve helicopter fuel. Only the women and children and those who were injured would evacuate via simultaneous multihelicopter trips from the facility to the ship. The Hawgs were given instruction to intercept the horde just a few miles away and swarm around above them in an attempt to stall or draw the undead in another direction. We do not know if this tactic will work, as there are only three aircraft with enough fuel to attempt the distraction operation. Over the radio, I heard one of the A-10 pilots say that he had to switch to manual reversion for his flight controls and that his hydraulics system had experienced a catastrophic failure. He declared an emergency and a few seconds later I saw him buzz over our heads, scramming back to base. I hope he makes it.

I'm sitting on back of a deuce and a half waiting on the remaining carrier helicopters to pick up the rest of the high-value assets before we roll. The current plan is to convoy southeast to the Gulf of Mexico and then rendezvous the USS *George Washington* via small boat. We have multiple hard cases full of intelligence to be analyzed onboard the carrier. John backed up the entire H23 mainframe before we welded the doors shut, turned off the lights and bugged out. The intelligence was marked for immediate review and dispatched with the first available outgoing helicopter.

CVN

0800: USS George Washington

The carrier is in poor shape. There is red rust everywhere, much more than the expected haze gray of a well-maintained warship. There is no safe way to perform material condition maintenance, as every dry dock port will most likely be overrun with the creatures. The convoy operation to the carrier did not come without a hefty price. We lost dozens of good men. We were being attacked on all fronts as we cleared countless old roadblocks and wrecks. Most casualties occurred as a result of waiting for the small boat that would take us to the ship. With the carrier's large size, she could not berth near the shore. She had to anchor out a distance and send smaller craft to extract us at a rate of two boats per trip.

The operation was delayed an hour due to choppy seas. We were forced to defend ourselves against hundreds of undead with our backs to the Gulf. Many retreated by jumping into the water, choosing the cold waters over being eaten. We set up chain-linked islands of LAVs floating offshore, providing crew-served weapon support from the water's haven. We did what we could until the boats arrived. The dead we were fighting up to this point were likely the leading edge of Swarm T-5.1. The information previously transmitted by Remote Six suggests that they have somehow tagged the known swarms in the United States and seem to be attempting to designate and track them from a distance. A rotating sortie of Hawgs did what they could to draw a line in the sand by cutting the horde down by about 0.001 percent at a time. In the end it might have saved our lives by buying us those extra few seconds we needed to board the boats. The pilots reported an undead stream for miles and miles.

We kept fighting, expending all small-arms and crew-served ammunition. We could hear the powerful sound of the small-boat diesel engines behind us as the undead broke our fifty-yard perimeter kill barrier. Just as they were overtaking our position and reaching our front-line defenders, the boats arrived. We quickly boarded. Some had to fight the undead hand to hand with bayonets and empty weapons to board. I tossed my Randall knife to one of the Marines just in time for him to unsheath it and brutally decapitate two nearly skeletal and naked creatures clawing for his flesh. He yelled a hearty thanks, wiped the blade off on his pants and gave it back as he boarded the boat.

We were safely moving in the water toward the carrier, stopping only briefly every few hundred yards to pick men out of the water who were still alive but going into shock. Some had already turned and reached for our rescue personnel as they attempted to save those that they could.

The day we arrived a mixture of military surgeons and volunteer AmeriCorps doctors that were onboard immediately checked us out. Although they were not military, they were happy to be here instead of on the mainland. As they patched us up they told us that the life expectancy in some areas of the mainland was one hour at most. Another sailor onboard told me that they had to make dangerous incursions hundreds of miles inland to places like Redstone and Pine Bluff arsenals to replenish ordnance and critical repair parts from time to time.

Tara and I were berthed in a stateroom together on the O3 level. I was more than happy to see her and find out she had made it onboard without problems. She gave me the stateroom numbers as well as deck and frame numbers of all former Hotel 23 residents, and I made a mental note to visit everyone I could when I had the time. When I was not writing an operational intelligence report on the past year's goings-on I spent all my time with her. She has seemed much more emotional lately. This is completely normal, considering the stress everyone has been through.

I truly missed her during my absence, and I finally had some time where we both felt safe enough to let our mental guard down a bit and have real conversations about what happened to me out there.

I'll never forget her words: "I can't believe you are here in front of me. I missed you so much. You were bringing back what *they* took away from me."

As we were moving deeper into conversation a messenger knocked on our door and asked me to follow.

My debriefing in the Aircraft Carrier Intelligence Center (CVIC) took an entire day and a half. I was going over documents with John and Saien when the ship's acting intelligence officer appeared on deck. He introduced himself as Joe from the Central Intelligence Agency. He wore one of those olive-drab "shoot me first" photographer's vests, gray T-shirt and cargo pants with desert combat boots. Using my journal, I pored over the details I thought would be of significance. I was told that the acting Chief of Naval Operations would be summoning me to his office soon, as he wanted to meet me and get firsthand ground truth about the situation on the mainland and speak about an upcoming mission that may need my consultation.

Joe quickly redirected me to anything and everything regarding Remote Six. I explained to him the nature of the technology I had seen—everything from the weapon laser designator that I still had to the button beacon and even the UAV C-130. When explaining the fiber-optic boxes connected to the avionics of the C-130 I was compelled to tell Joe that I felt the unusual technology was years ahead of the mainstream technologies that were commercially available at the time the dead started to rise. He took careful notes and asked precision-guided questions regarding the technology. It seemed he was much more interested in the communications and the technology coming out of Remote Six than in the undead situation on the ground.

Another subject of interest was the condition in which we had left Hotel 23. I explained that every piece of valuable intelligence was exfiltrated with the evacuation and that we had welded all access doors closed to prevent tampering by anyone or anything. Over his shoulder he ordered one of the intelligence personnel to ensure that the CVIC "keeps an eye" on Hotel 23 in the event that an attempt is made on the systems inside. He stated that it was worth diverting assets for at least a while.

I told him of a list of compounds that John had gained access to via the computer systems inside Hotel 23. I said that there were at least a dozen locations, and that the only location in the database I had recognized was Groom Lake, Nevada. I asked Joe if there was any significance to that location and why it would still be manned and in the green. He said that he did not know, but it seemed to me that he was being deceptive. While telling him about Project Hurricane technology, I had witnessed that he was interrupted by a phone call.

After nodding a few times and saying, "Yes, sir," he hung up the phone and said simply: "You're on."

I dropped off the debriefing report that I had invested the last two days writing and followed Joe to the admiral's in-port cabin. After I had stubbed my toes on three knee knockers and nearly hit my head on a leaking low-pressure steam pipe, we eventually arrived. There were two Marine guards standing in front of the cabin door and they stepped aside after seeing Joe. We knocked once and a gruff voice responded with only, "Come." On entering the cabin I saw the admiral sitting at his mahogany desk with a bottle of Chivas scotch and three glasses. I walked toward the admiral and stood at attention eighteen inches in front of his desk. I didn't recognize him. I introduced myself to the admiral and stated that I was reporting as ordered.

He laughed and said, "Sit down, son, I was only a senior fullbird captain a year ago. The stars were, how should I say—battlefield promotions?"

I sat down and he poured three glasses and handed two of them to Joe and me. He introduced himself as Admiral Goettleman.

He proceeded to offer his account of the past year—tales of his flotilla of small-boy ships and the littoral war against the dead that kicked off in the early weeks. After some major cities were destroyed by tactical nukes, his ships were charged with clearing operations. They would draw the dead to the coastline near major population centers and prosecute via full barrage for hours at a time in an attempt to thin the herd. There were times his destroyers and cruisers would sit at anchor for days with the ships' horns blaring intermittently to attract the dead in order to ensure high effect. He had personally witnessed .50 cal gunners throw red-hot barrels over the side into the water only to replace them with new cosmoline-coated surplus steel scavenged from various military arsenals around the United States He then looked solemnly into the distance—not at me but through me.

"Intelligence estimates credited my group with less than a one percent disposal rate. We got half a million at least. I know this 'cause we expended well over a million rounds. It turns out, the littoral war was of no more value than the nuclear campaign."

He then asked about my story.

After I had presented an executive-level debrief on my experiences of the last year, he took a long pause and then took a long drink of scotch and filled his glass back up three fingers. He went on to stroke my ego by saying that there are not a lot of men who could have saved so many people and survived that long on the mainland. He then stood up, walked over to the liquor cabinet and pulled it from the wall on one side. Behind the cabinet a safe was hidden. After spinning the dials back and forth he pulled out a thick file and placed it on his desk. As he unwound the string binding the folder, he informed me that he had a special team that he had put together for a very important, nationally sanctioned operation.

"The USS *Virginia,* a nuclear fast attack submarine, is currently en route to the Pacific side of the Panama Canal from the waters of Baja. Of course the Canal is derelict and nonfunctioning, but it is still the thinnest land mass between this ship and the USS *Virginia* on the Pacific side. I'll cut to the chase: We are sending an incursion team to China. Reliable intelligence suggests that the source of the anomaly resides in a defense research laboratory on the outskirts of Beijing. Our scientists think we may have a chance of finding a cure or at least a vaccine if we can locate and extract patient-zero or the research data associated.

"You and the civilians under your leadership survived for nearly a year on the mainland. The DEVGRU frogs and D-boys on this team I'm putting together can't boast that kind of experience statistic and probably wouldn't want to. China is, unfortunately, many times denser in undead population than the United

States, and over two-thirds of their undead population is walking on the eastern coast. In saying that, it is prudent to mention that they didn't deploy nearly as many nuclear weapons inside China to neutralize the dead. Luckily, Beijing was not destroyed. Taiwan was not so lucky. It was completely wiped out by the chicoms and will remain hot for years to come.

"The plan is to move the carrier to the thinnest point of the Atlantic side of the canal and fly the incursion team over the Panama land mass into the waitin' open hatches of the USS *Virginia*. She's relatively new and in much better shape than this ship. She has fifteen years or more until scheduled refueling of her reactors and currently has 'nuf food onboard for a six-month run."

I was starting to realize at this point what the admiral was leading up to.

"We intend to have the *Virginia* in the Bohai in three weeks. We've located airstrips with probably serviceable Chinese military helicopters at three different airfields near Beijing. Since the *Virginia* has no tactical requirement to run below periscope depth we can remain in constant data contact with her as she transits from CONUS to Pearl Harbor, Hawaii to the Bohai. After arriving in the Bohai, the *Virginia* will make her way upriver to Beijing and to the airfields we've identified. After arriving in the vicinity of the airfields, *Virginia*'s crew will launch Scan Eagle UAVs to recon the airfields and determine the best candidates for rotary-wing repairs and deployment.

"I'd like you to ride the *Virginia* to China as a technical consultant for the incursion team."

After letting the admiral's request (see: order) sink in for about ten seconds, I mentioned to him the obvious fact that I was no special operator. I am a naval officer and not a door-kicker or commando. I had no experience in this type of operation.

He replied callously with only: "I have been briefed in your background and I have decided that you will ride the *Virginia* to China and you will support this operation. I know about what you did in Texas. We screened all military message traffic leading up to the anomaly. Your name came up as, shall I say . . . *missing*?"

A line of seriousness appeared on the admiral's forehead and then he said: "Can't say that I blame you, son. There was no way to win at that time, but there may be a way to win now. There's space on the helicopter as well as the boat for an extra body, if you want to bring someone you know and trust. I'll leave that to you. You leave in three days' time. That is all, Commander."

All I could mutter was, "Aye, aye, Admiral."

. . . Then dismiss myself and walk out.

Leaving the cabin in a confused daze, I didn't realize until Joe congratulated me on my new promotion that I had been bumped up two ranks to commander. He also handed me the appropriate collar rank devices and wished me better luck than the man who had held these oak leaves before me. I tossed them in my pocket, never planning to wear them, and made way to my quarters.

BT

TS//SI//SAP HORIZON

BT

CRITIC FOLLOW-UP/I+274/

BT

Be advised this is not a finished intelligence report. Numerous COMINT intercepts originating from the People's Republic of China (PRC) leading up to the event reveal the probable anomaly source.

BT

One year ago VORTEX received communications revealing that the PRC had recovered something of great technological interest from the ancient ice of the Mingyong glacier in Yunnan Province. An object of ovoid shape (see separate enclosure 01: AURORA overflight imagery) about the size of a large passenger bus was discovered by the local population and reported to the local authorities. Chinese web precognitive awareness predictive language supports this intercept.

BT

At first the Chinese radiometrically dated the unknown alloy of the object back greater than six billion years (a geological impossibility). That was until they calibrated their instruments to the alloy's true decay rate. After instrument calibration, it was discovered that the object had been in the ice for approximately twenty thousand years.

BT

The vehicle (as it turned out to be) was not without damage to the outer hull. Imagery analysis indicated a two-meter hole in the top of the object that allowed the elements to slowly enter the inside of the vehicle during its glacial interment. The immense pressure of the ever-contracting and expanding glacial ice and the vast time span from crash to recovery was a direct factor that likely caused the outer hull to warp over the centuries. After weeks of careful excavation the Chinese advanced to the cockpit of the vehicle (see separate enclosure 02: HUMINT handheld imagery). It is unknown by this agency why the Chinese chose to excavate in the direction of the cockpit and not the assumed advanced propulsion systems of the vehicle. In the cockpit the excavators discovered what is known in the transcripts only as a creature assigned the Chinese code name CHANG.

BT

When discovered, CHANG was restrained in the cockpit seat wearing a thin exoskeleton of unknown technology that Chinese researchers postulated could function as a conventional astronaut environmental suit [REF 243B2]. CHANG was still mobile and seemed to react to the excavator's presence by moving its head from side to side inside the exoskeleton's helmet. CHANG was also encased from the chest down in ice. The scientists and security personnel were initially very disturbed by the movement of the creature and were given orders to keep it restrained by any means necessary. They were also given specific instructions not to remove CHANG's cranial helmet.

BT

TACNOTE: Some of the researchers were executed when central military commission cyber-defense agents discovered that they had PGP encryption keys installed on their personal computers and were in intermittent communication with unknown [to PRC] persons outside the PRC [covered in separate agency correspondence].

BT

According to intercepted initial magnetic resonance imaging, the creature is bipedal and has the rough appearance in mass and appendages of a young adolescent human.

BT

After securing and removing CHANG (still at this point in a relative block of ice), the Chinese began to excavate the rest of the vehicle. They discovered numerous artifacts, some destroyed by the ages and immense glacial ice pressure and some still very much intact. Most notable were the advanced propulsion systems that the Chinese recovered and took back to the same research facility in which CHANG was being examined (probably in Beijing). At first the Chinese took great interest in reverse-engineering the advanced magnetic levitation, propulsion and inertial dampening systems as well as the exotic power plant of the vehicle. The vehicle appeared to possess what PRC researchers hypothesized as a *crumple drive* module that might allow the vehicle to distort or crumple the space directly in front to an area twenty meters out (single-source HUMINT report). Also recovered were numerous handheld directed-energy weapons. Utilizing a transmission electron microscope with half-angstrom resolution capability, the Chinese were able to perform a cursory examination of the artifact internals. Much of the inner workings examined on the smaller artifacts indicated subnano technology advanced circuitry. When the PRC quickly came to a technological impasse with reverse-engineering attempts, their focus turned to CHANG.

BT

CHANG was being kept in a biohazard containment vault in the compound (probably in Beijing). He (unknown gender) was under constant security and observation but seemed to exhibit very little intelligence and made no attempt to communicate with the scientists or military officers charged with interrogation and study. It was decided after deliberations by Chinese presidential authority that CHANG be removed from ice and observed.

BT

The last communications intercept contained a distress call from the research facility that held CHANG (confirmed to be in Beijing, PRC, by this timeline of reporting). All HUMINT sources inside the facility have since gone dark.

BT

Remote viewing data is available via separate compartmented reporting channels.

BT

Assessment: This agency assesses that CHANG was infected with the Mingyong Sickness somewhere in transit between his star system and Earth. Judging by the acquired photos taken at the glacier site, it appears that the vehicle was at an abnormal attitude in the ice, which suggests an inverted crash landing. The hull damage score marks possess melted and deformed edges, which could indicate a blasting event by some great force, possibly a separate energy weapon event.

BT

Also of intelligence value: It is assessed that due to the timeline of the anomaly and the extreme complexity of the subnano circuitry, the Chinese were unable to effectively reverse-engineer the propulsion systems of the vehicle or even develop a theory about how the systems function. Beijing was the first city to be overrun by the creatures, thus halting research and development of advanced systems. Home Base and Utah Site 84-026 concur with this assessment.

BT

TF HOURGLASS is standing by to provide operational intelligence support to the Beijing incursion.

BT

TS//SI//SAP HORIZON

BT

DECLASSIFY ON: MANUAL REVIEW

BT

AR